COPY CATS

A CRAZY CAT LADY MYSTERY

BY MOLLIE HUNT

Copy Cats, a Crazy Cat Lady Mystery
by Mollie Hunt

ISBN-13: 978-1503258549

Editing and Design by Rosalyn Newhouse

Published in the United States of America

No generative AI has been used in the conceptualization, development, or drafting of this work.

Cover Art: "Incognito" by Leslie Cobb
© 2004 Leslie Cobb
www.lesliecobb.com

E2A

Other Books by Mollie Hunt

Crazy Cat Lady Mysteries
Cats' Eyes
Copy Cats
Cat's Paw
Cat Call
Cat Café
Cat Noel
Cosmic Cat
Cat Conundrum
Adventure Cat
Cat's Play

The Tenth Life Cozy Mysteries
Ghost Cat of Ocean Cove
Ghost Cat on the Midway

Other Mysteries
Placid River Runs Deep

Poetry
Cat Poems: For the Love of Cats

Cat Seasons Sci-Fantasy Tetralogy
Cat Summer
Cat Winter
Cat Autumn

Dedication and Acknowledgements

This book is dedicated to my husband, Jim Hunt, for accompanying me through the cat life; to my parents, Mary Elizabeth and Ernest, who regrettably never got to read this series; and to Mrs. Wilson, my fourth-grade teacher, for whom I wrote my first cat tale.

Grateful acknowledgement to Julie Sotomayor for all her help with cat breeder questions, something that as a shelter volunteer, I know painfully little about. If there are any inaccuracies in the story, it was on my end, not hers. Also to Jenny Martin and Rosalyn Newhouse for reading with a kind but erudite eye.

Special thanks to all the cats, real and imagined.

THE ROOM WAS SILENT. Not a breath, not a sneeze, not a cell phone ping sounded throughout the crowd. Attention focused on the woman on the dais as though she were the only star in the sky.

In a high-backed antique wing chair, its gold brocade at odds with the austerity of the convention room, she sat like a rock star queen. A single spot shone down on her generous proportions.

Her eyes were closed.

In her hand, she held a photograph.

Chapter 1

I am the crazy cat lady, but I'm not quite crazy yet.

Basically I'm just a lady who likes cats.

And has several cats.

And volunteers at a cat shelter.

And fosters sick cats.

Well, you get the picture, but I don't see how any of that makes me certifiable and certainly not nuts enough to believe one session with a pet psychic could break open a plot of abuse, perversion, and brutal murder. Ask my friends, though I'll admit they may be a bit biased, being mostly cat people, too. They'll tell you I went into this with only the best intentions. I had no idea at the time where it would lead or I would never have gotten involved. But I did and once in I had to see it through. As with cats, curiosity trumps my better judgment every time.

I don't know what I expected when I signed up for the Animal Communications Conference and Advanced Workshop given by the preeminent icon of pet whisperers, la Zoe. A little fun, some light entertainment. Not that I don't believe humans can commune with their animal companions—I do. I talk to cats all the time, and usually they *talk* back, but it's all pretty basic. I guess I just wanted to know if there were more to it than *feed me, pet me,* and *whatever do you think you're doing?* if I didn't perform the previous in a timely manner. An insight into feline philosophy, for instance? Or a catly consensus on world events? Maybe they could tell me the secrets of the universe, or even why they prefer one litter over another—that would be convenient.

Yes, animal communication would be a handy trick, though at the time I didn't hold out much hope of ever mastering it. And it certainly never crossed my mind that if I did, I might learn things I'd rather not know.

My name is Lynley Cannon, daughter of Carol Mackey, grandmother of Seleia Voxx, "mom" of Dirty Harry, Big Red, Solo, Little, Violet, Fraulein Fluffs, and my new and wonderful family member, Tinkerbelle. Those last seven are cats. I have a human daughter too, but when it comes to Lisa, I get along better with the cats.

I'm a busy person despite the fact that I'm nearing sixty. Sixty! It sounds so old! Except for the aches, pains, and intermittent memory loss, I don't feel like a *senior citizen* in the throes of my *golden years*. The *autumn of my life*—what balderdash! Of course my father said the same thing when he turned eighty. Eighty—now that's old!

Cats don't care how old you are. They don't look at your time-ravaged body, your wrinkling face, drying skin, gnarled knuckles, or veined hands. In fact, I believe they prefer older people. Less drama, less fear. It's true that cats can smell fear and it irritates them. They would much rather smell nice calm happy emotions, the ones they can take a nap on.

I spend a lot of time with cats. Some might think that's a bad thing, but my friends take it for granted. Besides caring for my own little clowder, I volunteer at Friends of Felines in my spare time, and since I'm retired, that means nearly every day. FOF, as we affectionately call it, is a small not-for-profit no-kill state-of-the-art cat haven. Built with love, sweat, tears, and many generous donation dollars, I am proud to say it's become a model for shelters all over the United States.

I find peace helping those homeless sweethearts transition to their new lives in caring homes. Why people give up their pets I will never understand. Oh, yes, I've heard all the reasons, and some are certainly valid. Death, for instance. And illness. Homelessness is a new one that we're seeing more and more these days. But excuses such as *it got too old* or *it isn't cute anymore* just make my hackles rise. To me, a pet is a life-long commitment, like a child, only pets don't grow up and go off to college; they stay and you love them. That's all there is to it.

And that brings up another reason I'd been looking forward to the Animal Communication Seminar. A good percentage of FOF's guests were strays with secret stories of the streets; many a time I'd wished they could tell me what happened out there to make them skittish or fearful or mad. Maybe with la Zoe's professional instruction, I might finally be able to find out. My motives were innocent, I swear. There was no sense of doom, no inner alarms going off. I didn't hear angels or see fairies or feel as if I were in the Time Tunnel. How could I have known that those few hours were going to change my life?

* * *

I may be a crazy cat lady, but I wasn't the only one there by a long shot. Cat daddies, dog dopes, bird buddies, gerbil guys—they all were drawn, just like me, to see the queen of pet communications. Most had come for the show, but an elite few would go on to a special session with la Zoe, herself. Frannie and I were to be among those few.

Frannie also volunteered at Friends of Felines where we had met several years back. We had developed an instant rapport, though to this day I don't know what she does when she's not socializing stray cats, cleaning out litter boxes, and performing the many ordinary tasks that make a shelter run. We often got together for drinks after our shifts, her place or mine, but our chit-chat rarely veered far from the day's work which both of us found to be infinitely interesting.

Frannie DeSoto is an amazing person. Though roughly my age, she has the air of a twenty-year-old. She is meticulous with hair and make-up, and whether she is volunteering at the shelter or attending a formal dinner, the platinum curls are always perfect, the bright pink lipstick never smudged or faded, and the nail gloss which invariably matches her whimsical eye shadow, sans chip or crack. I don't have a clue how she does it. My look tends toward the opposite: hair springing into a mess of gray-red snarls the minute I walk out the salon door, and aside from a little lip color of a nondescript plum, I don't wear make-up so that's that.

After la Zoe's introduction to Mindfulness and a short autobiographical narrative, the seer was scheduled to do actual readings from the audience. Everyone had brought a photograph or two in hopes of being chosen, and Frannie was one of the lucky ones. She was as excited as a kitten, which was cute to see on someone of retirement age. I was happy for her. She hadn't had a cat for as long as I'd known her because her apartment building didn't allow them, so the photo of the smiling tabby had to go back aways. La Zoe claimed she could speak to the dead so it wouldn't be a problem.

Frannie nudged me. "Teasel's up next," she whispered rapturously. "Finally la Zoe will be able to tell me how my baby's doing up in Kitty Heaven."

I nodded, examining the woman on stage into whom

Frannie was pouring her utter faith. She was large, manly even, reminding me vaguely of Darcelle, the famous Portland female impersonator. The long, concealing robes were classic gold; the unnaturally red hair was piled on top her head like a raspberry ice cream cone. I quashed a surge of skepticism; after all, if I had wanted to be cynical about the presentation, I could have stayed home and saved myself a hundred bucks.

We waited patiently for the spiritualist to finish up her current reading, a heart-wrenching attempt to locate a lost dog. Though la Zoe had found the pup's energy and could attest to the fact that he was alive, his thoughts told her little that would help with the rescue since the dog himself had no concept of where he was. Even la Zoe was helpless in this situation; the best she could do was to send calming thoughts and assurance that his family would never stop searching.

"I am sorry," la Zoe said in a sonorous voice that could have belonged to James Earl Jones. "Your Max is out there. He is healthy but afraid. Do not give up hope." She smiled broadly, a grin worthy of a Denobulan.

The couple who occupied the chairs next to the dais stood. Zoe handed the photograph to the man, then he and his wife shuffled somberly back to their seats among the audience.

The communicator took another picture from a neat pile on the little table next to her. "And now," she drawled, "Teasel."

She held the glossy page to her forehead for a moment—again I fought down the urge to scoff—then studied it intensely. "Ah. This one has crossed Beyond. Some time ago?" Her eyes grazed the room until they lit on Frannie. "Come up, my dear. Contacting those on the other side is always a bit bewildering for them. Teasel will need you close."

Frannie rose and scooched down our row. Though no one would guess from her confident demeanor, I knew she was scared. We had talked in depth before the program about animal communication, specifically communication with the dead. At the time I hadn't known she planned to submit her own passed puss for the reading. Now all those metaphysical debates, those half-formed thoughts, those dreams and nightmares we discussed made sense. Like myself, Frannie wasn't sure people could actually commune with their dead pets, but I guess she figured it couldn't hurt to try.

Frannie nodded a courtly hello to la Zoe, then sat down in the hot seat.

"I must have complete silence for this reading," the seer announced. "This is the most difficult of all contact. The thread to the Beyond is tenuous. So much as a sigh and it can be broken, just like that!" She snapped her pudgy fingers.

The room hushed; everyone held their breath.

"Teasel," the psychic crooned.

The silence reverberated.

It dragged out into a void of forever.

Then, finally and with great satisfaction, la Zoe smiled. "She is here!"

* * *

"Wow! That was amazing," I said to Frannie as we sat in the lounge having a much-needed cup of coffee.

Frannie was silent.

"Are you okay?"

She nodded slowly. "I think about her all the time, you

6

know. It's been nine years since Teasel—what did la Zoe call it? Crossed Beyond?"

I took a sip of my coffee. It was strong and lip-burning, just the way I liked it. "What did you think of the reading?" I said carefully.

Frannie's big eyes gleamed. "Everything she told us was right on. About the way Teasel meows when she yawns. And how she follows wherever I go. *Followed,*" she revised somberly. "I still miss her. Teasel was the reason I started volunteering at the shelter, you know."

"She must be very proud of you."

Frannie gave me a quizzical look. "You don't think la Zoe was making it all up, do you?"

I paused. That was a tough one. I still had my doubts, but Frannie was so happy to hear from her long-dead kit, I didn't want to step on her high. I was saved from my dilemma by the clear ping of a prayer bell. It pinged two more times—the summons to la Zoe's private session.

"Maybe we're about to find out."

* * *

We picked our way into a small conference room. A dozen chairs were arranged in a horseshoe with what had to be the queen's throne, a particularly large office chair, occupying the gap. Frannie and I took seats, and I looked around for somewhere to put my stuff. Finally for lack of a better idea, I shoved my laptop and purse under the chair. I saw others coming to the same conclusion, stowing books and carryalls underneath, then awkwardly balancing computers, notebooks, or in some cases, old-fashioned pen and paper on their laps. I wondered at the lack of desks but had a feeling it was all part of the show.

A door opened on the far side of the room and in swept

la Zoe. Her heavy robes rustled as she smiled and nodded to her much-diminished audience. Then without ado, she unzipped the front of her drape and shrugged out of the voluminous sleeves. Underneath she wore jeans and a Humane Society of the United States tee shirt, well worn, fading, with a few tiny holes at the hem. She undid the pins that held her red bird's nest of hair and shook it out as if shaking of the regal persona.

"That is better," she said, her deep, formal voice unchanged. "Now, are you ready to learn the secrets of life?"

There were titters and a cough.

"No, I am serious. Psychic communication is innate in all beings; it is merely locked away from our outward sight." She paused and looked around the class expectantly.

"I don't understand," said a young woman.

"That is alright, you will. Put away your writing gear, you are not going to need it."

There was the murmur of confusion, but eventually most everyone complied.

"Put away your pen, sir," she told a young man who was holding on to the implement for dear life.

"But, ma'am," he stuttered. "How am I supposed to take notes?"

"You will not be needing notes. Your heart will remember."

"But... what if it doesn't?" he persevered.

"Then it was not meant to be," she flipped. "What I am about to tell you comes from inside. No amount of notation can help you if you cannot accept that."

She bent down to reach into a banker's box beside her chair and pulled out an oversized paperback book packaged in plastic. "But if you are still unclear at the end of the session, you may purchase my book for a nominal fee. I will autograph it for you." Again she laughed. "Trust me, all will become clear once you begin to listen."

As with her first session, she began with a meditation, then moved on to a deep breathing exercise and a game of toss where we worked with a partner—to clear our chakras, she told us. After we'd had a few laughs chasing neon Nerf balls around the conference room, we got down to business.

I can't tell you the rest of what happened because, like the magician's assistant, we were sworn to secrecy. I wondered about the analogy at the time. La Zoe was right about one thing though: we didn't need to take notes. Everything that went on in that room that day is seared into my memory for life. I will never forget it, no matter how much I wish I could.

Chapter 2

Cats can be extremely stoic and are very good at hiding their pain. Often by the time their symptoms become apparent, the cause may be fairly advanced. Know your cat; note any changes in eating, sleeping, litter box habits, or general well-being. If there is any question, take kitty to your vet—it's always best to err on the side of caution.

It was only mid-afternoon when I headed for the bus stop by the Convention center, but the sky was smoky black, dark as twilight. Still, this was Portland in January, and I was just thankful it wasn't raining buckets. The weather wasn't foremost on my mind; the communication session had given me a lot to think about. The possibilities were endless. A part of me was predictably doubtful, but a more guileless element couldn't wait to get home and try it out on my cats. What would I ask them first? If they were happy? How they were feeling? Were they healthy? With cats, it's nearly impossible to know if they're sick until something's really wrong. Or would I just cut to the chase and ask what happened before we'd met? That's what I really wanted to know. Would they be able to tell me? Cats are very here-and-now creatures; would the past be important enough to recall?

Dirty Harry was the one who'd been with me the longest. The big black-and-white male with the distinctive white "petticoat" around his back end was a four-year-old stray when he came to me a decade ago. Where had he been before that?

Little and Tinkerbelle, a pair of unrelated all-black sisters, were also strays whom I'd adopted from Friends of Felines. What were their stories?

Big Red, the ginormous orange tabby, lived on my porch until I took him inside. He's afraid of feet; did that mean what I thought it did?

Violet, my sweet large girl—twenty-two pounds of pure love. What made her eat so much when other cats could pace themselves?

And Solo, the deaf white recluse who lived under the couch, was inherited from a needy friend; did she still miss her previous, if flighty, person?

Fraulein Fluffs was a hospice case I'd taken on. Thirteen years old with advanced renal failure, she was transferred to me by the Friends of Felines foster department to live out her few final days in the comfort of a real home. To note, that was several months ago and she's still going strong. Her blood work had improved—a mistaken diagnosis or a miracle? What could she say about her true state of health? As the bus chugged up Hawthorne toward my neighborhood, I couldn't wait to see.

My jacket buzzed and I jumped—no, it wasn't a mouse in my pocket but my cell phone announcing a call. I glanced at the woman sitting next to me but she seemed not to have noticed. I guess it would take more than a little flinch to get the attention of a seasoned Tri-Met rider.

Wrestling the phone from the denim, I looked at the caller's name. It was Kerry, the FOF Foster Coordinator.

"Hello, Kerry," I shouted over the noise of the bus.

"Lynley? That you?" Her voice was soft but urgent.

"What's up?" I knew without being told it was more than a social call to see how Fluffs was doing.

"I hate to bother you. I know you're already caring for the hospice kitty, but I have a special case I hoped you might consider."

"Okay, sure," I said without hesitation. I loved to foster and I liked a challenge; this sounded like both.

"I have a cat..." She paused. "A very special cat. He's going to need some serious attention."

"What kind of attention?" Usually my fosters had a physical ailment such as an upper respiratory infection, thyroid condition, or a surgery after which they needed some recovery time, but Kerry's somber tone made this sound like something more.

"His name is Meow, or that's what the team's been calling him. According to the collar he came in with, his name is Wichien-maat Prince Zoom Meow-Meow, CFA Registered."

"A purebred?"

"Yes and no."

"Yes and no? What does that mean?"

"Um, we're just not sure yet exactly what he is."

"I take it the info on the collar went nowhere."

"Disconnected number."

"Microchip?"

"Surprisingly, no."

"Did you check with CFA? Shouldn't they have contact information for the breeder or owner?"

"Cat Fanciers' Association has no record of Meow or of any cattery named Wichien-maat."

The bus began to screech to a clunky halt, and I stood, grabbing the yellow metal pole with my free hand. Sure enough, there was a final bone-jarring lurch before it came to light by the curb.

"Hold on, Kerry. I'm on the bus; this is my stop."

Without waiting for affirmation, I gathered my purse and laptop, the one I hadn't needed after all, and bumbled down the grid steps. I said thank you to the driver, a Portland custom, and watched as he pulled noisily away toward downtown. "Okay, I'm back. Now tell me all about Meow."

* * *

I was home just long enough to swap my computer case for my shelter bag and pick up my car. Now that I'm eligible for the senior citizen discount, I like to take the bus when I can, but the shelter was off the beaten track, and it was easier to drive. I'd forgotten all about communing with my cats; a quick pet and I was out the door. Little, my official sentry, sat at the window glowering as she watched me go, and it didn't take a psychic to know she was mad.

As I drove the winding streets, I wondered about Meow—Wichien-maat Prince whatever —and how he could be a breed cat and yet not. Kerry had told me he was part of an investigations case and therefore unadoptable. Surprisingly, he wasn't sick, just depressed, but depression could be a death sentence for a cat. He had stopped eating, and if he lost weight too fast, it could result in fatty liver disease, potentially lethal for felines. Kerry was hoping the change in environment would get him going; otherwise he would have to be force-fed or even fitted with a feeding tube, neither of which enhances a sad cat's attitude.

Kerry hadn't elaborated on the investigations side of the story. Friends of Felines often cooperated with the Northwest Humane Society's Investigations Department, a team of commissioned police officers who handled complaints of animal neglect, abandonment, and abuse on a daily basis. The humane investigators were pet heroes, their single job—and a big one—to keep Oregon's animals safe. While a lot of their work focused on education, they also had the authority to serve warrants, seize animals, cite offenders, and give highly respected testimony in court. Because of them, many bad guys had been convicted, and through their tireless efforts, uncounted animals had been saved.

All three of the agents were heroes in my mind, but Special Agent Denny Paris was someone I considered a friend. When I pulled into the parking lot and saw his big Ford truck out front, I felt my face flush. Besides being extremely good at what he did, he was seriously easy on the eyes. I may be decades his senior but never too old to appreciate a nice set of biceps and a perfect, manly smile.

Automatically I checked my face in the rearview mirror, frowned when I saw the old person staring back at me, then shook my head when I noted that the frown made me look even worse. *It is what it is*, I told myself as I touched up my lipstick. As I said before, the cats don't care.

"Lynley," Kerry exclaimed with her habitual enthusiasm—I swear the young woman's smile could light the world. "Thanks so much for coming."

I glanced around the office. Up against one wall was a bank of wire shelves filled with cat carriers in all shapes and sizes; from the yowls and mewls that echoed throughout the room, I guessed they were full. "Spay day?" I asked, nodding to the assemblage.

"Always! We're doing it every week now. Anyone on public assistance can get their cat altered for just ten dollars. And we even throw in a homemade kitty blanket, courtesy of the volunteer craft club," she added with a short laugh.

"I assume none of those are Mr. Meow."

She shook her head. "He's still in the kennels. I wanted to give you some background before you made your decision. And Special Agent Paris also has a few things to go over about the case. He's stepped out for a minute, but he should be right back. I'd rather wait till he's here to go into it if you don't mind."

She seemed nervous, and it didn't look natural on the tall dark-haired girl. I put my concerns aside; I was sure she'd get it all out when she was ready.

"I wouldn't mind checking the cattery if you think I have time. I always look in on Xena, the little tortoiseshell. She's been in such a grouchy mood lately, sometimes a few wiggles with a ribbon helps to bring her around." From my bag, I slipped a short wand with a waterfall of grosgrain ribbons attached to one end and gave it a cheerleader shake.

"Sure, go ahead. Take as long as you want."

I pushed out the heavy door and buzzed myself into the cattery with my key card. The feline scent hit me, and I breathed deeply, enjoying the musky mix. I know—it's weird and most assuredly an acquired taste, but to me, it always smelled friendly. Mind you, this was not the reek of a dirty litter box which I venture to say no one really cares for; the cattery was kept exceptionally clean, as were the cats.

Glancing into the stray cat room on my way by, I saw Frannie standing with her eyes closed. She held a huge black puss in her arms and was petting its head gently as she rocked back and forth. I changed my course and went in. Her lids lifted when she heard the clang of the door.

"I thought you were going home after the session," I said, taking the opportunity to don my Friends of Felines green volunteer apron and tie the bow at my back. "Did you decide to come test out la Zoe's lessons?"

"I meant to go home, but somehow I ended up driving out here instead." She put puss back in a lower kennel, gave him a final pet and whisker scratch and closed the door. Big Boy settled down on his blanket and blinked with obvious contentment.

Frannie went to wash up in the sink. "I kept thinking about all the things la Zoe told us. How to establish contact, to make the cat feel at ease, then finally draw him out, ask our questions and listen to his answers with our hearts instead of our minds. Well, I wanted to try it for myself."

"And did it work?"

She pulled off two paper towels and dried her hands. "As a matter of fact, I think it did. When I was doing Ronnie here, I suddenly had the clearest picture of a place, a countryside with grasses waving in the breeze and a big blue sky overhead. It was so vibrant, I could almost touch it. I could smell the dew on the hay. I felt like I was right there. It only lasted a moment and then it was gone, but I can still remember every detail, almost as if it were a memory of my own."

"What do you think it means?" I asked, clicking open a kennel to scratch the sideburns of a gregarious gray shorthair.

"Well, I really wasn't sure, so I went and looked at his paperwork, the questionnaire filled out by his previous owner. And you'll never guess! He was brought in to the shelter by some people who lived on a farm!"

"Wow," I commented, unsure what else I could say. Communication or coincidence? I'd just paid a chunk of hard-earned cash in favor of the communication side, but old habits die hard, and skepticism was one of my oldest. I tabled my disbelief, however, not wanting to spoil

Frannie's moment. Inconspicuously I offered up my mind to the gray, but either she didn't have anything to say, or I wasn't doing it right because I got nothing beyond the usual shelter confusion.

I said goodbye the old fashioned way—with words—and closed the kennel door. "I have to go back to foster care. I might be getting a new foster today, but Kerry wants to give me some info first. And Special Agent Paris is in on it." I paused, still wondering at the implications. "I'll call you later, see if you pick up anything else from the feline side."

"Okay, and let me know about the new kitty. It sounds mysterious."

I went to leave, then turned back. "You should try communicating with Xena. Maybe you can figure out what's got her so upset."

"We know what's got her upset," Frannie snickered. "She hates it here. She's been stuck in that kennel for over half a year, and she needs a home."

"Yeah, but every time someone wants to meet her, she hisses and spits. She's not going to find one that way."

"Okay, I'll give it a try," Frannie conceded. "Couldn't hurt."

I had been joking about the idea, but Frannie was right, it couldn't hurt.

Chapter 3

If, like most of us, you're not a cat psychic, you may still be able to understand what your cat is thinking. Body language—eyes, ears, whiskers and tail—convey many messages of their own.

Special Agent Denny Paris was already in the foster office by the time I got back. Through the large display window that looked in from the spacious lobby, I studied the young officer. He was tall and sturdy, immaculate aside from a few brown curls escaping from under his NHS baseball cap. In his uniform, he looked like any other cop until you got to the face. There was a sparkle to his cat-green eyes and an optimism in his handsome countenance that belied the usual hardened police crust. Here was a man who believed he could make a difference, and with good reason. Denny and his team, Frank Dawson and Connie Lee, investigated over a thousand cases each year throughout the Pacific Northwest.

Denny and I got to know each other last summer when he helped me straighten out a bogus murder charge by tracking down the real killer, but I still called him by his official title of Special Agent, partly because I liked the sound of it and partly because he deserved the respect, every little bit.

Denny was head to head with Kerry. As I opened the door, he was saying, "...another homicide. That makes three."

"I know," Kerry answered. "You never think that sort

of thing can happen so close to home, do you?"

"And the method, it's like something out of Law & Order: Grisly Victim's Unit."

"Hi, guys," I said, feeling a little like I was interrupting. "Everything okay?"

The two looked up guiltily. "Oh, Denny and I were just talking about the news. Bad news, of course."

I waited for her to elaborate, but she smiled passively, lips tightly shut.

I looked at Denny. "Special Agent Paris, good to see you again. How are you doing?"

"Good, Lynley." He smiled, but his thumbs remained looped in his utility belt, a signal that he was running in one hundred percent official mode.

Kerry stepped out from behind her desk. A medium-sized carrier hunched on the laminated surface, and she ran a loving hand over it. I peered in through the grid door and saw two huge blue eyes staring back at me. The pupils were widely dilated so I blinked a reassuring cat smile and backed off, not wanting to push the greeting.

"Is this Meow?" I asked unnecessarily.

Kerry picked up a sheaf of papers and tamped them on the desk. "That's him. He's a beautiful cat and I think he'd be really very loving, if only..."

Denny held up a hand. "Whoa now. Let's not get ahead of ourselves here, Kerry. We have no assurance this cat can ever be resocialized."

"Why?" I asked. "Is he feral?" I gave another glance through the grid, checking out a dark brown nose, wide brown ears and those deep blue eyes, so dark as to be almost purple. "He looks Siamese to me."

Kerry and Denny looked at each other.

"Looks can be deceiving."

* * *

For the next half hour, Denny and Kerry went over Meow and his special circumstances, but when I came away, carrier, fluid bag, and supply of special cat food in hand, I knew little more than I had going in. The three-year-old male wasn't sick, but for some reason, he wasn't eating, hadn't had a thing for at least two days. He wasn't drinking either, hence the fluid bag; I would be giving him subcutaneous fluids until he decided to take water on his own.

Meow was what breeders call a traditional, or Applehead Siamese, a muscular, athletic cat with a round head unlike the modern Siamese which tend to be long and lanky with a head like a pointy shovel. It still wasn't clear if he were actually pedigreed or merely purebred. Apparently he was part of a case against a breeder, but he didn't look neglected or abused so I didn't know what the problem was, and Denny had elected not to enlighten me. My job was to try to get him eating again so he would live long enough to tell his story, whatever that may be.

Before I'd even made it through the front door, I heard my phone ringing. It was the land line in the kitchen, so I guessed it was either a sales pitch, a wrong number, or someone I knew only formally; my friends called on my cell. I said a quick hello to Little who was waiting on the side table like a tiny panther and shuffled my burden to the kitchen. Depositing Meow's carrier on the dining table where he wouldn't be bothered by my own feline welcoming—and sometimes not welcoming—committee, I picked up the handset.

I fully expected to hear the pause and click of a recorded message, but it was Fiona, event coordinator for the Clan MacKay Society of which I'm a proud member.

My mother is a Mackey, one of the variations on the clan name, and I had been brought up from an early age to cherish my Scottish heritage, kilts, pipes, haggis and all. Well, maybe not the haggis, but I did like steel-cut oats and Finnan haddie; bagpipes made me cry; and I won't even begin to say how much I loved a braw Scotsman in a kilt.

The second I heard her soft highland "Ged afternoon," I knew what she was calling about.

"I didn't forget," I fudged. "The pot-luck tonight at the Scottish Rite Hall. I've been looking forward to it."

"Ye put your name down tae help set up, if ye recall. Shall we say five-thirty?"

I looked at the Kit-Kat clock wagging its metronomic tail on the wall. That would give me just enough time to get Meow squared away and run to the deli for a salad. "That would be fine, Fiona."

"Come to the back, now mind ye. Geordie will be lettin' you in. I appreciate the help."

"No problem. I'm not going to be able to stay for the presentation though. I have a new foster cat who needs to settle."

There was a pause. "Ye'n your moggies, Lynley!" She gave a little chortle. "But Alistair will be doin' the recording so you can purchase the CD if you care to. Seumus MacKay is tellin' the tale of his ancestors' migration to the New World in 1736."

"I'll be sorry to miss that," I said sincerely, having enjoyed tracing my own Scots ancestry back several generations. "Definitely put me down for a CD."

"Just tell Alistair when ye come in. He'll be handling all the sales."

"Okay, Fiona. See you soon," I said to the hang-up click on the other end. I sighed. Fiona McGillis McKay was a busy woman, but she got things done, and I wouldn't want to trade places with her. The Portland faction of the Clan MacKay was a large and demanding group if the breadth of her martyrdom was any indication.

I heard a light knock at the front door, then a screen door click and a "halloo" as footsteps crossed the hardwood floor.

"You left your front door open," said Halle as she ambled into the kitchen. "I thought you knew better, Lyn."

I gave her a little hug. "I do, but the phone was ringing."

"Ah, the ever-demanding social network. Still, hon, you of all people should know to be careful. You don't know who might take that as an invitation to come in."

I nodded in contrition. She was right; though the Mt. Tabor district was a relatively nice part of Portland, one never knew what crazies lurked among the Victorian homes and century-old arbors. "I know I'm early, but I didn't have time to go home after work so I figured I'd kill a few minutes with my clan mate. Catch up on things," Halle said, shedding her coat and seating herself comfortably in one of the mission oak dining chairs. "If you're busy, just pretend I'm not here."

I smiled. That was just like Halle; with her expansive personality she was about as ignorable as a tiger.

Halle MacKay Pratt was a sixty-eight-year-old semi-retired criminal lawyer. She always dressed meticulously, though in manly fashion as befitted her sexual preference. Today she was sporting a red Gaultier suit, white silk shirt, and a fine pair of Clark boots. The crimson wool clashed slightly with her flame-red spiked hair, and on her short and stocky frame, made her look a little like a beach ball, but one well-dressed and formidable beach ball all the same.

"Coffee?" I asked. "Or tea? I think we have time."

Halle fished in her pocket and pulled out her cell phone, a state-of-the-art contraption that probably did everything but her laundry. "We've got an hour and a few. How about tea? Earl Grey if you have it."

She knew I did. "I need to be there a little early. Fiona's enlisted me to help set up."

"Lucky you."

I put the kettle on and gathered the tea things on a floral tray. "Can you watch while I put Meow in the kennel room?" I gestured toward the carrier.

Halle raised a lavish eyebrow. "Meow? That's original." She peeked into the gloom of the carrier, began to stretch out a hand and then thought better of it.

"Meow's only a part of his name, but I don't remember the rest. He's not sick, just depressed. I'll be right back. It shouldn't take long."

Grabbing the carrier and a few cans of food, different flavors in hopes of exciting his appetite, I made for the back of the house. The old Victorian had five bedrooms, and I'd turned this one into a kitty care unit, complete with a bay window that looked out onto the garden and a large kennel where I could house a new cat until it got used to its situation.

Cats don't take change well, and they like to start small. In a few days, Meow would be ready to explore, but for now, a soft bed, a litter box, a scratcher, food, and a few toys were all he needed. He could watch the birds or the clouds or the stars, safe and warm, from inside his very own space.

At least that's the way it usually worked; Meow had a different idea. Before I'd even got the carrier open, he threw his muscled body against the latch and leapt to freedom. I was so surprised that all I could do was stand in horror watching him rampage around the room. Luckily I'd closed the door behind me, but he gave the small area a thorough going over in a matter of a minute: under the counter; in and out of the towel shelves; up the boxes in the closet, and over top of the kennel. Suddenly I realized what the term *climbing the walls* really meant.

I thought about trying to catch him mid-flight but knew that would just scare him even more and possibly send me running for the first aid kit, so I stood quietly while he got it out of his system. I hoped he wouldn't end up wedged behind the dresser or ensconced in one of the high cubbies that ringed the old-fashioned Victorian ceiling at the good height of thirteen feet.

"Meow dear," I said gently. "Settle down now. You're safe. Whatever bad things happened to you will never happen again, I promise."

As Meow continued to fling himself from wall to wall with no sign of slowing down, I suddenly recalled my new communication training. Closing my eyes and taking a deep breath, I recited the mantra that's supposed to clear the psychic path between our two minds. I exuded good thoughts, quiet thoughts, thoughts of naps and sleeping.

Cracking an eyelid, I looked to see if my soothing attempts were having any effect on the subject. Both eyes popped open, and I gave a gasp as I saw a sandy blur coming straight for me, claws extended, ears flat back, and mouth open in a wide, toothy hiss. Instinctively I stepped aside, then realized I hadn't been the Siamese's target after all. He landed on all fours in the cat kennel, gave himself a little shake, then stalked purposefully to the bed and lay down, blinking his huge blue eyes in all innocence.

"Wow!" I gasped. "You okay now? Feel better I hope?" Cautiously I held out my hand for him to sniff, then, passing the test, petted him gently on his head. His fur was soft as the finest silk. I became a little bolder as he began to purr, finally ending up in a pet-fest that was enjoyed by all. As I cracked two cans of food, one a thick, pungent pâté and the other shredded free-range chicken in an aromatic gravy, I felt like we had made progress, and it didn't bother me one bit that it almost certainly had had nothing to do with telepathy.

Chapter 4

Siamese cats have many defining characteristics, but one of the most legendary is their voice. Siamese are thought to have a distinct "vocabulary." When upset or seeking attention, their loud wail is sometimes compared to that of a human baby.

Since I'd spent so much time with Meow, Halle had made the tea and we drank it on the fly. My own cats were sulking as they always do when I bring home a new foster. Though they had not yet seen the intruder, they could smell him, and in this case, hear him as well. When I got back from the dinner, I'd have to spend some quality time with them to prove their authority was not about to be usurped by an alien.

Halle drove in her Maserati Quattroporte since she also planned an early night. We breezed by the Hawthorne Deli where I jumped out to grab an antipasto salad—the best in town with pepperoncini, mozzarella balls, and big strips of cotto salami—while she cruised around the block. We were a few minutes late arriving at the Scottish Rite Center, but now that there were two of us, setting up the chairs and tables for the potluck went extra fast. We were done in time to get drinks from the no-host bar—beer with a Jack back for Halle and ginger ale for me since I had drunk my life's allotment of booze earlier in my career—and chat with friends as they arrived.

The delicacies began to amass on the sideboard: meats, casseroles, soups and salads, and an assortment of desserts that would be the envy of any bakery. At seven o'clock on the dot, Fiona stepped up to the podium. She adjusted the microphone upward to accommodate her lofty height, then gave a smile so brief one might have missed it with the blink of an eye.

"Welcome, Clan MacKay. I'm so pleased ye could all be here t'night."

Fiona was dressed in full Scottish raiment: the long skirt and sash in the MacKay colors—green, blue, and black—and a white cotton blouse. Her sash was pinned with the largest clan crest brooch I'd ever seen. I could almost read the MacKay motto, *Manu Forti* (With a Strong Hand), from where I sat several tables away. There was a huge green cut stone set into the hilt of the crest sword, and it was hypnotizing the way it caught the light. I have to admit that watching those emerald facets twinkle, I'd totally lost track of what Fiona was saying.

Suddenly and to my absolute embarrassment, my phone rang. I nearly jumped out of my seat trying to pull the thing out of my purse and silence the trill of church bells that was my ringtone, but it was too late. Fiona ceased mid-sentence and glared at me, as she had every right to do.

"Sorry," I whimpered. "Forgot to shut it off I guess."

All eyes were on me as I muted the ringer and glanced at the caller's name. With a start, I saw it was Patty Herbert, my young next-door neighbor. There was absolutely no reason for her to call unless something was wrong at home, so with another round of apologies, I made my way out of the dining room to the empty foyer where I could talk freely.

"Hello?" I said cautiously. "Patty? What is it?"

"Oh, Lynley!" the soft voice moaned. "I didn't think

you were going to answer."

"I'm here," I said. "What's going on? Is there a problem?"

"Well, I don't know. I wasn't sure whether to call you. I tried your home phone. I thought you might be there, considering and all... but no one answered. It may be nothing, but..." Her energy fizzled.

"But what?" I said as patiently as I could with adrenaline shooting through my every vein.

"Well..." There was a pause. "Here, listen."

Her end of the line went quiet and then I began to hear it, an eerie wailing. As it grew closer, I knew.

No, it wasn't banshees in the night or someone being strangled; it was the howl of a Siamese cat in distress. Though it sounded like the poor thing was being tortured, I knew from experience it could just as easily be a case of loneliness, frustration, or hunger.

The wails cut off. "Did you hear it, Lynley?"

"Yeah. Where are you?"

"I'm standing outside your house." She hesitated. "Lynley?" she asked tremulously. "What is that awful noise?"

She sounded so frightened I almost had to laugh, but that would have been callous. Patty, as much as she liked cats, had very little working knowledge of them, having only recently come on as my part-time cat sitter. She had been an enthusiastic and fast learner, but screaming Siamese were a lesson we hadn't come across until now.

"It's okay, Patty. What you're hearing is the very vocal complaints of a Siamese. It's my new foster cat. There's probably nothing really wrong, but thanks for letting me know. You did the right thing. I'm at a dinner, but I'll be home as soon as I can get a cab."

"Do you want me to do anything? I still have your key."

"If you don't mind, could you go inside? He's in the kennel room at the back of the house. His name is Meow. Just make sure he hasn't got caught in something or hurt himself. Talk to him, but don't try to touch him. I'll be right there. And Patty," I added, "thanks again. I really appreciate it."

When I returned to my table, the speech was over; everyone had served themselves and had begun to eat. The food smelled delicious, but alas, for me it was not to be. I scooched in beside Halle and took a calming swig of ginger ale, setting the glass down a little too loudly.

Halle took one look at my face. "Problem?"

"I have to go home. Cat emergency. But don't worry, I can just pick up a taxi."

"No need, hon. I don't mind ducking out early. I really shouldn't have come at all; I have a deposition in a criminal case first thing tomorrow morning, and I still have to get my questions straight. I'll probably be up half the night as it is."

"Oh, no, I don't want to inconvenience you."

She wiped her mouth with the maroon cloth napkin and pushed out her chair. "No bother, just give me a minute."

"Well, if you're sure. I need to go make my apologies to Fiona or I'll never hear the end of it. Meet you up front?"

I gathered my coat and purse and looked forlornly at my empty plate. I found Fiona at the head table and briefly explained my circumstances.

"Weel, my dear, we'll miss ye and hope tha the next time you'll be stayin' a bit longer."

"Oh, I'm sure I will. I still want to get a CD of the

presentation, of course."

"Since you've got the wee emergency, ye can jist give me the money and I'll place your order with Alistair. That will be ten dollars."

Rummaging in my purse, I pulled out a ten, which I thought was a bit expensive for a home-made CD, but I knew it went for a good cause; it wasn't cheap to keep the seven-hundred-year-old Scots clan alive and well in Portland, Oregon.

As if she could read my thoughts, Fiona said, "Now that includes postage right to your door, mind you." She snatched the bill and tucked it into her bodice, a move straight out of a romance novel. I wondered what the handsome Alistair would think of the retrieval; Fiona was a lovely woman even if she was nearing fifty. But then Alistair was no spring chicken either.

Halle came up, a paper carryout box in each hand. She gave me one and shouldered her purse.

"What's this?" I asked in surprise.

"Can't go home without our supper," she said. "Isn't that right, Fiona?"

Fiona stuttered a surprised but positive reply.

"Ready?"

"Yes, thanks, Halle. Sorry, Fiona. I'll talk to you soon I'm sure."

As we walked out of the old hall and into the crisp winter night, I gazed up at the moon, nearly full and ringed with a crystalline umbra. It seemed the epitome of cold. I snuggled inside my woolen coat, but the chill wouldn't quit. I knew it was impossible, but on the sweeping, frozen breeze, I thought I heard the echo of a Siamese wail.

* * *

When we reached my house, all was quiet as a country lane. Halle let me off and waited considerately until I was inside before screeching away to her own destiny. All the lights were on, but aside from that, things seemed just as I had left them only an hour ago.

Patty came into the living room from the back, followed by her husband, Jim. The struggling but optimistic professional couple lived in the apartments next door and had proved a lifesaver when it came to emergency cat-sitting. Patty, young and kitten-like herself, seemed to have an instant rapport with the cats. Jim wasn't so sure-footed, but he supported his wife completely, and together they made a good team.

"Oh, I'm so glad you're back, Lynley!" she burst out. "He's stopped now. We looked in on him and couldn't see anything wrong, but I didn't want to take any chances."

"He sounded like he was dying," Jim put in. "Or worse!"

"I'm so sorry," I said as I dropped my things on the couch and headed for Meow's room. "Siamese can be unpredictable. And I only got Meow from the shelter today. It's my fault—I shouldn't have gone out until I knew he was going to be okay."

I stopped mid-stride, looking around for members of my own brood. There was not a cat in sight.

"Oh, your kitties are all fine," said Patty, catching my concern. "I really couldn't do anything for the new one beyond making sure he wasn't hurt, so I spent some time with the others. Little, Red, and Fluffs are on the bed in a big pile." She began counting off her fingers—one, two, three. "Violet's in the kitchen on her pillow; Solo's under the couch as usual." Four, five. "Tinkerbelle's on the back porch, looking out the window." Six. "Harry was a little restless so I let him out into the backyard. I know it's completely cat-fenced so I figured that was alright, even if it is after dark." Seven. She closed her palm with a sigh of relief at getting them all.

"Thanks so much for doing that. You really are good with them. Another person might not have noticed."

Patty smiled with the praise.

"Oh, I'm pretty sure someone would have noticed Mr. Meow screaming his head off," Jim said. "You're lucky the police didn't show up thinking there was a murder being committed!" The young man laughed nervously, unsure if it were a joke or not.

The doorbell rang, a nasty, jangly nineteen-forties clamor that made me jump every time.

"Oh, that might be your friend, Frannie. I called her when I couldn't get hold of you, before I reached your cell. I hope that was okay. It really did seem like an emergency at the time."

In the quiet hominess that surrounded us now, it was hard to imagine the urgency, but I took her word for it. When it came to my cats, better safe than sorry.

"That was a good idea," I assured her on my way to open the door. "But I think we can take it from here."

"Everything okay?" Frannie asked worriedly. She must have come from the shelter because she was still wearing her green volunteer apron.

"I think so. It was a Siamese incident, my new foster making a ruckus. You know how they can be."

"Well, we'll be off then," Patty said. "I'm glad everything's fine."

"Thanks again for calling me. I really owe you one. Hopefully Meow will settle down now and we won't have any more episodes."

The four of us indulged in a few minutes of easy, non-cat-related conversation before the Herberts said their final goodnight. By the time Frannie and I finally got in to see the wayward Meow, he was fast asleep in his bed, a seal-brown paw covering a seal-brown nose, the picture of innocence. I turned out the light and we tiptoed out of there before he had a chance to wake up again, as if he were a napping baby.

"You might as well have a cup of tea for your efforts," I told Frannie. I was feeling a little guilty about Patty calling her over, but Frannie didn't seem to mind.

The sound of the kettle must have roused Little and Red, because they appeared out of thin air thinking it was dinnertime. Violet always thought it was dinnertime; even though her strict special diet had got her down a couple of pounds, she was still a big girl with an appetite to match. Tinkerbelle haunted my feet like a rotund black shadow. Harry returned from his outside adventure and demanded I come up with a round of nutritious treats for all.

"Where's Fraulein Fluffs?" Frannie asked. She had a special love for the elderly cat who continued to defy her dubious prognosis. "Never mind," she said, lifting a tiny gray form off the chair where she had been about to sit and resettling it on her lap. Fluffs gave a little purrumph and lay her head back down as if nothing had happened. Frannie stroked the long fur thoughtfully.

"So what do you think about these murders on the news?" she asked out of the blue.

I broke off pouring hot water into a squat Chinese teapot. "You're the second person I know to bring that up today."

"I'm not surprised. It's got everyone on edge."

Finishing the pot, I brought it, along with two cups and

a tray of shortbread cookies, over to the table. "I really haven't thought that much about it. I don't watch the news—it's always bad. And besides, aren't there always murders in a town this size?"

"Sure, but these are strange, Lynley. They seem to be serial but random. A lawyer, a student, and a homeless man: nothing in common with each other that the police can come up with except for the way they were killed, raked to death with some sort of giant claw. It's like something out of *Criminal Minds*."

I inadvertently shivered. Though I enjoyed the gritty crime drama that often bordered on gruesome fantasy, I wouldn't like to think those things could happen in real life.

For a moment, we both were silent, lost in our thoughts. The room was quiet too, the kind of winter quiet that comes from having all the doors and windows shut tight, closed to the outside world. The furnace clicked on with a cozy hum; the Kit-Kat clock lazily tapped out the seconds; Fluffs sighed a little kitty sigh and fell back to sleep.

Suddenly a chaos of screeches split the night. I leapt to my feet and ran to the window, fully expecting to see a jet screaming out of the sky or an out-of-control car careening through the bushes at the back of my house. The sound came again but this time I placed it.

"Meow!" Frannie and I exclaimed in unison.

We made it to the kennel room in record time, though by now my logical mind was realizing it was probably nothing but noise. And sure enough, when I switched on the light, there he was in all his Siamese glory, sitting up in his bed, wailing up a storm.

"Meow!" I said loudly, then softened my tone. "Meow dear sweetie cat..."

I flipped the latch and began to open the kennel. "Frannie, close that door behind you. This one is a runner."

Frannie shut the door, and just in time, too; Meow had seen his chance and pushed out of the kennel contemplating a repeat of his earlier rampage. This time he skipped the lower regions and went straight to the top of the floor-to-ceiling shelves. Burrowing into a tiny space between a row of shoe boxes labeled *Taxes*, he turned, gave us a withering stare, and began the yowling all over again.

I looked at Frannie. "This has got to stop."

"Any ideas?" she asked.

"Wait here, I'll get the step ladder."

I slipped out of the room, fast so the wayward Siamese couldn't zoom through behind me, but he seemed perfectly content where he was, if you can call howling his heart out the mark of contentment. I knew at the bottom of that disturbing behavior lurked something terrible. I felt confident that if I could just get him to feel safe, the behavior would diminish and hopefully desist, at least until he went back to the shelter. I wasn't going to think about that right now; one step at a time, and this step was up a ladder where I could try to soothe him and bring him down.

When I came back, I gave a soft knock on the door to make sure he wasn't about to bolt as I entered. He had quit crying, I noted, so maybe this wouldn't be so hard after all.

"Come on in," Frannie said in a whisper, "but you don't need the ladder. At least not right now."

I set it aside and cautiously opened the door where I stopped in my tracks.

"I think it's okay, but I wouldn't leave that door open if I were you. Don't want to give him any ideas."

I did as she suggested, then stared wide-eyed at the

scene of peaceful domesticity before me.

Frannie was seated in the rocking chair with Meow on her lap. The big Siamese was purring so loudly I could hear him from across the room. He was rubbing his chocolate sideburn against Frannie's hand in apparent ecstasy. His ears were forward, his eyes squinted closed, and his lips curved into a smile; it could have been a whole different cat.

"Wow," I commented, sinking onto the footstool beside Frannie. "What happened?"

"I'm not sure. I just sort of started the communication mantra, to see if I could get anything from him, and before I knew it, he stopped yelling. He stared at me for a moment, then jumped down and curled around my ankles. When I sat in the chair, he hopped up. You can see the rest."

I reached over and petted the dark brown head. The big Siamese leaned into it with a resurgence of purrs. "So what did you do with Meow, Frannie? You've obviously switched cats on me."

She laughed and shook her head. "I can't explain it."

"You don't have to—he's a cat, after all. Privileged to act any way he pleases. I'm just glad you got him calmed down."

I gazed at the beautiful purebred. Now I'm not into breed cats for two reasons, the first being that there are about a zillion unwanted cats in the country already, and in my opinion, people should take care of those before they start creating more. My second concern had to do with what breeding for show does to the species, creating undesirable traits along with the desired. Persians for instance, who are bred to have that flat, squished face, are prone to tear duct overflow and conjunctivitis. Siamese tend to have neurotic temperaments, as displayed by our own specimen, Meow. But there was no denying how gorgeous he was.

"Did you get anything?" I said abruptly.

"Get what?"

"Anything from Meow? Any contact?"

"Oh, no, not really. Once he settled down, I quit trying."

I smiled mischievously at the woman. "Want to try it again?"

Chapter 5

It is important that a cat doesn't suddenly stop eating. In a very short time, the lack of food can start the body sending fat cells to the liver, causing it to become clogged and begin to fail. This is known as Fatty Liver Disease.

"That's amazing!" I exclaimed.

"Well, that's what the cat told me," Frannie chuckled.

"Oh. Yeah. Right." Who could say how accurate this Frannie-Meow communication may have been?

Frannie and I had taken ourselves into the living room where I served her a much-needed cup of tea. Meow had zonked out after the session, and it looked as though Frannie would like to do the same. I was tired myself; it was nearly midnight, but the fact that Frannie had come up with something solid from the big Siamese was endlessly fascinating.

Frannie slumped on the couch, head back, staring up at the ceiling. I sat at the other end with Harry on my lap. Since it was winter, he had taken to setting himself as close to a living body as possible; later in the year when the weather got warmer, he'd retire to his fleece donut on the floor or his cubby by the television set, but for now, we both enjoyed this seasonal affection.

"So what was it like?" I pushed one more time. Okay, I'll admit it—I was a little jealous of Frannie's casual success with animal communication. We had both been to the same seminar, after all, but I had yet to get a telepathic peep out of a cat where she was already sharing their deep dark secrets. I couldn't quite see that as fair. On the other hand, I felt lucky to have her help with Meow; otherwise I'd still be at square one.

"I told you. It was only flashes and feelings. The one scene that came across the strongest was a barnlike building, but huge—maybe a warehouse of some kind." She closed her eyes, as if to catch the phantom image. "Big and isolated, out in the boonies," she said slowly. "It seems to be abandoned—wait, no! I can see a sign..." Her brows knit and she frowned. "P-e-n-d-l... Pendleton? Pendleton Mill, maybe? The sign looks old and some of the letters are gone, but that would fit the spaces."

Frannie's eyes popped open, and she sat up. "I recognize it now!" she exclaimed. "It's the old Pendleton Woolen Mill, over near Mt. Hood. Mother used to take us there to buy our school uniforms."

"Everyone went there back in the day. My mum bought wool remnants to make clothes for the family. A long drive but pennies on the dollar for Pendleton products and closer than the town of Pendleton where the main factory was located. But that place closed years ago when the new building went up here in Portland."

Frannie sighed and shrugged. "It's what I saw."

"Don't take this wrong, Fran, but how do you know your flash isn't just a memory of your visits when you were a child?"

She leaned forward thoughtfully. "Well, Lynley, it's hard to explain. This felt different than a memory, that's all I can tell you. And it wasn't just the image itself; there was the perspective, too, as if I were looking up from a very low angle. I would have had to be flat on my stomach to have viewed it that way. Or small."

"Perhaps cat-sized?"

She nodded. "Then there was the feeling that went along with it," she said with a shudder. "A horrible feeling. Not like anything I've ever experienced before."

I scratched Harry's ears, soft as velvet though for the most part he was a coarse-furred cat. "Can you describe it?"

She looked at me sheepishly. "Do I have to?"

"No, but it might help to get it out."

"I guess you're right." She deliberated for a moment, then stood and crossed to the window, taking her teacup with her. As she stared out at the bleak winter rain streaking across the feeble glow of the street light, she began. "The only thing I can call it is palpable terror. As if fear was something you could taste and feel; a gas that choked your lungs and gagged your throat and made your fur prickle."

I wondered at her reference to fur but didn't want to interrupt her train of thought.

"A noxious liquid in which you were drowning," she went on. "A pressing, squeezing weight, slowly pushing down into the filthy, tainted ground."

She swung around, the fear still reflected in her face. "Heavens, Lynley, I don't know. If that poor cat experienced anything like what he was sending to me, I feel awful for him."

"I need to find out more about his circumstances. All I got out of Denny was that Meow was part of an investigations case. Maybe if I tell him about this, he'll be a little more forthcoming."

Frannie laughed. "Tell Denny Paris what the cat says? I don't know about that. Besides, it could be all my imagination. The workshop was..." She hesitated. "Wow, was that just this morning? Seems longer. But still, it's not like I've really done this before."

"La Zoe said some people are just naturals. Maybe you're one of those."

"You believe I actually connected with him?"

"Don't you?"

Frannie didn't answer right away, then in a barely audible whisper, she said, "Yes."

She returned to the couch and sat heavily, as if she weighed a thousand pounds. Both of us were beyond words. The minutes stretched out as the clock struck midnight. Big Red stalked into the room, saw someone was occupying his place on the couch and stalked back out again; Fluffs gave a little twitch to remind us she was there.

"You want to go check it out?" I asked.

"What?" Frannie replied.

I stared at her and smiled.

"You mean, to the old mill? What would you hope to find?"

I shrugged. "I don't know. But we have to start somewhere, don't we? If someone made Meow feel the way you described, then something needs to be done."

"Yes, certainly, but..."

"Just think about it, okay? And call me tomorrow afternoon. I should have had time to talk to Denny or at least Kerry by then."

Frannie looked thoughtful and then shook her head; her platinum curls, which had been looking a little weary after the night's work, immediately sprang back to perfection. "I'll think about it, but no promises. It's been a long day. Right now I feel like I could sleep for a week."

She got up and looked around for her bag, found it stashed under the coffee table, and slung it over her shoulder.

"Oh, and Lynley, you might want to take a look at Meow's tail. I felt a rough patch at the base. Did Kerry say anything about that when you picked him up?"

"No, she only talked about his not eating."

"Well, you might want to get someone to check it out. It felt funny."

"Funny how?"

She shrugged. "Just... not right."

* * *

After Frannie left, I rushed to the kennel room to check out this mysterious tail ailment. Frannie was not a vet, but she knew when something was off with a cat.

Meow was still in his bed. He cracked one cobalt eye when I came in but there was no panic in it.

"Hi, Meow," I crooned in the soft, melodic kitty-speak that promised my intentions were harmless.

I noted with a leap of joy that his kibbles had diminished, and the bowl of pâté was halfway gone. The level of his water had shrunk as well; the fact that he was eating and drinking on his own after only a few hours away from the shelter was beyond promising. It took everything I had not to call Kerry immediately with the good news, but though I knew she would be as pleased as I was, she would be more pleased if I didn't wake her in the middle of the night.

Besides, I had a tail to check.

Gently I massaged the Siamese in little circular motions, beginning at his head and working my way down; that way I could feel for lumps, bumps, and anything else that hid underneath the lush fur. Around his left ear I felt something, a sticky coarseness that should have been totally foreign to a Siamese. I continued on, planning to come back to it later and have a look. The long back bone was smooth and the underside as well, but when I came to the base of the tail where the seal-brown fur began and right where Frannie had said it would be, I found the same discrepancy. It didn't feel like a wound, just something sticky that had got into the fur. I smelled my fingers, thinking it might have been pitch. There was a faint order, not of pitch however, but of paint.

I switched on the high-wattage overhead light, and Meow blinked accusingly at me.

"It's for your own good," I told him. He turned away with that *que sera, sera* look that cats do so well.

On examining the ear and tail, first with my naked eye and then with a magnifying glass, I was left at a loss. The young cat had definitely got himself into something he shouldn't have but it didn't seem to bother him. It would probably wear off in time, but I figured I'd ask Kerry about it in the morning when I dropped by to tell her Meow was eating. I also planned to discuss Frannie's revelations and find out if there was anything she could add to the story. Maybe the strange substance had a connection to where Meow had been before he was stray.

"Okay, sweetie. I promise not to bother you any more tonight. Sleep well." I refilled his kibbles, topped off his water, and flicked off the lights.

As I turned to leave, I saw out of the corner of my eye a shadow flit across the window. I started. The kennel faced my back garden which was completely surrounded by a high, cat-proof fence that was latched from the inside; no one should have been there. For a moment I froze in place, then I leapt over to the pitch-dark glass and stared outside. In the glimmer of the street light I could see the pool of ragged grass, the spikes of spent summer flowers, and the skeletons of trees and bushes. On the climbing rose, a last few brown blossoms clung for dear life. In a shadowed corner by the garage crouched a hulking shape, but after a short zing of trepidation, I realized it was only the compost barrel.

I snorted. "Nothing there," I said to Meow, more to convince myself than him.

I left the room, closing the door behind me. In the gloom, the Siamese turned unblinking blue eyes toward the night.

Chapter 6

Tortoiseshell cats are often gifted with something affectionately known as tortitude. *The tri-colored females tend to be extremely sensitive to stimuli. Noise, action, even the touch of a hand can suddenly become too much for them, at which time they may lash out like the little divas they purport to be.*

The next day blossomed into one of those crisp winter mornings that make Oregonians break out of their wet, soggy fog and come alive. The sun was bright, and the air was so clear it sparkled. Mt. Hood was visible in the east, a majestic reminder that the city living in its shadow was just borrowing space, an alien sprawl in the magnificence of its natural surroundings.

In spite of the late night, I was up at daybreak and off to the shelter. I liked being there before the public when doors that were kept closed and locked during the day were propped open wide while energetic cattery staff flitted around feeding cats, cleaning kennels, and giving medications. There was the buzz of happy chatter and the trill of laughter. Somewhere in the back, a radio played; I recognized the tinkly sound of salsa music though not the song itself.

Friends of Felines cat shelter is very modern, having wisely used grant and donation monies to the very best of its ability. There was a large, airy lobby with a glass-enclosed kitten room where patrons could watch the ever-fascinating antics of baby cats at play. The cattery itself was a bank of spacious kennels encircling an inner office so cats could be viewed from the outside and accessed from the inside by employees and volunteers.

On my arrival, I liked to make the rounds, see old friends—feline, that is—and check out who had come in since my last visit. I stopped by Xena's kennel, but she was asleep, and I thought it best to let sleeping cats lie, especially ones as feisty as Xena.

A new face peered out at me from the space next door, another tortoiseshell, and I wondered briefly about the wisdom of putting the two torties in such close proximity. Tortoiseshells tend to be divas and often don't play well with others, especially others of their breed. Still I had to admit the two looked impressive together.

The newbie's name according to her kennel card was Carlotta Que, most likely a product of cattery staff. They had the job of naming the strays, and with several hundred per year, their imaginations were taxed. Often they would go with a theme—cheeses for example. I remember last month we had a tuxedo cat named Roquefort, a red tabby named Cheddar, a white called Philly, and a husky Russian Blue they tagged with Gorgonzola. The month before that it was classic movie stars: Betty Grable, Kirk Douglas, Lana Turner and such. Sometimes it seemed like they were stretching the envelope—I mean, who would want their cat stuck with a name like *Princess Sara von Sassy Kat*? Why they just didn't ask us volunteers for some input I could never understand, but there seemed to be some unwritten edict that names were the sole privilege of staff.

"Hello, Carlotta," I said to the new cat, omitting the "Que" on general principles. Opening the kennel door, I let her sniff my hand, then when she accepted me, smoothing her sideburn along my proffered fingers, I petted her head gently. I ran my hand down her back once or twice but didn't press my luck. Torties can be unpredictable given the sensitivity of their fur.

From Carlotta's kennel, I could see down the hall to the foster office. Kerry was just getting to work, a heavy pack slung across her shoulder and her arms loaded with files. I said goodbye to C. Q. and caught Kerry at the door, unlocking it with my badge.

"Thanks, Lynley," Kerry puffed as she dropped her load onto the desk. "This may be a paperless society, but word hasn't reached FOF yet!"

"Are all those foster cases?"

"Yup," she nodded.

"Wow, I had no idea there were so many."

"There are probably as many cats in foster at any given time as there are cats up for adoption. Most are recovering from an illness or a procedure, but these big files here..." She fingered a couple of bulging folders. "...are part of ongoing investigations."

"Like Meow?"

"Like Meow." She paused and smiled but her eyes remained serious. "How's he doing?"

Well, she asked, so I told her. She was thrilled to hear he had begun to eat but became a little concerned when I filled her in on the cat fits, and downright skeptical when I mentioned the outcome of Frannie's session. I don't blame her. As I told the story that had seemed so feasible in the wee hours of the night, I saw that in the light of day it was more than slightly farfetched.

"I can't say about any of that," she told me diplomatically when I had finished my tale, "but here's what I do know. Meow is one of a group of cats who might be involved in a serious scam. Someone out there is simulating breed cats, falsifying their papers and selling them for hundreds to thousands of dollars to unsuspecting entrepreneurs in the show market."

I leaned against her desk. My back hurt and I hadn't even done anything yet; one of the curses of age. "How can you fake a breed cat? Anyone in the business must be able to tell the difference by the markings." I stopped to think. "Wait a minute. Can the markings be touched up? Painted?"

"Exactly." She dug through the pile of files and came up with an orange folder. Inside was a sheaf of eight-by-ten glossies, close-ups of cats and fur details. She rifled through them until she found a grainy black-and-white. I recognized it as a microscope shot.

"What am I looking at?" I asked as I studied the page.

"The scammers are using a complex type of dye to touch up near-perfect specimens and pass them off as their stock. It's incredibly toxic—the smell alone is carcinogenic and has been linked to lung cancer—but it's cheap and long-lasting. Once on, there is no solvent that can remove it without damaging the hair itself. The dyed parts have to be shaved and a pharmaceutical compound applied where it's seared into the skin. Luckily, it doesn't cause lasting damage to the hair follicles and the naturally colored fur eventually grows back on its own.

"I think we found some on Meow."

"Around the ears and tail?"

I nodded. "You said it was toxic. Will it hurt him when he grooms?"

Kerry's dark eyebrows furrowed. "Dr. Angela doesn't think so. It's worst in its liquid form. Breathing it when it's applied is where it does the damage."

"So you knew about the dye? How come you didn't

treat it?"

"It was a difficult call. Meow was so traumatized, we would have had to put him under just to shave, and Dr. Angela didn't think that was a good idea if we could possibly avoid it. There's always a risk with anesthesia, you know. We hoped a few days with you would make a difference, and it looks like it has. You can bring him back whenever you think he's ready and we'll take care of it."

I pictured Meow flying around the room like a tiny cyclone. "Will it hurt him to wait a little while longer?"

"No. We want him to be relaxed. Check in with me tomorrow and we'll set it up some time soon." She read the doubt in my face. "Only if he's ready, Lynley. A day or so won't make any difference since the damage has already been done."

Kerry stared down at the photos and began to riffle through the big orange file. I started to leave, then turned back.

"So honestly, what do you think about Frannie's vision?" I asked, laying all cards on the table.

Kerry looked up and smiled indulgently. "You know I believe in animal communication. Our own Jennifer has helped a lot with the cats. But one thing I've learned from her—and she's been doing it for years—is that the impressions you get are not necessarily true scenarios or all that factual. Sometimes they are more like metaphors, and cat metaphors at that.

"Still," she added. She ran her fingertips across her desk, then suddenly sat down in front of the computer and began typing like mad. "Still," she mused again.

I tried to follow along on the screen, but she was moving too fast. As one window opened on top of another, then another, I got the gist of what she was searching for but nothing more.

Then she stopped and leaned back in satisfaction. "Special Agent Frank Dawson is in charge of Meow's investigation. He's going to take a look at a possible site later on today. It says here," she grinned, "it's an unused warehouse."

"The old Pendleton Woolen Mill?" I exclaimed.

"Doesn't say. I guess that's classified," she joked, then swung around to face me. "But it could well be. Or as I mentioned, Frannie's images may have been a metaphor for a place with a similar feel."

"Can I go along?"

Kerry gave a little snort. "With Frank? I doubt if he'd let you, but you can try. I can tell him I recommended the ride-along for you as Meow's caretaker."

I wasn't quite sure if she was serious; I doubted being Meow's foster mom would give me much clout in the investigations world, but it might be an edge.

She leaned into the screen again to study the fine print. "Looks like he's set to roll at two o'clock. Want me to send him an email?"

"No, that's okay. I think I'll just surprise him."

"Frank doesn't like surprises," she warned amicably.

"He might like this one," I told her with a wink.

She raised an eyebrow but let it go. Instead she asked, "Do you need anything else for Meow, more food now that he's eating again?"

"He liked that tuna pâté if you have some of that."

"Think so." She clicked an intercom button and asked if someone could bring it up from the back. There was a nebulous, crackly confirmation and a click as they went to search the bowels of the storeroom for those itty bitty cans.

"One thing, Lynley," Kerry said slowly. "If you do end

up going along with Special Agent Dawson, be careful. I don't know much about this case, but Northwest Humane has been tracking these perps for a long time. NHS is working in concert with other states, since apparently these counterfeiters like to move around a lot. They're associated with some instances of violence as well as fraud. I'd hate to see anyone get hurt."

I began to smile but then hesitated as I considered her warning.

A cute young girl in powder-blue scrubs brought in the cat food cans and put them on the desk.

Another foster parent came into the office and began talking to Kerry about a batch of sick kittens.

Dr. Angela breezed through with a cat in a leg cast clutched to her breast.

The phone rang; a beeper beeped.

I was still considering.

Chapter 7

"The Portland metropolitan area has reduced euthanasia in local shelters by 65% from 2006 to 2012, thanks to the efforts of the Animal Shelter Alliance of Portland (ASAP) and their Spay & Save program which alters cats for owners in need of financial assistance. No healthy, social cat or dog has been euthanized since 2010." The Oregon Humane Society

I had a few hours to kill before I planned to show up at Northwest Humane Society and solicit Special Agent Dawson for a ride-along. There were some errands to run: groceries, the pet store, a good sale at Shoes Plus. I crossed off that last; one of my New Year's resolutions was not to buy things made in China unless I absolutely had to, and I knew without looking that Shoes Plus was Chinese import right down to the American Flag shoelaces. Good deals though.

I had just got into my little car, a ten-year-old cherry-red Toyota (made mostly in the USA in spite of the Japanese trademark) when my phone chimed.

"Lynley Cannon?" came an official-sounding voice on the other end. "This is ADT Home Security. We've received notice of a possible break-in at your home. Can you verify your code word?"

The adrenaline shooting through my brain made me draw a blank for a moment. "Attila," I finally spit out, then spelled the name of one of my most notable cats, "A-t-t-i-l-a."

"Thank you, Ms. Cannon. Are you at your house currently?"

"Nnno," I stuttered with predictable panic.

"The police are on their way."

My heart raced. "What should I do?"

"Would it be possible for you to meet the officers at your residence?"

"I can do that. It'll take me about twenty minutes to get there. I'm leaving right now."

A break-in! I revved the motor and beat it out of the FOF parking lot, speeding toward my house on the other side of the city. The police were coming, I told myself. They'd get there long before I would; by the time I was home, it would all be over and everything would be fine. That's what I paid those security people for, I told myself sternly. My lead foot let up a little, but the surging jolts through my nervous system didn't abate one bit. I knew what it was like to be the victim of a home invasion—it had happened to me only months before. I didn't ever want to feel so helpless and violated again in my life.

When I got to my street, two police vehicles were already parked kitty-corner blocking the house. "Officer!" I cried as I leapt out of the car. "What's happening? Did you catch them?"

A surly young man turned, then came toward me. "Are you Lynley Cannon?"

"Yes," I panted.

"Officer Jakes. It looks like someone tried to jimmy a back window."

"Did they get it open?" I blurted, thinking of my cats who could slip through incredibly small gaps if they had a mind to.

"No, they abandoned their attempt when the alarm

went off. Long gone by the time we got here though we have men and cars out searching. Good thing you had security because it's doubtful anyone would've seen them back there in that garden."

"I'm really thankful myself right about now."

"You're going to need to fill out some forms." He nodded toward his patrol vehicle.

"Of course I am," I sighed, relief restoring my sense of humor.

He smiled, a move that transformed his surly countenance into that of a young boy.

I unlocked the front door; I didn't need to punch the security code because that had been turned off at the source. I would need to contact the security company to reset it as soon as we were done with the formalities. Little greeted me with eyes the size of Frisbees; she had been sitting by the window watching my every move and wanted to tell me all about it. I scooped her into my arms and asked Officer Jakes to show me where the man had tried to enter. As I suspected for no good reason except an intuitive flash, he led me straight to the kennel room. Depositing Little in a convenient cat bed, we slipped inside to look.

Jakes leaned into the window and peered outside. "Had to be this one." His gaze turned toward the cat in the kennel who was watching him intently. "Woah!" he exclaimed. "Big Siamese! The intruder probably saw him and thought better of breaking into this room."

I instantly recognized Jakes as a cat person. "This is Meow," I introduced. "I'm fostering him for Friends of Felines Cat Shelter."

"Hey, my wife volunteers there," exclaimed the young officer as he reached out and scratched Meow's sideburns through the grid. "Her name is Beth. Do you know her?"

I shook my head. "I might by sight, but the name doesn't ring a bell. FOF has hundreds of volunteers, you know."

"She mans the phones for the Spay & Save program. I'll have to tell her we met."

"Spay & Save's great!" I said with honest high praise for the inter-shelter program that was helping alter cats for poor people. In just six years, I'd watched their efforts change the face of cat overpopulation without condoning euthanasia as a solution.

"You'd better come on back outside and assess any damage that might have been done," Officer Jakes said, all business again.

He turned, and I followed him. The sun was still out, but I noticed dark gray clouds lurking on the horizon. I remembered something in yesterday's weather forecast about another storm on its way and hoped it would hold off for a few more hours, at least until after the ride-along with Agent Dawson. I don't know why, but the idea of touring a lonely, abandoned warehouse in the dark of a winter storm seemed the epitome of ominousness. Ominicity? I remembered it might well be a moot point if I didn't manage to convince Frank to take me with him.

Officer Jakes and I slid out the back door and into the garden. Around the side of the house, a detective was already measuring and photographing footprints. Sure enough, a huge gouge showed raw in the sash of the storm window where it looked like a crowbar might have been none-too-gently inserted. I reached up and touched the splintered wood as if it were a wound.

"Clumsy job," said the detective, slinging the wide strap of his camera across his shoulder. "And stupid too."

He motioned to the fly screws that held in the removable window. "He coulda just undone the screws and taken this one off. Wouldn't have got him inside but he woulda been a step closer." The older man shook his head. "Idiots!" he grumbled.

"Maybe it was kids," I offered.

He scrutinized me as if he were seeing me for the first time and unsure if he approved of what he saw. "Yeah," he finally said, "but I don't think so." He gave a nod at the gouge. "Too high for kids. Teens, maybe." He shrugged. "Who knows?"

"I hope you do," I said bluntly. "At least I hope you find out."

Again the shrug. "Yeah, whatever." Hefting the camera a little more snugly on his shoulder and cupping a protective hand over the lens, he turned and strode away.

I looked at Officer Jakes, my mouth open.

"Don't pay any attention to Morris there," the young cop said quickly. "What he lacks in people skills, he makes up for in investigational savvy. If anyone can pull some clues out of the information here, it'd be Detective Morris. He's an expert on this stuff."

"Good to know," I conceded, though I didn't see why people had to be rude just because they were experts.

"Don't think it's going to be enough for your insurance to get involved, but you might want to give them a call, a heads up."

"Then again I might not," I replied. "It seems like every time I report something, my premiums go up."

"There is that." Jakes laughed. "Come on back to the car and I'll get that paperwork for you."

"Can you give me a minute?" I asked.

He hesitated, then nodded and left, pushing through

the overgrown ornamentals toward the front of the house. I really need to get out and prune, I told myself, then promptly forgot about it.

Standing quietly in thought, I studied the rough evidence of the attempted assault on my home. That sort of violation gave a horrible feeling that stabbed at the heart of a person's serenity. But as horrible as it was, I couldn't help but think there was something more to it. I looked up at the window, into my dark reflection. Suddenly a pair of eyes appeared, then a face, dim and floating in the ripples of the antique glass. I blinked a cat smile at Mr. Meow and touched the window gently. He just stared as if seeing right through me. He had to have been upset by the noise of the attempted break-in, and I needed to go spend some time with him. It's a lot for a kitty to take on his first day in his new foster home.

I gave the area one last look around: the crushed sword ferns; the boot marks in the dirt; the white wood splinters poking out of the crimson sash like bone protruding from flesh. Now I was getting morbid. Wrapping my arms around myself to ward off a sudden cold gust of wind, I turned and walked back the way I had come.

Meow's eyes followed me; for a moment, he pressed his face to the glass and watched me go. Then he pulled back, ears flat and mouth opened in a fearful, warning hiss.

Chapter 8

Cats depend on their sense of smell for survival, to sniff out food and mates, and to alert them to danger or potential enemies. A cat's sense of smell is about fourteen times as powerful as a human's; they have twice as many scent receptors in their noses.

By the time I finished filling out the paperwork, basically a form in quadruplicate that I had to read and sign in several places, it was getting on toward one o'clock. It took me about twenty minutes to drive to Northwest Humane Society from my house so that left half an hour to come up with a proper bribe for Special Agent Dawson. I knew he had a sweet tooth and momentarily thought about baking cookies, but aside from the time restriction, I was not the best baker in the world, and it would be a shame to waste those precious moments on something that turned out black or bitter or hard as concrete. The bakery was the better option; I could pick up something yummy on the way, leaving time to pull myself together before I needed to take off.

Plans set, I reheated a cup of the morning's coffee in the microwave, careful not to overheat it to the point of having it blow up in my face as the myth goes, and took it into Meow's room. The other cats seemed to have taken the attempted break-in and subsequent police visit in stride; I doubted Violet who was napping on her pillow in the kitchen or Solo who lived her solitary life under the sofa even knew anything had happened. Dirty Harry had stalked out his cat door into the enclosed backyard where he was doing an investigation of his own. Little was still at the window but now fast asleep. Red was in his sanctuary—my bedroom upstairs—where I think he believed nothing could touch him. Fraulein Fluffs was up there too. They looked the odd couple curled together on the quilt: his seventeen pounds of red tabby muscle and her six pounds of silver-gray fleece.

When I came in, Meow was resting in his bed, sphinxlike, looking like a normal Siamese. Closing the door behind me, I cautiously cracked the kennel gate. Thoroughly prepared for Meow to spring through on a rampage like the night before, I was pleased to find him much calmer. Fact was, besides his eyes, which followed mine right down to the blinks, he made nary a move. I sat in the rocker and took a few sips of my coffee. It was somewhat rank, being several hours old, but I was used to it. I had grown up with a fanatical "waste not want not" mother and had come to find the adage sound and wise.

It was quiet in the room, peaceful. Immersed in the warm, homey ambiance, it was hard to believe that an hour earlier, thieves had been trying to gain access there. I put that out of my mind.

"Well, Meow," I began out loud. "I'm going to visit your warehouse in a few minutes. Is there anything you want to tell me before I go?"

Meow blinked innocently.

"I don't know what happened to you, but there are a whole bunch of people set on finding out. If somebody hurt you, Frank and Connie and Denny'll get them, you wait and see. No one's ever going to hurt you again."

Meow rose slowly, stretched—first front legs, then back—and with an effortless leap, landed lightly in my lap.

I gave a little squeak as my coffee sloshed onto the floor, then put the cup aside and petted the silken fur. With an instant purr, he settled comfortably into a circle, making my legs twinge with the unexpected weight.

I looked at him and he looked at me. I found myself whispering the contact mantra from the communication session. It just sort of flowed out of me like a song stuck in my head. Meow purred and rubbed, then suddenly he stopped and held completely still. I could feel his body tense, and he began to shiver. I clasped him loosely, trying to send him my warmth. He calmed down, and the next moment, it was as if nothing at all had happened. The purr took up again, the blue eyes squinted closed. He gave a last rub against my hand, then jumped down to the floor. I let him explore for a little, sniffing out the new digs, and was just beginning to wonder how he would react to being reinstalled in the kennel when he jumped up on his own. He sniffed at the fluid bag that hung by the gate, then as if he knew the implications, went to his water bowl and drank of his own accord. After a long wet one, he got into his bed, curled into a silken ball and went to sleep. I could even hear little cat snores.

I took this as a good sign and checked the clock. One-twenty. I had just enough time to hit the bakery and make it to Northwest Humane to ambush Special Agent Dawson before he left for his investigation.

* * *

Armed with a white striped box of delicacies—chocolate chip cookies, macaroons, and a donut or two—I waited in the parking lot beside the investigations truck. I didn't want to disturb the agent in his office, and I also figured it would be harder for him to say no if I were there and ready.

When he hadn't come by two-ten, I began to wonder if I'd screwed up somehow—maybe he was taking another vehicle; maybe the time had changed. I was just about to go inside and check when, to my relief, he came through the gate and down the steps to the gravel lot.

Special Agent Frank Dawson was a tall, lanky man in his early forties, older than his two partners, Denny Paris and Connie Lee, who were both late twenties. He had an oval face and a long nose, which, with his military haircut, made him look a bit like one of the larger birds—an eagle or hawk. He didn't smile much, at least not that I had ever seen, but I didn't know him that well.

A shiver of anxiety coursed through me as I readied myself for potential rejection. I really wanted to go along on this trip, but it was an official Northwest Humane investigation, and there was a good chance he'd say no. In fact, there was a good chance he'd laugh at me or even be ticked off by my presumption. Frank wasn't famous for his chumminess, but I had to try.

"Special Agent Dawson?" I said as he approached, key fob in hand.

He peered at me for a moment. "Lynley?" he asked as recognition surfaced. He beeped his car open. "How are you?"

"I'm fine. I was wondering..." My confidence faltered as Frank, in a single, seamless movement, opened the heavy door, swung himself into the driver's seat, and shut it again with a substantial thunk. He rolled down his window to continue our conversation, but I could see how antsy he was to get on his way.

"You're investigating my foster cat, Meow, aren't you?"

"The Siamese case? Yeah. What about it?"

I pushed on. "I was wondering if I could ride with you,

see the place he may have come from and all?"

Frank continued to stare; his brow wrinkled slightly. I took it as a sign that, if nothing else, he was considering my request.

"Kerry said it might be okay," I added quickly.

"Kerry said that, eh?" he muttered.

"Yeah. She thought maybe I could be of some help, knowing cats as I do."

"You a cat expert?"

"Sort of." I held out the bakery box, my last persuasion. "I brought goodies."

His face didn't change. The seconds stretched, and I felt like I was in the hot seat. Then he smiled.

"Sure, why not? We don't expect any trouble. Get in."

I ran around the other side of the truck and was up in the passenger seat before he could change his mind. The box I placed between us on the console.

He eyed it lasciviously, then opened the flap. I could almost hear a moan of desire. He closed it again, started the truck, and crunched slowly out of the lot toward the street. "We better have coffee for this."

Chapter 9

In 1879, thirty-seven cats in Belgium were used to deliver mail to villages; however, they soon found that the cats were not disciplined enough to complete the job.

Frank was upbeat as he made his way to a little independent drive-through coffee place and positively jovial as he consumed two macaroons, one large chocolate chip cookie, and a donut. I nibbled one of the macaroons, a little too excited to fully enjoy the rich coconut treat.

"Kerry said something about someone simulating breed cats?" I mentioned, hoping to get the conversation rolling.

"Yeah, that's right," Frank mumbled through a mouth full of cookie and latte.

I waited for him to elaborate, but he didn't. "So how does that work?" I went on. "I don't know much about breeding, being an advocate for the adoption of shelter animals, but I thought that people who bought a breed cat were pretty careful about its pedigree. How do you fake that?"

Frank shrugged and inhaled another goodie. "Like anything else, I guess. The counterfeiters prey on the inexperienced and less intelligent buyer. It's just like P. T. Barnum said."

" 'There's a sucker born every minute'," I finished, amused he chose a quote attributed to a nineteenth century con artist. "But how do they get away with it? One cat show and they'd be found out, wouldn't they?"

"Sure. But by that time, the scammers are long gone. Apparently this group moves around a lot. They've been traced through several other states."

"But would it be worth it? I mean, I know pure-bred Siamese and such can go for a pretty penny, but it isn't into the millions or even the thousands, is it?"

"Not usually, but it's a reasonable income for not a lot of work and almost no overhead."

"You said it was a group. As in more than one or two?"

"Not necessarily, but that's what we think. What we've caught them doing is all over the map. Too much for just one person."

"Do you have any idea who they are?"

Frank frowned. He put his empty coffee cup in the bakery box, also empty. "No," he said flatly. Nothing more.

* * *

It was a long drive, a little more than an hour, out into the wilds of rural Oregon. The first leg was freeway where Frank was intent on passing everyone in sight. At Troutdale, we turned off and headed for Mt. Hood. The sky was still overcast but the rain had held off, for which I was grateful; Special Agent Dawson drove that winding highway a little faster than I'd like to have seen in a rainstorm.

The old Pendleton Woolen Mill was not in Pendleton, or at least this one wasn't. The now-famous textile manufacturing business made its start in the Eastern Oregon town but soon branched out to other locations in both Oregon and Washington. Special Agent Dawson hadn't confirmed that as our destination, but he was certainly heading in all the right directions.

Fields and pastures whizzed by, bleak with winter. Tree farms, their bounty merely a dark regiment of twigs this time of year, a few windswept houses, and a gas station or two—the old fashioned kind that consisted of a shabby storefront instead of an acre of blacktop and lighted signage—were the only relief. On both sides, the land climbed gently toward the green-blue hills. Occasionally before us we would catch a glimpse of the sharp, white face of the mountain.

"How did you find out about Meow?" I asked. "Was it a tip?"

Frank was quiet.

"Never mind if it's classified or something. I'm just curious how these things happen."

"No, it's not really classified," he said finally, "though we don't like to say much about an ongoing investigation just on general principle. You never know what might be an important fact later on."

I held up my hand, palm out. "I won't tell, I swear."

He glanced over at me and smiled. "That's okay, Lynley. I promise not to divulge any state secrets. Usually we do get tips: a neighbor who senses or sees something wrong; a witness to cruelty or abuse; or in the case of a business, someone who's purchased an animal who turns out to be sick. But this one was different. We've been working with a detective from Missoula, Montana. He had traced these perps here to Oregon. They'd dropped off the grid for a while, but luckily we knew what to look for when they resurfaced again. That's the good part; the bad part is they caught on fast and pulled up stakes before we could figure out who they were."

He paused, reached for his coffee, then remembered it was long gone and scowled.

"A stray cat with a collar that says he's CFA-registered yet there's no record of cat or cattery," Frank continued, "well, that raises questions. When Meow was relinquished to Friends of Felines, they called us to see if he matched the profile, and he did."

"Which is?"

"These people tend to pick cats who, physically, have all the attributes of the breed they're trying to simulate. Then they touch them up, dying the fur to correct any imperfections. Siamese are the easiest—there are lots of good-looking Siamese mixes running around, and all the counterfeiters have to do is fill in the dark markings so they fit the breed standard, fake the papers, and voila! A five-hundred dollar cat. Some breeds they have to go a bit farther. The Bombay cat for instance. Are you familiar with that breed?"

I nodded. "A little too familiar," I said before I could stop myself. Last year, I'd had a misadventure that entailed Bombay cats, chocolate diamonds, and murder. Not a good mix.

"So you take a black domestic short hair with the right body structure and fur density, touch up any white he might have, such as a pendant, and slip in a couple of copper contact lenses."

"Contact lenses?" I gasped. "That's horrible!"

"Yeah. Cat's eyes aren't built for contacts, and it's a sure thing nobody's going to keep them clean if they don't even know they're there. Luckily the folks who buy breed cats would take them to their vet when the eyes become inflamed, which they inevitably will. Then the show's over, so to speak, and they find out their kitty is no more Bombay than Garfield. But when they look for the sellers, they've vanished into thin air."

"What other breeds do they counterfeit?"

"Persians, absolutely. Usually that just entails forging papers since they can't fake the face. Russian Blue and British Shorthair when they can find a gray cat with the right proportions. Even Scottish Fold or Japanese Bobtail with a little minor surgery—whatever the market will bear. A British Shorthair can go for up to fifteen hundred dollars; a Scottish Fold, three thousand. Some Persians go for more than five. And our Siamese, well, you can guess, since they're one of the most popular show breeds these days."

I shook my head. "Surgery? I can't believe the things people will do for bucks!" I said under my breath.

"Amen," Frank agreed, "but that's what we're here for. We'll get them. Trust me."

* * *

The highway had straightened; to either side stood tall Douglas firs, sighing in the winter wind. Ahead Mt. Hood loomed like a snow-covered triangle. Then suddenly we broke from the woods and came to a crossroads, the first for many lonely miles.

A small green sign proclaimed it Sharon, Oregon. On one corner was a near-vacant micro-mall and on another, a run-down Chevron station. Frank turned right into the tiny town, and we cruised through at a lawful twenty-five miles per hour.

Sharon was a mix of old and new. The buildings and storefronts ranged from turn-of-the-century gothic to turn-of-*this*-century plastic. Some of the more ornate holdovers such at the Guild Theater and the skating rink had been fixed up and refurbished in grand style. Others had been left to decline.

Then in the proverbial blink of an eye, we were out the

other side. Frank made a quick left at a road so small I didn't even see it coming. We bumped along the unkempt gravel for a ways and there we were.

I remembered the Sharon Pendleton Woolen Mill from when I was a kid, some half a century ago. Back then it was a busy place, loud with the clacking of the shuttles and the laughter of the ladies who worked them. When the noon whistle blew, they would stream out the massive doors in their cotton dresses and head scarves with their brown bag lunches. There was a little store, not much more than a wooden outbuilding, where remnants and seconds were sold. My mum would sift through the bins to find just the right piece for a skirt or a school dress. I could almost smell the hot wool from those bygone summer days.

Whatever nostalgia I may have had for the old place, Frank was all business. He jolted to a stop in the empty parking lot among the grasses and dried teasel that had sprung up there.

"Lynley, you're going to have to stay in the truck," he commanded as he sprung out the driver's side.

"Hey, wait a minute," I blurted. "I didn't drive out all this way just to sit in the car. You've got to let me come with you, at least for a look inside. I promise not to get in your way or touch anything."

He slipped on a pair of teal latex gloves. "Tell you what. Let me go in first and check it out, see if it's safe. Then you can come in for a quick once-over, okay?"

"Yeah, okay," I conceded. Safe? I thought that might be a little melodramatic, but this was his moment, and I was pretty sure arguing wasn't going to get me anywhere. "Can I at least get out and stretch my legs? I think my butt's asleep."

He laughed. "Of course. But I wouldn't wander off.

This shouldn't take long."

With that, he grabbed a black, boxy case from the back seat and was off. When he got to the door, he produced a key to the oversized padlock, and in a matter of seconds, had disappeared inside.

I'm not really good at waiting. You'd think at my age, I would have developed a modicum of patience, but no. When I've got something on my mind, like wanting to see where my foster cat was held hostage, there are only so many songs I can hum, lists I can check, or phone calls I can make (in this case, none, since we seemed to be out of cell range) before I get nervous. I studied a couple of interesting weeds and looked for pretty rocks among the gravel. I gazed at the sky which had gone white as linen and then got back into the truck when I realized how cold it was. It seemed like Frank was taking his time in there. I couldn't help but wonder what could be so engaging.

The quiet was almost ear-numbing. I cracked the window, but the silence remained. No birds, no cars, no city hum that I was so conditioned to hearing. Then there was a sound. First one, then a few, then a tattoo of taps upon the roof: the rain had come.

In Oregon, we have at least twenty-seven names for rain. This one classified as a shower, a little heavier than a sprinkle but certainly not as dramatic as a downpour. Its rhythm was hypnotic. I leaned back against the high neck-rest, closed my eyes, and without any thought, nodded asleep.

I woke with a start, wondering where I was, then wondering what had wakened me. The memory of something loud echoed in my ears, though now it seemed as soundless as before.

I checked the clock; half an hour had passed while I'd

been in peaceful repose. That made forty-five minutes since Special Agent Dawson had gone into the mill. That was a long time, and a bad feeling crept over me. It was beginning to get dark; the parking lot was awash with gloom. The old, abandoned structure looked like a bunker from a fifties science fiction flick, the kind where right when you think you're safe and alone, the aliens come bursting out the door, ready to eat you.

As I stared at the flat black facade, I thought I saw movement. I sighed with relief. Frank was finally returning.

Except he didn't.

The shadow-man, which was all I could see in the dim, dodged around the back of the building and disappeared. *Rats,* I swore to myself. *He's still on the prowl.* I was getting truly sick of waiting for the special agent to finish playing Magnum, P.I. of cats. My previous concern had morphed into agitation which was quickly working itself into annoyance. *How dare he leave me sitting and worrying? Me! Lynley Cannon, cat aficionado! This was all about cats, and I could be helpful in there if he would just let me. Who was he to tell me I had to wait in the car?*

He was the detective, of course, and in charge of an official case, but I didn't let facts interfere with my mental tirade. I'd had enough sitting. Without another thought, I shrugged on my coat, leapt from the truck, and pulled the hood up against the rain which was more of a driving type now.

I hesitated when I reached the door but only for a moment. I'd just slip inside and take it from there. What could that possibly hurt? Frank really couldn't fault me for coming in out of the rain, now could he?

I ducked in and closed the door behind me, pausing to

let my eyes adjust. The twilight of the diminishing day translated into near pitch black in the little office. One small, besmeared window showed a lighter patch of gray, but it gave no illumination. The place smelled of disuse, dust, and damp. It wasn't all that warm outside, but I could swear, in that room, it was a good five degrees colder.

I was beginning to get my bearings; I could see shadows. Then the shadows solidified: a desk, circa nineteen fifties; a coffee table, complete with dog-eared magazines; a mousy couch stacked with boxes; a wooden chair flipped on its side. A few pictures hung at odd angles on the walls along with an old calendar. I peered closer at a fly-spotted photo of a proud yellow tractor; the date was September 1975.

A second door at the back of the office stood open. Beyond it gleamed a tiny, faraway light. Between me and that pinpoint bloom of radiance was the gaping cavern of the mill, itself.

"Special Agent?" I called uncertainly. Then again with a little more resolution: "Frank?" I waited for an answer and when none came, wondered if he were still outside. Where had he been going? As far as I knew, the only outbuilding was the old store, but that was in the front near the truck, the opposite direction. Oh, well, he'd be back, I figured. It's not like someone could get lost.

The light beckoned. I began cautiously across the old plank floor, initiating a series of creaks that popped and echoed through the silence. The old machines were gone, leaving the room empty except for a few crates draped with dusty canvas—forgotten storage.

When I reached the lighted room, I saw the glow that had seemed so brilliant from across the gloom was actually only a dim bulb hanging from the ceiling on twisted cloth wire—twenty-five watt, forty at the most. It gave everything a shadowy sameness, like a washed-out photograph; the corners faded into obscurity and only the central portion was even the least bit discernable. It seemed to be a second office, but this one had been stripped of everything except a wooden table, a primitive battered swivel chair, and a disheveled metal file cabinet. The table was bare; the chair looked like it hadn't been occupied since the last World War. If Frank had been there, he certainly wasn't there now.

I turned back the way I had come and raked my eyes across the cavernous mill. I strained my ears for a noise, any noise, though my personal preference at the moment would have been the gruff rasp of Frank's voice in cheerful greeting. Nothing. Not even the rain. It was as if all sounds had been left at the door, as if I stood in a time warp, between the seconds where the senses could not go.

Okay, I admit it, I'm a bit of a sci-fi fan, but it really was eerie. I shifted my attention back to the little office, searching for something I'd missed. So far, I hadn't seen any sign of the cat counterfeiters. No shop or holding area. I sniffed the air: only dust and age. No cat.

Maybe the mill had turned out to be a bad tip. Maybe Meow—or Frannie's interpretation of Meow—had been mistaken. Maybe Frank was already out in the truck waiting for me, ready to write this one off as a dead end.

I was about to give up when I noticed something peculiar. The linoleum floor of the office was covered in a few decades of dust, enough to show a set of footprints that traveled from where I stood at the doorway to the table and then around the room. Frank's, I assumed; I had seen them before. What I hadn't picked up on was another set of prints, actually more like a jumble, in one of the dusky corners. I peered through the dark. Half hidden behind the file cabinet, I thought I could see a strip of vertical molding. The edge of a secret door?

I crossed for a closer look, and sure enough, in back of the rusty cabinet was a narrow, paneled doorway. The privy? But why would someone bar the way to the bathroom with the heavy cabinet, unless...

I really began to wish Frank were there; I didn't want to mess with something that might hold a clue to Meow's abusers. Besides, I doubted if I could move the cabinet without help. Had Frank even noticed the door or the muddle of tracks nearby? Maybe he had but had discounted it. Maybe it was just what I'd thought in the first place—an old and most likely disgusting toilet.

In my frustration, I slumped against the cabinet and nearly fell on the floor. The thing rolled! On well-oiled wheels, my little push had sent it sashaying across the linoleum to twirl to a stop against the tumbled chair. It had made barely a sound.

Had Frank noted this in his go-around? I now recognized a few sets of the cabinet's distinctive skate-like marks among the footprints, though none as far-reaching as the ones it had just made.

My attention returned to the narrow door. Without anything that could be considered rational thought, I gripped the black ceramic knob, pulled it open, and stepped inside.

Chapter 10

*If a cat is frightened, the hair stands up fairly evenly all over its
body; when the cat is threatened or ready to attack, the hair stands
up only in a narrow band along the spine and tail. This is called a
piloerection.*

The smell hit me instantly; not the dust and mold smell that
saturated the other parts of the building, and not the ick
smell of someone's dirty bathroom either. This was the
smell I'd been searching for earlier: cat. Urine, feces, and
fear, so strong my eyes burned. And there was something
else as well—biting, chemical—and I knew even in my
blindness, I had found the counterfeiter's lab.

The room was dark; the weak glimmer of the office's
low-wattage bulb made little more than a thin stripe that
petered out a foot or so from the doorway. I felt the wall for
a light switch and found one, old but functional. With a flip
and a prayer, the lights went on.

I gaped at what can only be described as a kitty
chamber of horrors. The mass of fluorescents shone cruelly
down on the large space; it had never been a bathroom, that
was for sure. Against the wall to the left stood a bank of
cages, empty I was thankful to see. Across the back of the
room ran a continuous workbench with shelves above and
below. To my right hunched a huge set of concrete sinks. In
the center of the room stood a stainless steel groomer's
bench the size of a banquet table.

I took a few steps into the room, then moved

automatically to the cages, horrid tiny wire coops lined with filthy newspaper. There were twelve total, but only about half of them had been occupied. Those now contained nothing but the soiled paper—no food, no water bowls. The likelihood that someone had come along and cleaned up those items when the cats left was ludicrous, implying that the animals had been terribly neglected. I peered closer at a specimen of scat and judged it as recent. At least one of the cats had been there not that long ago.

I turned to the work bench. Strangely enough, the white Formica was unexpectedly clean though cluttered, as if someone had been working there. I picked out a few standard items—combs, brushes, scissors, and claw clippers—alongside things I would hope never to see at my local pet salon, such as wire cutters, spray paint, epoxy glue, and a rusty razor knife. The shelves, again spotless except for a light sprinkling of dust, were filled with bottles, jars, and cans of miscellanea. Some were labeled; others, ominously unmarked. A quart jar oozed a black-brown slime; a number six can with its lid partially pried open held something that reeked of ammonia.

I headed for the sinks to complete my circuit of feline hell and stumbled. As I caught my balance, I looked down to see what had tripped me and faltered again, this time reeling from shock.

A booted foot stuck out from behind the sink. Instantly I was on my knees, heart racing. Half under the groomer's table, in the shadows, Special Agent Dawson lay unmoving. Blood pooled on the tile floor from an ugly wound near his temple, strangely crimson in the green-blue light. There was a lot of it, and it looked as if it were still running.

I felt for a pulse, afraid of the worst. Not being the

nursey type, it took me a fearful minute to locate one. The beat was weak, or so it seemed to my untrained touch, but it was there.

"Frank!" I cried. My voice echoed raucously in the stillness, and I sucked in my breath, realizing after the fact that whoever had taken down the special agent might still be lurking nearby, ready to make it a twosome. "Frank!" I hissed urgently into his ear, accompanying it with a cautious shake.

I waited for a reply, a moan or movement, but it didn't come. I put my hand on his; his fingers were like ice. "Frank, wake up," I whispered dismally. "You need to wake up now. I don't know what to do."

I sat up and closed my eyes. I had to think. Nine-one-one was the only thing that came to mind, and I was almost sure that wasn't an option. Pulling my phone out of my coat pocket, I tried anyway, but sure enough, no signal. There were still places where the long microwave arm of mass communication didn't reach; I'd have to mention it to my carrier, assuming I got out of the old mill alive.

Fear crept over me like a frozen claw. What to do? I didn't want to move him; if he had a head or neck injury, any maneuvering could make it worse. Besides, though wiry, Frank was much heavier than I could lift, I was certain of that. And where would I move him to? The truck, some half-mile away in the big, empty parking lot? Totally out of the question.

Should I bathe the wound? Staunch the bleeding? I peered closer at the mass of blood and hair; it had slowed even since I'd found him which had to be a good sign. Still, a little first aid couldn't hurt. There must be a first aid kit in the investigations truck.

Suddenly, like a flash, I remembered that the truck was also equipped with a radio. Would that work where a cell phone would not? I didn't understand the laws of those particular physics so I could only hope and try.

Bounding to my feet—okay, at nearly sixty, it was more like pulling myself up with a grunt and the aid of the groomer's table—I ran to the door, then turned to look back. From there, Frank was invisible. I hated to leave him alone in that cold, hateful place.

"I'll be right back," I told him, hoping that somewhere in his conked-out brain, he could hear me. "I'm going for help. You're going to be alright.

"Everything's going to be alright," I added, knowing full well it was a lie.

* * *

The rest of the night had been a blur: I remember running to the truck, fiddling with the communications set until I finally roused someone with my ineptness, then going back into the mill to sit with Frank despite my better judgment which kept telling me that whoever hurt Frank might still be there. The ambulance and local police came quickly; I filled them in with what little I knew. A nice lady EMT wrapped me in a victim blanket as she and her partner took the unconscious humane investigator away to the nearest hospital which was back in Portland. Special Agents Denny Paris and Connie Lee showed up at some point in the smaller investigations van—I knew it must have taken them at least sixty minutes to make the drive yet it seemed like no time had passed at all. I repeated my story to them, then Connie bundled me into the van and we headed back to town. Special Agent Paris stayed to finish up with the locals and then return the truck to headquarters.

Stress always makes me sleepy so within minutes of sinking into the warm, soft seat of the van I was nodding off. Connie was quiet, probably practicing some Wiccan meditation which I knew she enjoyed so much. Either that or planning a craft party, deciding which off-road spot she would visit on her next vacation, or coming up with six vegan recipes for kale. Her tastes were many and varied. I don't think I'd ever seen the young woman disinterested or bored.

At one point in the drive, I woke with a start, not recalling where I was. The agent smiled her huge smile and said in that gruff voice of hers, "Get some more rest, Lynley. We got a few miles to go."

Connie Lee was a muscular, short-haired ball of energy, all positive unless you were harming an animal at which time she morphed into a storm with handcuffs and a Taser. I felt completely safe with her and took her advice, falling back to sleep until the journey was over.

We made it to the house a little after midnight, and I wandered around checking on the cats until the wee hours of the morning. They were all fine, sleeping like babies, even Meow who was tucked up in his bed, one stockinged paw stretched long and the other curled underneath him. I guess no one ever told them cats were supposed to be nocturnal.

Finally I sacked out on the couch with Little on my back and Fluffs draped across my legs. It was a thankful, dreamless slumber, and the next thing I was aware of was the ring of the phone, way too early I thought until I looked at the clock and realized it was nearly eleven. It was Frannie, asking if I wanted to go to lunch before her shift at the shelter. My first inclination was to decline and go back to sleep, but I knew I'd only toss and turn and think of the things I should be doing when I wasn't visualizing Frank on that cold lab floor, so I gave her a drowsy yes.

Frannie had allowed me an hour to pull myself together and meet her at the local watering hole, the Pub & Pony up the street from my house. They served British Northwest fare such as steak and kidney pie with yam fries and fish and chips with arugula slaw instead of good old cole. They also made a respectable veggie-burger which was what we had both opted for, Frannie with a side of Walla Walla onion rings and me with a cup of free-range chicken and wheatless noodle soup. They were taking their time in the kitchen, but that was fine with me. I had ordered automatically because it was what people did in restaurants around noontime, not because I had any interest in the food itself.

"Did they find Special Agent Dawson's attacker?" Frannie asked as she sipped her hot chocolate.

"Not that I know of," I replied, hugging my coffee for dear life. "How did you hear about the assault? It can't have hit the papers already."

"Facebook, our FOF volunteers' group. It was all over my email this morning. Lots of comments about how Frank was rendered unconscious in the line of duty and how a brave Lynley Cannon called the cops."

"Do they know how Frank's doing?"

"He's going to be fine once he gets over a monster headache. No serious concussion or anything like that."

"I'm surprised," I said, then added quickly, "and pleased, of course. But he was out for so long. He never did regain consciousness as far as I know, even when they put him in the ambulance."

"Apparently he had been drugged, shot with some sort of animal tranquilizer."

"You're kidding! That explains it. I suppose someone who spends their time spray painting cats would have to have some good drugs around."

"Was that the place, do you think? The breed simulator's lair?"

"It had to be. Oh!" I exclaimed, ransacking my purse for my phone. "What time is it? I nearly forgot, I'm supposed to go to Northwest Humane this afternoon to give them a statement."

Frannie casually checked her watch. "It's twelve-twenty. When do you need to be there?"

"Three," I signed, hanging my bag back over the arm of the chair.

"Plenty of time."

"As long as we get served in the next few hours," I said with unnecessary sarcasm.

As if on cue, our wait person—server? Back in my day they were plain old waitresses—arrived with a cheerful disposition and a tray of dishes, making me feel properly ashamed of my slight. She presented us each with a large oval plate stacked with burger fixings: a curly leaf of butter lettuce, a thick slice of tomato, a ramekin of sweet onion bits, a dill pickle the size of a cucumber, and the veggie-burger itself, crisp and hot and fragrant.

"Who gets the soup?" she asked. I raised my hand. By power of elimination, she handed Frannie the Walla Wallas. "Condiments are on the table. Can I get you anything else?"

"This looks great," I told her honestly. Frannie nodded agreement. "Maybe a little more coffee?"

"Back in a sec." She turned and streaked off, giving full display of an elaborate tattoo at her waist. It was perfectly situated between her low rise jeans and her high rise tee shirt, a sun-moon-star-dragon-smoke design in several colors. I respect tattoos, especially the beautiful ones such as hers. I would probably get one myself except there aren't any parts of my wrinkled, elderly body that I'd care to draw attention to.

A thought hit me. "Where did they take him? What hospital?"

"Frank? OHSU, up on the hill."

"Maybe I'll grab the tram and visit after the debriefing. Or will he be out by then?"

Frannie began building her burger. "You never can be sure with hospitals," she said with a knowing tone.

I nodded, being no stranger to the green-walled halls myself.

Frannie was obviously hungry and tucked into her fare without hesitation. I spooned at the soup but couldn't quite get into the burger, maybe because I'd just got up and it wasn't really what I would call breakfast or maybe because after last night, I wasn't sure I'd ever be hungry again. It was shock, I knew; a mini form of PTSD, and not my first. It would wear off sooner or later—sooner, I hoped—but until then, I just had to take it easy and treat myself with respect.

As if she sensed my dilemma, Frannie steered the conversation away from treachery in cold, abandoned warehouses and toward fuzzier subjects. I was happy to chat for a while, and by the time lunch was over, we had come up with a plan to get long-time shelter resident Nelson on a TV pet news spot, figured out a possible reason why Zooks wasn't using her litter box, and batted around some strategies for the upcoming spring bazaar.

Eventually I gave up on my untouched burger, and when our server came with the check, asked for a box. We paid the bill and left a tip. The day was overcast but relatively warm for Portland in January. No rain at the moment, just an airy gray that seemed more like mist than cloud. The sun was a white coin overhead; it might yet win the battle and shine through. Frannie and I said our goodbyes; she went to her car bound for the shelter, and I began the short walk home.

As I ambled down the side street, I pulled out my phone to turn the ringer volume back up and saw I had missed a call from the foster department. I lingered by a budding plum tree while I sent for the message and heard Kerry's voice on the other end.

"Lynley? Sorry I missed you," she said. Then there was a pause, as if she were uneasy. "Can you call as soon as you get this?" Another hesitation. "It's Kerry. 'Bye."

Something about her tone left me unsettled. My inclination was to phone her back that very moment, but just then, an obnoxiously huge SUV roared by with the racket of a freight train, and I decided that however important it might be, it could wait the two minutes it would take to get back to the quiet of my living room. I'll admit, though, I picked up my pace and made it in one.

Without taking off my coat, I pressed the reply key. "Hi, Kerry?" I said when she answered. "I got your message. What's up?"

"Oh, uh. Can you hold for a moment?"

"Sure," I said tentatively. The line went to music, some rather nice classical that I might have enjoyed had I not been in panic mode.

The music clicked off. "There. That's better. Thanks for getting back to me so quickly. I was away from my desk."

"It sounded important."

"It is. There's been a development in the breed simulation case. They found more cats. Three to be exact."

"More like Meow? Where?"

"Actually they'd been chucked in the dumpster behind the Pendleton Mill."

"Oh, no! Are they okay?"

"They seem good. Dr. Angela thinks they couldn't have been in there for long. Special Agent Paris speculates that the person who assaulted Special Agent Dawson took the cats out in an effort to hide them. They were cold and a bit dehydrated. Hungry as all get out, but that probably points to treatment way before last night. Apparently the place they were being held was pretty rough—well, you saw it for yourself, didn't you?"

"Yes. I saw it," I said, barely restraining the hostility I felt at the thought of a sweet cat incarcerated in those horrible, filthy cages at the whim of some monster that cared nothing for its tiger soul. Then I went melancholy. "I thought the place was abandoned. I had no idea there were still cats there. I should have known. I'm so sorry."

"It's not your fault, Lynley. You had your hands full with Frank. It was the special agents' job to do the search. And Denny found the cats, no problem, so all is well."

"I suppose," I conceded though I didn't really feel it in my heart.

"Anyway, we're going to need Meow back in the office now. A detective from Missoula is flying in today, and Investigations needs all four cats here."

"But," I stammered, "he isn't ready! I've just managed to get him calmed down. You should have seen him that first night—he was crazy. If he goes back now, we might undo all the progress he's made."

"I know, but it's a chance we'll have to take. We'll try to keep things as calm and quiet as possible. And you can visit him whenever you like. We've got the others housed in a room of their own, very limited access. It's all we can do for now."

I knew they would do their best; they always did. I also knew there was no point in arguing; it was their cat, after all.

"When do you want him?"

"Can you come right away?"

I sighed. "Be there in half an hour."

Chapter 11

Cats have two sets of vocal cords and can make over one hundred different sounds.

The house seemed exceptionally quiet with Meow gone; believe it or not, I missed his wild Siamese squawk. The other cats were so settled that they spoke only rarely: when they were hungry; when they wanted out into the fenced backyard. Little always had a few words to say when I came home, but those had been said hours ago and now she was fast asleep on her carpeted cat tower.

It wasn't that late, not past ten. For all the things I'd done during the day, you'd think I'd be tired, but I was wide awake and restless. I had been debriefed at Northwest Humane which took far longer than I thought it should for the little that I'd seen of the lab at the old mill, then I'd taken the tram up to the Oregon Health & Science University Hospital to visit Frank. He was in the process of being discharged so I sat with him until the doctor came around to sign him out. His room had a spectacular view of Portland: the vivid blaze of downtown lights; the obsidian strip of the Willamette River, crisscrossed by strings of luminescent pearls—the bridges; the east side, a diamond grid that dwindled into the distance like the play board in Tron; and finally on the horizon, the silhouette of Mt. Hood, a lopsided pyramid black against the moon. We'd talked about the view, about Portland, about the weather—anything besides the experience we had shared

MOLLIE HUNT

the night before. He didn't say anything, and I wasn't about to bring it up.

Now though, as I paced my living room brimming with questions, I wished I had pushed a little more. I wanted to know if Frank had heard or seen anything before he was knocked out. I also wanted to know what had led him to that mill in the first place—it wasn't Frannie's psychic ramblings, that's for sure. But most of all, I wanted more information about the investigation itself and the interstate circumstance that had brought a detective all the way from Montana.

On impulse, I went to the phone in the kitchen, the land line, and dialed the foster number. It was a little late for Kerry to be in the office, but she was known to work all hours. No answer though. I put the handset back in its cradle and stood for a minute. My mind was suddenly racing; if I couldn't talk to Kerry, maybe I could do the next best thing.

I grabbed my coat, keys and shelter bag where I kept my apron, badge, and other accoutrements for my role as FOF volunteer. I paused by the front door, wondering if I were insane. Then I gave up wondering, deciding that I probably truly was, and headed for my car and the shelter.

* * *

Friends of Felines cat shelter stayed open to the public until nine o'clock, so I wasn't surprised to see a few cars still in the parking lot. It took an hour or so to clean up, feed cats, give nighttime medication, and leave everything ship-shape for the morning. My badge would key me in at any time, day or night, a privilege awarded to only a few volunteers and of which I was very proud. It had happened one dark and stormy night many years ago when the river flooded its banks, and the shelter was awash with six inches of mud and muck. I was one of the first to respond to the emergency call, and for that I earned the trust and respect of the powers that be.

I keyed in to the side entrance and walked down the long hallway toward the cattery. Open doors to either side revealed darkened conference and meeting rooms, the media room, the behavior center, and the real life room with its comfortable couch and lounge chairs where we could take the cats for a much needed simulation of home. I had to key in a second time to get to the cattery itself. The lights were low, but I could see the glow of wide eyes watching my every move. It was quiet; so far, I hadn't encountered a soul though I could hear the low moan of a vacuum somewhere in the building.

"Hi, everyone," I said automatically as I passed the banks of kennels. I would stop by later for a more mannerly greeting but right now I knew exactly where I was going. I wanted to see Meow and the new ones. I had to see them. I had to check out my poor returned foster and his wronged brothers and sisters.

Instead of turning right into the public section of Friends of Felines, I veered left toward the bowels of the shelter. More offices, the foster care center, the ICU, and the enclosed investigations room. I peered through the thick window and counted four pseudo-Siamese kitties in various states of repose. One was curled up in a donut while two others sat like bookends on a throw rug. One was at the feeding station solemnly crunching kibble. They all stared up at me, even though to my knowledge I hadn't made a sound.

At first, I couldn't discern which was Meow, then the cat in the donut gave me a little blink smile. Bingo!

"Hi, sweetheart," I said through the glass. I touched the pane lightly with my fingers. "I'll be right back, I promise."

Zipping up the hall and into the foster room, I went to the cupboard where the supplies were kept. I hadn't seen a notice that any of the cats were on a special diet so I chose a few cans of the best food I could find among the donated assortment, a plastic pitcher which I filled with fresh water, a stack of clean stainless steel bowls, and a soft brush. I started to leave, then turned back and picked out a few pouches of cat treats.

I stuffed the treats in my apron pocket. I still had my shelter bag slung over my shoulder and was glad no one was watching me try to balance my load as I shuffled down the hallway. With the help of some stabilizing angel, I managed to make it back without mishap, but then I saw the problem. The investigations kennel opened with a separate key, a real one I kept in my apron pocket. I'd have to set my things down in order to get it.

First the cans, then the pitcher of water went on the floor by the door. I began to fumble, but I had unthinkingly put the treat bags on top of it, and now the key on its Humane Society of the United States key ring was lodged underneath. As I dug, one of the pouches came open, spilling fish-shaped pellets out across the polished floor.

"Bother!" And I still couldn't reach the key.

By the time I got the elusive thing out, I'd had to put everything down. Using a paper towel as a broom, I corralled the treats which had scattered to the far corners of the hallway and shoved them back in my pocket; the cats couldn't care less about the thirty-second rule.

Noting a sign that said *Authorized Personnel Only* and assuming as Meow's foster mom I was about as authorized as anyone, I pulled open the heavy door. None of the cats looked like they were going to bolt, but I wasn't taking any chances. Greeting them calmly, I quickly shifted my load inside and closed up behind me.

The investigations room, though large for cats, was somewhat small for humans. The plethora of beds that scattered the floor made it an obstacle course, but I was used to that. Besides, I needed to acclimatize the cats to my presence first and foremost. I slid to a crouch with my back against the wall and took a deep breath.

"Hello, kitties," I said out loud. "How's everybody doing tonight?" Okay so it wasn't the wittiest chatter you've ever heard, but believe me, the cats aren't particular. They just like the sound of a friendly voice.

I picked the treats out of my pocket, checked them for dust but found none, and held a handful out to the brood. Meow was up and out of his bed in a heartbeat since he'd already done the research and deemed my offerings delectable. I put his treat on the green tiled floor—cats, unlike dogs, have no desire to eat out of your hand—and he snapped it up in a move that was both elegant and efficient. I gave him a long stroke from head to tail and another treat, chit-chatted a bit more about nothing special, then repeated the whole effort with the others.

I didn't know any of their names but most English-speaking cats answer to "kitty, kitty" and these were no exception. They studied me, then one by one, they came. By that time, Meow had settled on my lap which the others must have taken as the okay signal because there was no shyness in getting those treats.

"I brought you food and fresh water," I told them, "but as you can see, I'm a little occupied at the moment." I looked down at Meow who for all intents and purposes seemed to be asleep. I slid my hand down his long back and thought what a beautiful cat he was. I touched the base of his tail, now a patch of sandy stubble where the fur had been shaved. There was a bare patch on his head as well. With the colorant removed, the pale skin that would produce light fur extended up from his cheek to meet his dark ear in a divergent sweep, very interesting but definitely not on the list of true Siamese markings. I liked him all the better for it.

I studied the others. They all had the athletic body profile and round head of a traditional Siamese, at least as far as I could tell with my unprofessional eye, but each had noticeable atypical marks: a ringed tail, an uneven sock. What an idea, I thought to myself, taking these near-perfect specimens, and with a little cosmetic assistance, passing them off as the real thing. I didn't have a lot of sympathy for the rubes who were deceived by the ruse. In my opinion, there are far too many unwanted cats on the planet to be going around breeding more. The real victims in this crime were the cats who were forced to endure toxic procedures, a hostile environment, and who knew what else the simulators put them through. These offenders had to be stopped, whatever it took.

I found myself getting madder and madder the more I thought about it. I heard a petulant meow from my lap and realized I had been stroking Meow so hard his fur was electrified.

"Sorry, sweetie," I said, pulling my hand away, not before a tiny shock crackled between us.

Meow was up and stalking toward the food bowl. Time to open the cans.

"Which kind would you like?" I sorted through the stack I had brought from the foster office. "We have Fancy Feast, Kitty Delight, Spot's Stew."

I hefted myself up off the floor. My foot had fallen asleep, and I staggered, not significantly but enough to tip a food bowl before I could catch my balance. In that millisecond of uncertain movement, the four cats were gone. It was almost like a vanishing act except I had seen them go. Ears back, stomachs to the ground, they had scuttled to various hiding places as best as they could find in the small space. Two sets of huge eyes stared out from under a low shelf; a cat-sized lump sat perfectly still under a blanket; Meow had scorched up to a high platform in the farthest corner of the kennel where he huddled glaring as if I were a wild coyote instead of the familiar person with whom he had just been sharing a nap.

Quickly I sank to my knees. I knew what the behavior meant; there had been abuse somewhere in their lives. I had seen it many times in rescued animals but never with such similitude. They had moved in perfect concert, their sad ballet poignant and beautiful at the same time.

"I'm so sorry," I said softly. "I didn't mean to scare you." I took one of the cans and flipped the pop top. Even the friendly sound didn't quite convince them of their safety, and only after another several minutes of soft talk, good smells and—yes, I'll admit it—a little meditation on serenity that we'd learned in the animal communication class did they creep in utter, profound silence from their hideaways to the bowls of food.

I was just settling back against the door with the cats munching, somber and mute, when there was a knock. I scooted over a little and reached up to the knob. As my fingers tightened on the faux brass and turned, I had two thoughts.

The first was, *why didn't whoever was outside use their key, seeing as it was way past closing and anyone with authority to be in the building must have one?*

The second was, *maybe I should see who's there before letting them in.*

The door slammed open with a sound that echoed through the empty halls like a gunshot. The cats again hightailed into hiding. A strong hand grabbed my arm and pulled me to my feet. For a split second, I was staring into the face of a large, clean-cut white man wearing the ever-suspicious hoodie; then he swung me around and pushed me hard. I stumbled and fell, my head clipping the sharp corner of one of the wooden shelves with a crack. Pain blinded me, just like they described in the stories; I pivoted with the impact and tumbled to the floor, cracking the back of my skull on the hard tile. My eyelids winced closed, but my consciousness continued to process for a few seconds longer. Between the drumbeats of pain, I made out a sound that wrenched my heart in two. I struggled to rise, to help, to open my eyes, but it was beyond my control. All I could do was lie there totally helpless, listening to the haunting, terrible cries of the anguished Siamese.

* * *

Even before I opened my eyes, I knew there was a problem. First of all, I had a killer hangover which was wrong for so many reasons, the most obvious being that I didn't drink, at least not anymore, and I had a coin with the Serenity Prayer on the back to prove it. Also, though I seemed to be in a prone position, I wasn't on anything resembling a bed. My back had stiffened on the cold, hard surface, and pinpoints of agony radiated from all other body parts that pressed into the unforgiving ground. My cheek was damp and sticky as I tried to turn my head.

Then I remembered.

Images pulsed in time with my headache: The face of a clean-shaven man—pulse! Falling backwards into an abyss of pain—pulse! The screams of the assaulted cats—pulse. Someone yelling something about... about...

But there the memories fragmented, becoming glimmers of nonsense that faded into crimson obscurity.

I forced my eyes open and saw the small dim room. Staring around, I confirmed my fears that it wasn't all a dream, and the cats were truly gone. The place was in shambles: blankets crumpled on the ground; food bowls overturned; kibbles strewn like sepia confetti across the emerald floor. Those little kitties must have put up a brave fight, I thought with a flicker of satisfaction. The reprieve was brief, however, as I recalled those four small vulnerable and already traumatized animals, again at the mercy of their captors.

A thought skimmed across the puddle of my mind: *Why?* I was assuming the abduction linked back to the breed counterfeiters, but why would they bother? Could it have been someone else? Were no felines safe anymore?

My head hurt and my hair was gummy with drying blood but there was no nausea so it wasn't a concussion. A bath, a Motrin, and a good rest in my own bed was all I needed, and I couldn't wait to get home. I had to call someone about the cats first. I didn't know how much time had passed; it was unlikely the thief—or thieves?—could be traced at that point but we had to try.

With the effort of swimming through syrup, I sat up. Half-crawling half-slithering, I crept toward the door. It was time—past time—to get out of there.

I reached for the knob and turned. My hand slipped, and I tried it again. I knew I was weak but not so weak I couldn't open a door. Something was wrong. Somehow the cat thieves had locked me in.

No need to panic, I told myself, even though my adrenaline said otherwise. I had the key. I rummaged in my apron but found nothing but fishy-smelling crumbs. Oh, right! Since my pocket was full of treats, I'd tossed the key ring into my shelter bag when I came in. Still no problem. Once I located the bag, I'd be free.

I surveyed the small room, then when I didn't see it right off, I made the rounds again as if it might be hiding behind a Kong toy or under a catnip mouse. The results were the same. This time I did panic. There was no doubt about it—the bag was gone.

I did a quick inventory: my purse was locked in the trunk of my car, something they say one should never do but, in this case, would save me from the hassle of reporting lost credit cards and a plethora of miscellaneous I.D.; my car keys were clipped to my belt loop as usual. But my phone had been in my bag as well, so plan C, calling for assistance, was over before it had begun. I couldn't comprehend how the door had got locked, but the whys were moot. Without help, I was stuck there for the duration.

Angrily I grabbed at the door knob and swung to my feet, ignoring the painful pounding the movement brought to my head. With both hands, I choked and rattled the brass handle. I had no way of knowing what time it was. Had I been out for minutes or hours? I didn't wear a watch because why bother when I had the World Time at my fingertips on my phone? But now my phone was gone, and I suddenly missed my trusty Timex more than I had in years. I could no longer hear the whine of the vacuum, but maybe the cleaning crew had moved on to a quieter job. For

Chapter 12

It is common knowledge that a cat's purr can reduce anxiety and lower high blood pressure in human companions, but studies show that the low frequency vibration of the purr may also induce bone growth, promote pain relief, and help heal tendons and muscles.

Next thing I knew, I was being pulled upright by a man I couldn't place. At first, I thought he was the cat thief returning for a second round. I'd only seen my assailant for the briefest moment, but it was a face I'd remember for all time. Then my vision cleared, and I realized with relief it wasn't him at all. Though similar in build, this man was older by at least five years. I'm a terrible judge of age, but I'd say mid to late forties. And where the cat thief had been clean-shaven, this face was rough with stubble and not in the fashionable way either.

I continued to stare at him. His sooty-black hair was short and lackluster. I imagined it would be wayward if he didn't use that gooey product to slick it down. His eyes were mousy in both color and size. His mouth was turned down in a frown that looked as if it might be perpetual.

I shook my arm against his grip, but his hand just clenched tighter. "Ow! You're hurting me."

"Quit squirming and it won't hurt so much."

"I appreciate your assistance," I said with the crisp formality I reserved for rude people, "but I'm fine. You can let go now."

"You're not going anywhere until you've answered a few questions." He began to propel me out the door.

"Where are you taking me?" I demanded, but he ignored the question.

I noticed a little crowd had gathered. Kerry stood front and center between Special Agent Paris and Special Agent Lee. As my escort shoved me through, they stared at me as if I were a stranger.

"Kerry!" I called as the man hauled me away like a sack of kitty litter. "Denny! Help!"

The trio looked uneasy but made no move to assist. In another moment I was being thrust through a heavy door into oblivion. I glanced back as my fan club disappeared behind. The lights were full on now and glared into my eyes. I still had a dull headache and needed a drink of water something awful. I was getting angrier by the moment; what right did this man have to take me away from my colleagues? And what power did he hold over them that they hadn't even blinked an eye?

I was maneuvered through another door into a part of the shelter where volunteers didn't go. Another hallway, but not so nice on this side. The lights hanging from the ceiling were strictly utilitarian; the floor, gray concrete; the walls, cinder block. A final door landed us in a room about the size of the holding kennel but not nearly as pleasant. A folding metal table, three metal chairs and a laptop computer were the only furnishings.

"Sit down. Please," the man added through his teeth.

I thought about defying his will on general principle, but my knees felt weak from the night's maltreatments, and I didn't trust myself not to fall on my face, the only part of my head that didn't already have bruises.

I took the chair.

He stood.

We stared at each other with tangible dislike.

"Why have you brought me here?" I said finally. "If it's about the theft of the investigations cats, I'll be happy to tell you everything I know."

He produced a small recorder from his suit pocket and clicked it on, police-like. It suddenly occurred to me that it wasn't his only official feature.

"You're a cop?" I stammered.

"Detective. Garrison."

I held out my hand. "Pleased to meet you, Detective Garrison. I'm..."

"I know who you are," he interrupted. "Now tell me. What's happened to the cats?"

It took me a moment to get what he was saying and even when I got it, I didn't comprehend. "You think I had something to do with the disappearance of the Siamese?" I laughed. "You must be joking. I was in the kennel when the thieves came."

"Thieves?"

"Yes. A man. Or men. I don't know for sure."

He hesitated as if trying to grasp the concept that the perp was not conveniently in his custody, and he would now be forced to go back to work.

"What makes you think there was more than one?" he said finally.

"I don't know. I thought I heard voices, but I only saw the one man."

"Did you get a good look at him?"

"Not really. He pushed me down, I hit my head and must have passed out. Why are you standing there accusing me when you should be calling the paramedics to look at my injuries?"

He didn't answer.

There was a knock on the door. For a moment, it seemed as if Garrison were going to ignore it the same way he was ignoring me, the truth, and everything else pertinent to the case, but he clicked off the recorder and answered. I saw Denny Paris's handsome profile in the doorway. The two spoke in hushed tones and then Garrison turned. "You stay here," he commanded. Stepping out into the hallway with Denny, he closed the door behind him.

"And where do you think I'm going to go?" I asked the drab, gray walls.

I sat for a while and waited, growing more perturbed with every second. Finally I couldn't stand it anymore. I should be giving evidence and getting checked out by a young, handsome EMT—not rotting in the Tank like a common criminal! I got up and headed for the door, making my plans as I went. If it were unlocked, I would leave; if locked, I would bang on it until someone came, and this time they would because according to the round battery clock tick-tocking away on the wall, it was now nine in the morning and the shelter would be busy busy busy. As I circled the table, however, I caught a glimpse of the laptop's glimmering screen. I forgot both plans and went for another objective altogether.

There were several windows open on the desktop, the topmost being what looked a lot like a rap sheet with my name at the head of it. Once I had ascertained that it was still thankfully blank, I quickly minimized it to peer at what lay behind.

Some of the documents seemed straightforward enough: a report summarizing the breed simulation case, dated over a year before and referencing cases in Florida,

Michigan, Montana, and Oregon; a letter from Northwest Humane Society. Others were more obscure: several forms and an Excel spreadsheet with long lists of large figures but no references as to what they represented. The very last window was the beginning of an email on a secure messaging site from Detective Garrison to someone named Thomas. First name? Last? I couldn't tell. What I could tell was that I was never meant to read those words:

Have traced Bannock to Portland, Oregon. Up to his old tricks again. Must stop him before someone else does. Pretty obvious Londale is loose. That's dangerous. Wait for my note...

There it ended as if he had been interrupted. I glanced at the return address in the banner, Rxgarrison@mpd.gov, and made a mental note. Not that I had any intention of emailing the ill-mannered detective. I wanted to help with the investigation— I wanted to see those cat abusers behind bars. But this man who for no good reason was accusing me of the crime? He was someone I could live without.

The door opened abruptly, banging against the wall. It seemed like everything that man did was rude, loud, and excessive. "Hey!" he yelled, crossing the distance between us in two long strides. "What do you think you're up to?" He slapped the laptop shut and pushed me back toward my chair. "Sit down. I'm not through with you."

"Now hold on!" I spat, finally reaching the end of what little patience I had left. "Whatever you want with me, tell me and get it over with so I can get out of your obnoxious presence!"

I realized the moment the words sprang from my lips that they were over the top, but maybe it was just what was needed; Garrison stood as if struck dumb. He swayed slightly, then looked away.

"I apologize, Mrs. Cannon. Please," he said, this time

without the malice, "have a seat. Let's talk about what happened last night."

Still panting with ire, I stared at him, waiting for some sign that his civility was a ploy, but none came. He sank into his chair and reopened the laptop, punched a few keys, and looked at me. His beady eyes seemed quieter than before.

I sat. "You want to know about last night?"

"Yes."

"The truth?"

"Yes."

"Do you still think it was my fault?"

He hesitated. "I'm just here to get the facts, Mrs. Cannon. I have no opinion on your guilt or innocence. That would be for a judge to decide."

It wasn't altogether the answer I thought I deserved, but it would do for the moment. I wanted to give my statement and be gone. I was tired and everything hurt and I still thought somebody ought to check out my head wound, just in case, so I took a deep breath and told him what I knew, from my late night visit with the cats to the man who pushed me down. To Garrison's credit, I'll say that he listened respectfully, making notes on his laptop to augment the tape recording. When we were done, he said a generic thank you and got one of his men to escort me back to the foster office. I was never more pleased to put someone behind me.

Detective Garrison had told me I needed to report my stolen bag to the Portland Police and to call my cell carrier right away about the missing phone. Kerry was out, but her volunteer assistant, Jack McCahery, was at the desk. Aside from giving me a once-over as if I were some sort of freak, which I probably had earned after my night in the investigations kennel, he was courteous and helpful and even dialed the numbers himself. He probably thought me incapable, and he might have been right. I'll admit I was fading fast.

Kerry came back just as I was finishing up with the phone company. She handed me a cup of strong coffee. "I have someone to look at your head, Lynley. Is that okay?"

I smiled as I gazed into the deep blue eyes of a crisply clad medic. The fact that it was a woman and not a man didn't bother me one bit. She took my pulse, peered at my pupils with a little light, and looked at my head wounds. She wanted me to go to the hospital to have them checked further, but I declined and she didn't argue. Producing an expansive metal first aid kit, she cleansed the gash on my forehead, applied antibiotic ointment, and covered it with a large bandage. She said the goose egg on the back of my skull was a hematoma, in other words, a bruise; it would be sore for a while but not to worry.

When she was done, Kerry said, "Come on, Lynley. I'll drive you home."

I thought about declining—after all, it would mean I would have to bus it back to pick up my car at a later date—but I realized I didn't have the energy to quibble.

"That would be great," I said. "That is, if you're really sure it's not too much trouble."

"I'm sure." She grabbed her coat and wallet from the locked cabinet under the desk. "Jack, you can handle things for an hour or so?"

"Sure, Kerry, take your time. It's almost lunch hour anyway. I'll go when you get back."

Lunch hour? I looked at the clock after quelling the impulse to pull out my nonexistent phone and saw it was eleven forty-five. Where had the time gone?

"We have to go by my car and get my purse."

She gave me a quizzical look, then said, "No problem."

"Can I ask another favor?"

Kerry nodded.

"Can we visit Xena for a minute? She would be mad if I was here and didn't at least say hello."

Kerry laughed. "We wouldn't want Xena to be mad, now would we?"

I snickered, the joke being that the feisty tortie was always mad.

* * *

I leaned back in the seat of Kerry's Toyota Yaris and closed my eyes. I had that spinning feeling that comes after a night with not enough sleep and too much coffee which was pretty much the whole of it. I gave her directions to my house, and we drove in silence. I think I was nodding off when she said, "Lynley?"

"Yes?"

She hesitated. "What happened to the investigations cats?"

A rush of anger coursed through me, and I sat up. "Not you too? You can't think I had anything to do with their abduction."

"No, we don't. We got the guys on our surveillance tapes. There wasn't much detail, just a couple of men wearing hoodies coming in with a big dog carrier on a roller dolly, then leaving with same, filled with the cats, I assume. I... Well, it's just that you were there, which is a little surprising. I left around nine forty-five, so you must have come in after that. That's awfully late for a shelter visit. What were you doing, if you don't mind my asking?"

"I have privilege," I justified. "And it wasn't *that* late. I just wanted to see Meow and the new kitties."

"It's okay, Lynley. I'm not accusing you. I totally understand wanting to drop by. It was just a little irregular."

"I know," I sighed. "It was stupid. Maybe if I hadn't been in the room, they wouldn't have got the cats. I let them right in, you know."

"It's not your fault. The shelter is supposed to be a safe place. They shouldn't even have been able to get into the building, but they did. They would have got to those cats one way or another."

I looked at her. "You think?"

She smiled reassuringly. "I'm sure of it. They're crooks after all."

"Are you thinking it's the breed counterfeiters again?"

"That's the unofficial assumption. Why would anyone else go for those exact same cats?"

Kerry pulled to a stop to let a pedestrian across the crosswalk. I gazed at the scenery, an ultra-modern storefront flanked by starkly contrasting residential houses.

"But why?" I blurted, surprising myself as much as Kerry. "Why should they want the cats back? What's so important about those particular cats that they would break in, risk getting caught? Why not just cut their losses and steal some new ones?"

Kerry shrugged. "I don't get the whole business. Breed cats aren't cheap, but the ones they've sold, the ones we know about at least, didn't bring all that much. Not like they're going to get rich off their troubles. But no accounting for crooks."

"And that's the other thing."

"What's that?" Kerry asked, starting across the intersection and back into the flow of traffic.

"Detective Garrison. I don't get why a detective from Montana would follow an animal abuse case all the way to Oregon. If it were a perfect world, yes, all animal abusers would be chased down like drug dealers or murderers, but that's just not the way it is."

"It's getting better."

"I know, but really, Kerry? Doesn't it seem a bit suspicious to you?"

She frowned but didn't answer. I turned to watch the houses go by, the big trees, bare bones in the white winter sun, gardens of brown stalks and black decomposing leaves. I'm usually optimistic this time of the season, having made it through the holiday hump and knowing spring is on its way, but for some reason, this time it felt too much like death. I closed my eyes again and didn't open them until Kerry pulled up in front of my house.

I got my purse and dragged myself stiffly out of the small car. Amazing what a night on the floor can do to old bones. I reached back for my shelter bag and then remembered it was gone.

"They took my bag, you know," I growled. "And my badge. I'll need to get a new one."

"I'll have it for you next time you come in. You can just pick it up at the front desk."

"Thanks. And thanks for the ride. I appreciate it."

"You're welcome. See you soon." She paused. "We will see you soon, right?"

I smiled. "You bet. It'll take more than a knock on the head to keep me away from the shelter."

"I'm so sorry." Her dark eyes misted. "I hate that something so terrible happened on my watch."

"I know, but it's certainly not your fault. Maybe now that we have a detective on the scene, the jerks will be caught."

"Here's hoping."

She watched me heft myself up the short flight of steps and onto my front porch, then pulled away. I plucked the key clip from my belt loop, uttering a short prayer of thanks that they had not been stolen with the rest of my stuff. I unlocked the door, picking up the morning paper on my way in. I was about to toss it onto the side table when through the film of the plastic bag, I caught the headline.

There had been another murder.

Chapter 13

Cat behaviorists suggest we play with our cats for at least ten minutes a day. A little one-on-one time with a string or a toy can keep kitty happy and healthy, to say nothing of our furniture, our breakables, and our plants.

Despite what I told Kerry about my whole horrible experience not turning me off to the shelter, I found myself a little reluctant to return to the scene of the crime, if you'll excuse the cliché. It wasn't that I was afraid it would happen all over again; the chances of that were next to nil. It was more of a feeling, like a dark, hovering shroud that threatened to suffocate me whenever I thought about being there. I knew it was irrational; I also knew it would go away, eventually.

It was taking its sweet time, however. After Kerry dropped me off, I'd slept for a day and a half, then napped away a few more in front of the TV surrounded by cats. It didn't help that the local news was filled with reports of the latest in the series of Portland killings. I hadn't known the person—a woman this time, brought down near her car in the Lloyd Center parking lot—but because the murderer was simulating an animal attack, specifically that of a wildcat, the media fluffed their story with sensationalist footage of cats gone bad. If I'd watched one more clip of a cougar jumping an elk, I might have thrown myself out a window!

After giving up on television as a form of restorative

therapy, I'd progressed to putzing around the house, still doing next to nothing and certainly avoiding tasks requiring serious brain work. Kerry and Jack had convoyed my little car to my front door, but I had no desire to go out. That lasted another week, until finally I had decided enough was enough—it was time to rejoin humanity.

Even if I wasn't quite ready to face FOF, I had lots of other things to do. I hadn't seen my granddaughter, Seleia, for way too long, so without another thought, I grabbed my brand new smartphone and texted her, by far the best way to get hold of the busy sixteen-year-old. I'm not great at texting, and it took me a full five minutes to type out my simple message, complete with errors courtesy of the phone's autocorrect feature: *Hi luv been to long want too go to lurch?* Within a few seconds, she had texted me back. Her message read: *Hi Lynley. Glad to hear from you. I'd absolutely love to go to lunch. Classes are heavy so it would have to be on the weekend. How about Saturday, same time same place? Love you :).* I don't know how she does it!

Same time was eleven o'clock before the lunch rush, and same place was Huber's, one of Portland's fine old restaurants. I had been taking her there since she was a child, impressed by the tablecloths and linen napkins, tea from a real tea pot in real English tea cups with saucers. The wait persons were still decked out in black with white aprons, but in spite of the highbrow aura, they were never stuck up. A grand old institution, I prayed I'd be dead before it ever slipped totally into the twenty-first century.

So that took care of Saturday. And then I had some catch-up work to do on my family tree. I had recently discovered a new great-uncle on the Mackey side through a Scottish Genealogy club I had joined and was excited to research him and his line across the Pond.

And of course, there were my own cats to be considered. Sometimes, what with the fosters and my time at the shelter seeing to others, they didn't get as much attention as they would have preferred. I tried to play with them every day, but lately it had been more like every other day, and I'll admit that since the Meow Mystery, I hadn't been the best playmate, my mind wandering away from string, balls, and catnip mice to pseudo-Siamese and all the implications.

Actually it had been doing that a lot; out of the blue I'd find myself staring into space, my thoughts miles away in a dirty warehouse or an empty midnight kennel. In fact, I was off on one of those introspections when my phone rang. For a moment, I didn't recognize the ringtone, a ding-dong doorbell sound that I would have to change when I figured out how to do it. I liked the new upgrade Verizon had sent me to replace my stolen model, but it had embellishments the old one could only have dreamed of. Some I was finding convenient; others seemed more trouble than they were worth.

I clutched the slick black oblong, noting the caller was not among my contacts. "Hello?"

"Lynley?"

"Yes?" I panted, not quite placing the basso female voice.

"This is Pinky, volunteer coordinator for Oregon Hospice. You got a minute?"

"Oh, Pinky, how are you? What's up?"

"Haven't heard from you in a while. Would you and Tinkerbelle be interested in a new assignment?"

My heart jumped. "Sure. We'd love it. Actually this is perfect timing."

"There's a lady on hospice," Pinky stated. "She's in an

assisted living facility and misses her cats desperately. She had two older kitties, and they have both passed on now. So sad. And of course it's impossible for her to get another at this point. She has end-stage liver disease and is basically confined to her bed."

"How's her..." I wavered.

"Her mind?" Pinky finished for me, familiar with the concern. "Sharp as a tack. And she's had quite a life which she enjoys talking about at great length to anyone who will listen. I'm sure you'll get an earful if you go. What do you think?"

"Sounds good. Let me check my calendar." I looked around for my engagement book, spied it by my computer. "When do you want me to start?"

"Soon. I'll email you the details. Then you can make the arrangements whenever it suits your schedule."

I flipped the pages. Though there was a scattering of commitments, most of the coming weeks were a little bleak. "I can probably get by within a few days."

"Good. I knew I could count on you, Lynley. Call if you have any questions."

"I will."

She hung up and so did I. I bristled with excitement. The idea of a new Pet Partner visit was motivating and just what I needed to get me out of my funk. Tinkerbelle seemed to know instinctively what was up. She put her little paw on my leg and meowed expectantly.

"Want to go on an adventure?" I asked her, scooping her into my arms. She purrumphed in assent.

We hadn't been on an assignment for quite a while so the first thing to do was check my gear: Tink's cat-sized vest with the Pet Partners insignia; the harness and leash she was required to wear; the soft brush; the special treats she was allowed at the end of the visit.

I pulled the shiny foil pouch out of my carryall and shook it. A puny rattle came from inside. I tried to recall when last I had opened them. Since I couldn't, I decided it was high time to get some new. I needed to buy a few other things at the pet store, and I had a coupon that would expire if I didn't use it soon, so that was settled.

I distributed the last of the treats among the clowder that, with the rattle of food, had materialized from out of nowhere, then bade them farewell. Jumping into my long-forsaken car, I headed for the Pet Pantry, a small, locally owned pet supply store where, though they might not have aisles and piles of every item, they were always well stocked with the things I needed.

When I got there, the owner, Harlene Meadows, was behind the counter. She was one of those women whose age was hard to guess. With her round, timeless features, she could have been anywhere from early thirties to a well-preserved fifty-five. Her hair was bottle blonde and cut in an indeterminate style. Her eyes were the sort of blue that made one think of summer skies or colored contact lenses. Her clothing preference tended toward oversized dresses, usually in a loud floral print or calico which made her look heavier than she really was. When she was working, she wore her neon peach *Pet Pantry* apron, the pockets of which invariably bulged with an array of useful items such as pens, pencils, tape, and scissors. She had been known to carry staple gun and staples when she was reorganizing her bulletin board and even a small knitting project, complete with needles, when business was slow.

Harlene smiled when she saw me. "Lynley! How are you? How's the kitties?"

"We're all good," I answered. "And you?"

"Great. Great." She nodded furiously. "Business gets a little sparse sometimes, you know—people can't afford as much as they used to, but we get by."

"I pass out your business card wherever I can. I know at least a few people have stopped in."

"Oh, bless your heart, dearie! I hope they had a good experience."

"I've had only good reviews, Harlene. What's not to like about this place?" I gestured to the small, cozy reading area with its library of animal-related books and the nicely arranged shelves brimming with stock. The homey atmosphere spoke for itself.

"Well, we like it," she said modestly. Though Harlene Meadows was the sole owner of the Pet Pantry, she always spoke in the plural. Those of us who knew her assumed she referred to her cat, Scout, as a full partner.

I looked around. "Speaking of Scout, where is the little lady?" Scout was a small female kitty with an old lip injury that had left her with a perpetually quizzical expression. She had been scrawny and nearly furless when Harlene had rescued her from a shelter in her home town of Washougal, Washington. With love, care, and hypo-allergenic cat food, Scout had grown into a luscious sweetheart with fur like a mottled seal. I spied her on one of the easy chairs in the reading area. She was gazing at me and gave a welcoming blink. I blinked back—the polite thing to do. Her golden eyes closed, having done her duty, and she returned to her kitty dreams.

"Can I help you find anything?" the proprietor asked.

"No, I just need some treats and food, the usual."

Taking a small cart, I gathered up my supplies: an eleven-pound bag of dry food; a case of cans. I mulled over the treat section—so many choices! Should I go for dental, hairball, hip and joint, or just plain yum? I decided on one hairball and one yum and added them to the basket.

A soft red tube about two feet long and eighteen inches in diameter caught my eye. I peered inside at the plush interior and saw a galaxy of puff balls hanging from a dark blue sky.

"That's the greatest thing," Harlene said, coming up behind me. "We just got them in. It's called a play tunnel. Do you have one yet?"

I laughed. "We have climbing trees, scratching posts, and carpet-covered hideaways, but no tunnels I'm afraid." I touched the soft plush. "It seems nice, but would they really use it?"

"Scout does! She has one upstairs that doubles as a toy, an exercise place, a cozy covered bed, and a hide-away—whatever mood she's in. They come in other colors," she added, pointing to a showy stack of donuts on the floor. "There they are, all folded up."

"Wow! They just collapse down like a slinky? That would make it easy to store."

Harlene laughed. "If you ever wanted to store them, that is. Scout's has been set up from the first, she uses it all the time, but it would be easy enough to move if we went somewhere. We'll probably take it along when we go to visit Mom in Klamath Falls next month."

"Really? She likes it so much you'd take it on a trip with you?"

"Sure! You bet. Why not?"

Since I couldn't answer that and here was a cat toy I had yet to have, it seemed only fitting that I should choose one. I picked sage green to match my living room decor since according to Harlene, that was where it was destined to reside, and added it to my cart.

"Will that do it?" Harlene asked as she returned to her place behind the counter.

"A couple of sparkly balls and I'm set." I grabbed the tiny toys from a bowl by the checkout and presented her my coupon. Harlene began to ring up my booty.

She gave me the total and ran my debit card. The flimsy receipt chugged out of the machine. Harlene tore it off and handed it to me. "Thanks, Lynley. Always great to see you. I hope your kitties like the tunnel. If they don't, you can bring it back, but I'm pretty sure that's not going to happen."

"I have a feeling you're right."

I turned to go when my eye landed on the bulletin board next to the front door. A shot of adrenaline hit my system as I zeroed in on the photo of the lovely Siamese. Underneath was penned in a neat hand: "Pedigree, papers. Can't keep him. Needs a good home. Call for details."

Though the Pet Pantry absolutely did not support puppy or kitten mills, they did sometimes have ads for animals for sale from private parties. I peered at the photo again: the sapphire eyes; the sable fur; the dark brown points of ear and nose. For a moment I'd thought it was Meow.

"Where did this come from?" I asked cautiously.

Harlene thought about it. "A man brought it in, an occasional customer. Why? You're not thinking of going for a breed cat, are you?"

"No, of course not. I just wondered... Are you sure it's all on the up and up?"

"What do you mean? Is he truly a purebred?" She shrugged. "That's for the buyer to confirm, and I always advise them to do just that, but I think he is. Why wouldn't he be?"

I stared for a moment longer. Definitely not Meow, nor did it really resemble any of the other investigations cats who had been housed at the shelter. "You're right. Why wouldn't he be?"

I started for the door, resolving to put it out of my mind. After all, not every Siamese in the city could be part of a counterfeiting scheme.

Could they?

Chapter 14

I can't say enough about the Pet Partners Program (formerly the Delta Society). Through the unflagging efforts of their volunteers, cats, dogs, bunnies, alpacas, miniature horses, and other animals bring joy, comfort, and compassion into hospitals, nursing homes, hospice situations, schools, libraries, and more.

The next couple of months were blissfully uneventful. My trepidation had waned, then evaporated altogether, and I was back volunteering at Friends of Felines, reaping the joy that comes of doing good for cats and people alike. Tinkerbelle and I made weekly visits to Lenore, my hospice patient, which we would continue to do until she died. That could be a while since Lenore showed no signs of slowing down. Whenever I saw her, she was happy and vivacious; though she moved only between bed and wheelchair, she projected an aura of strength and serenity. She knew what fate held for her and was entirely ready to meet her maker when she was called, but until that day, she intended to spend every moment living, learning, and pursuing the things she loved the most.

And she loved Tinkerbelle. I felt privileged to be able to provide her with that simple feline touch so precious and otherwise inaccessible to someone in her circumstances. I sympathized; the thought of living out my final days without a kitty to love seemed utterly unbearable.

Tinkerbelle and I had only been actively volunteering with Pet Partners for about a year, but my first contact with their program had come a decade before. A close friend of my mother's had fallen ill and gone into a home. As fate would have it, the one time I happened to visit, a woman was there with her cat. She was going from room to room, and being the cat person I am, I followed. Not everyone was interested, but most were overjoyed to see Tillie the tabby. The looks on their faces said it all, and I knew I had opened the door on a new dimension of cat companionship. From that moment, I began a quest to find a cat whose personality would accommodate the rigors of the job: the bathing and cleanliness regimen; the travel in the car; the multiple contacts with strangers in strange places. Finally I came across my lovely black lady, Tinkerbelle. I immediately adopted her, pushed through the training, and we were registered. I find great satisfaction providing a cat to the catless, and I like to think Tink gets something out of the hour-long pet-fest, too.

We had just pulled into the narrow parking lot of Lenore's facility when Carla, one of the more mobile residents, rushed up to greet me.

"Lynley! Lynley! You'll never guess what!"

At first, I was alarmed—one never knew what sad news may come out of those places—but then I saw the wide smile on her face.

"Hi, Carla. What's up?" I got out of the car and started around to the passenger side.

The elderly woman grinned widely. "Did you bring your kitty?"

"Yes, I did." I retrieved Tinkerbelle's carrier and my Pet Partners carryall containing the paraphernalia I needed for our visit. "She's right here. Want to see her?"

"Ooh, yes, please!"

I held the carrier up to her eye level, and Carla peered

through the grid. "Oh, pretty kitty. You going to visit Lenore?"

"Yes, that's right."

She wiggled her fingers through the wire. "I've forgotten kitty's name, honey."

"It's Tinkerbelle."

"What?"

"Tinkerbelle, like the little fairy in Peter Pan."

Carla cocked her head, sending a wisp of gray hair flying across her brow. "Peter Pan? I thought you said her name was Tinkerbelle."

I laughed. Carla and I had had the conversation before, though she never remembered. I assumed whatever she had been about to tell me had gone that way too, but I was wrong.

"You'll never guess what!"

"What?"

Carla gave a sly smile. "She'll tell you when you get there." She turned and shuffled toward the garden where I could hear voices and laughter from behind the lilac hedge.

Tinkerbelle was a round, fluffy pixie of a cat. She only weighed eight pounds, but added to the bulk of the carrier, it was a good, shoulder-wrenching load. Thankful she wasn't Big Red at seventeen pounds, or worse, Violet, at twenty two, I went into the building and down the brightly lit hallway to Lenore's room. Her door was ajar so after a token knock, I let myself in, closing it softly behind me.

Lenore was sitting up in her hospital bed reading. Per protocol, I gave her a once-over to see how she was doing. With a sigh of relief, I noted she seemed no worse than the last time I was there.

The eighty-seven-year-old was rail-thin with the yellowish complexion that accompanies liver difficulties, but her brown eyes sparkled every time she saw me. She always wore a colorful silk turban—I didn't know whether she was bald underneath or if it was a fashion statement. She had the largest collection of silk bed jackets and robes of anyone I'd ever known, and since I had run with an antiques crowd in my younger days, that was saying a lot.

Today she sported a voluminous paisley print in rust and mocha that complimented her eyes. She looked a little like a butterfly—tiny body and huge, beautiful, showy wings.

"Good morning, Lenore," I said, putting Tinkerbelle's carrier on the floor. I try not to ask the banal, *How are you,* of hospice patients; as long as they were alive, that was all that mattered.

Lenore marked her place with a satin bookmark and put the book aside. "Hello, Lynley. How's my kitten?"

"She's good." I opened the carrier to let Tinkerbelle out. First a cautious black nose, then a paw appeared. She stood poised for a moment, then deciding she was in friendly climes, strode from the box like the queen of all she surveyed. I clipped the leash onto her harness, scooped her up, and placed her on the bed beside Lenore. She sniffed the old woman's proffered hand then smoothed her sideburn against it, claiming it for her own.

Tinkerbelle circled and found just the right spot to lie down. I had learned long ago that when it came to pet visits, I was merely the chauffeur, so I sat by the bed and let Tink do her thing.

Usually, for the first few minutes Lenore was so wrapped up in the cat that she basically ignored me, but this time after only a cursory stroke or two, she said in her soft cultured tones, "I have some news, Lynley, that I think you will appreciate."

"Oh? What's that?"

"My nephew has bought another cat," she said with obvious satisfaction.

"Well, congratulations." I smiled, trying not to let my preference for shelter animals over the purchased kind affect my reaction.

"Yes, it is very good. The boy is nearly sixty and had never had a cat until this year. Now he has two. Can you believe it?"

"That's amazing. Was he a dog person?"

"Not really. He traveled a lot. He was an airline pilot, you see. He figured he didn't have time for a pet. But when he retired, I made it my business to convince him to consider a cat." She beamed conspiratorially. "And being a smart boy who listens to his wise old auntie, he did just that."

"Good for you."

"Well, you know I adopted all my cats from sanctuaries—either that or they adopted me." She snickered as the visions of cats-gone-by danced in her rheumy eyes. "But Bill had his heart set on a certain breed. I told him to wait until one showed up at your Friends for Felines—they always do eventually."

"People don't realize how many purebred cats end up in shelters," I agreed.

"And there are breed rescue groups too. But once Bill decided he wanted a cat, he had to have it right now. No patience, that boy. Still, I can empathize with his enthusiasm. Why wait when you never know what tomorrow may bring? And once he had the one, he concluded he needed another as a companion. He still spends a lot of time away from home and was concerned that Bonnie might get lonely."

"So he got a second kitty?"

"Yes, a male. He picked him up last week. Very expensive, I take it. Even more expensive than the first which he bought at a cat show." She harrumphed. "But he has all his papers and apparently comes from a long, important line."

"Have you met him yet?"

"Not yet. Bill is still acclimatizing him to his new home. He doesn't want to do anything out of the ordinary at this time. And though I can tell you I am a little disappointed, I do agree with him."

"It's a good idea to let them settle. A week isn't very long for a new cat to get used to such a big change. I'm sure he'll bring him soon."

"I'm sure he will." She stroked Tinkerbelle's silken fur and gazed out the window. I knew she was wondering if she would still be around by then.

"What did he get?"

Lenore turned wide eyes to me. "Pardon?"

"You said he was a breed cat. What breed?"

"Oh yes." She waved a bantam hand. "There are photographs. Look on top the chest of drawers."

I rose and crossed to the antique waterfall dresser, keeping hold of Tinkerbelle's leash per Pet Partners protocol, though by the looks of her, all curled up in the crook of Lenore's arm, she wasn't going anywhere. Spread out on a Battenburg lace runner was a handful of color glossies. Smiling, I gazed at professional quality pictures.

My smile faded. With a prickle of alarm, I stared at them dumbly.

"Pick them up, dear, and bring them over."

Robotically I did as I was told. My hand trembled as I handed them to Lenore.

"Siamese!" she exclaimed. "I don't know why perfectly common words escape me sometimes. Siamese, obviously, silly me. He has a long, fancy show cat name, but Bill calls him something for short—oh, I should remember this. Yes, I know, it's..."

"Meow?" I finished for her.

Her keen eyes flicked from the photos to me. "Meow? No, that's not it at all. Let me think. Ah, yes! Bill calls him Zoom. You know, the cat in the sweet children's series."

I took back one of the pictures and held it up close. I studied every satin hair, every sable whisker, the familiar blue-on-blue eyes gazing at me through the celluloid. I paid special attention to what I could see of his ears and tail; they were fully furred and perfectly tinted as a seal point Siamese should be. The last time I'd seen Meow, those parts had been shaved, the noxious colorant removed and cleansed by the FOF doctors, but that was two months previous, and the fur would have grown back by now. The crooks could easily have re-applied the dye.

I looked again. Yes, if the smiling Siamese wasn't Meow, it could have been his twin brother.

"Where did your nephew get this cat?" I asked a little too abruptly.

Lenore stared at me quizzically. Not much gets by her. "Why, Lynley, is something wrong?"

I pushed myself to relax and glanced once more at the image. Was I so absolutely sure this was my Meow? "No, it's nothing." I forced a smile. "He looks like a perfectly wonderful cat. Maybe I can meet him sometime when he visits."

"Do you think Tinkerbelle would appreciate that? Does she like other kitties?" Lenore petted the wide black back, and Tink purred in ecstasy.

123

I had to laugh. "It depends on her mood. She'll either play prima donna or give him a bath."

"Well, we will see." She handed me the pictures. "Please put them back on the dresser for me, dear."

I flipped through the images once more and pulled out a full body shot with a good close-up of the face and head. "Do you think I could get a copy of this one, Lenore?"

She hesitated, then gave a little wave. "Take it. Bill will bring me more. Lots more!"

I stuffed the photo in my bag, took a deep breath, and turned back to Lenore.

"And what's been happening since I saw you last?"

* * *

I walked into my house, set Tinkerbelle's carrier on the carpet, and opened the flap. Tink emerged, somewhat faster this time since she knew she was home. I clipped off her harness, then switched my shoes for slippers and tossed my coat and carryall on the chair by the door.

"Treat?" I asked her, making my way to the kitchen. It was part of the visit ritual to give her a treat when the job was finished. I was allowed to give it to her onsite but had learned that she won't eat anything when she's out working, so we wait until we get home.

She gave a short purrumph and followed, feathery tail sailing through the air like a wisp of brown-black smoke.

Grabbing the foil bag from the orange Bauer bowl on the high shelf, I fished out a few gray-green pellets. They looked like pebbles to me, but she seemed to like them.

When she was happily munching, I made myself a cup of coffee. Glancing at the Kit-Kat clock on the wall, I realized it was already four o'clock. We had stayed with Lenore a little longer than usual, but she had begun telling me about her work as a costume designer for *Transpose*, the gay men's theatre. That was back in the eighties: wide shoulder pads, big hair, and enough sequins to signal an alien spacecraft. Lenore had led quite a life. I could become morose, thinking how all that wealth of experience and knowledge was about to come to an end, but I preferred to celebrate what she was and is and leave it at that. None of us can ward off the inevitable, so we just have to do the best we can, one day at a time.

But I digress. Which is exactly what I did as I sat at the old oak table and sipped my coffee. I thought about Lenore, about the gay men's theatre, about my former career as an antiques dealer who often ran with the same crowd. Then I began to reflect on things I needed to do, things I wanted to do. I had myriad craft projects in varying states of incompletion, and since I had no plans for the rest of the evening, there was ample opportunity to tackle any one of them.

Or I could work on my never-ending family tree project.

Or watch that new String Theory DVD I'd borrowed from the library.

Or read a book.

Or do the dishes.

Anything but brood upon Lenore's nephew's new cat who, in my eyes, was a dead ringer for Meow, the stolen Siamese. I thought about the advertisement I'd seen at the pet store a few months back. Siamese were a popular breed; was I merely noticing them more than usual because of what had happened in my recent experience?

Coincidence, that's all. It had to be.

But as a life-long mystery buff, I knew deep down in my heart that there was no such thing.

Chapter 15

By nature, the big cats are elusive and reclusive, preferring to avoid all contact with humans. Though they will fight to protect themselves and their kits, there have been only 88 confirmed attacks on humans between 1890 and 2004 in the US and Canada, and of those, only twenty were fatal. Though cougars were once found in all forty-eight states, now only fifteen are home to them.

From that moment on, I began to count Siamese cats to see just how often the breed showed up in day-to-day living. Over the next few weeks I discovered:

Seven at Friends of Felines.

Six owned by people I knew.

Eight references in books.

Four on TV human-interest stories.

Two on the popular cat behavior show, *My Cat From Hell*.

Fourteen incidentals on other television episodes.

One on the radio, though I had to take the announcer's word that it was a genuine Siamese and not a Siamese impersonator.

Twenty-seven miscellaneous pictures in magazines and newspapers.

I lost count on the internet and Facebook.

And one stray cruising my backyard.

All of them looked more or less like Meow, with exception of the radio cat which, of course, I couldn't see. This exercise was supposed to put my mind at ease, and I guess in some ways it did. I found over time I was not as compulsive about the count, then it fizzled altogether. I still noticed Siamese but it would be more like, *Oh there's another one,* and I'd go on with my business.

Then there was another murder, and my Siamese statistics were forgotten altogether.

It was Frannie who called me at four in the morning to give me the news that the serial killer had struck again, this time right by Friends of Felines. All shifts had been canceled, and the shelter would be closed until further notice. We immediately made plans to go over there and check it out anyway. I don't know what we were thinking: That the closure didn't apply to us? That they would take one look and say, *Oh, it's Frannie and Lynley,* and let us in? Maybe Frannie could offer her services as cat communicator to ask the cats if they'd seen anything untoward. All I knew for sure was that we were drawn to the place as surely as a cat is drawn to an open door.

When we pulled into the parking lot a little after nine, the grounds were crawling with cops, detectives, crime scene photographers, and forensics people in purple vinyl gloves and blue paper booties. News trucks with all their high-tech equipment were parked at odd angles near the entrance, and newsmen slunk at the edge of the red police tape like wolves near downed prey.

We weren't alone in our curiosity: a little knot of green-aproned volunteers huddled against the spring chill under the old maple tree at the west end of the lot, out of the way of the action but close enough to see what was going on. Frannie and I, bundled in coats, scarves, and fleece hats, joined the group. I only recognized a few faces, but that never mattered among volunteers.

We made introductions in hushed tones, befitting the

solemnity of the situation, then got caught up on what the others knew, which wasn't much. A body had been found on the footpath down by the lake, apparently a random stranger who had been strolling the forested area we nicknamed the Wilds. It wasn't really that wild, what with its paved pathways, manicured lawns, budding azaleas, and string of pole lights that came on at the first hint of dusk, but that was where we walked the cats in their bright little harnesses, and to them, scampering behind bushes and pouncing on bugs, it was about as wild as it gets. Why someone would be out there at four in the morning was a mystery. A jogger? A druggie? A criminal? I felt both thankful and guilty it was no one we knew.

There seemed to be no doubt it was the same killer that had committed the other four gruesome murders. The media was calling him the Panther, which I personally found insulting to an absolutely regal line of big cats. I had to admit, however, that the pretense of mutilation by a wildcat was disturbingly accurate. Whoever was doing this had a fearsomely intimate knowledge of the real thing.

A large ambulance truck stood at the ready beside the west gate.

"Is he..." I nodded toward the vehicle.

"Not yet," said a young woman who had introduced herself as Maryell. In spite of the cold, she wore only jeans and a tee shirt, exposing arms banded with labyrinthine tattoos. "At least not that we've seen."

"Do we know for sure the victim was a man?" Frannie asked.

"That's what the lady on the news said. She's standing out front doing a running commentary." Maryell pointed to the arched entrance where a well-dressed woman in a lovely but inappropriately thin suit was standing like a statue, microphone in hand. I could see her lips move and strained without luck to catch the words.

"You can hear her from here?"

Another volunteer named Terra pulled a smartphone out of her apron pocket. "No but we've been watching on this." She punched a button and slid her finger across the small screen, and sure enough, there was the newswoman, front and center.

We all crowded around.

"...for those of you just tuning in, there looks to be yet another Panther murder, bringing the count up to five. This is Rebecca Russ, live from Friends of Felines Animal Shelter where the body of a man was discovered early this morning."

"Friends of Felines. Now that's a cat shelter, correct?" asked a voice attributed to the anchor in the newsroom. "Could it in some way be connected to the work of this Panther? You know, cat versus cat?"

"That's an interesting question, John," said Rebecca Russ in those dry-yet-dulcet newsperson tones. "The police maintain they have no reason to believe the shelter, itself, has any connection to the crime."

The camera panned as a solemn officer stepped self-consciously up beside the news lady.

"We have Sergeant Louis Hooper of the Portland Police Department with us. Sergeant, can you tell us if this killing was in fact the same *modus operandi* as the other murders?"

"As far as we can tell from initial examination, yes. The body was mauled by claws, big claws. We can almost certainly rule out a copy-cat crime, if you'll excuse the pun." Sergeant Hooper allowed himself the briefest of smiles.

"As we've seen in the previous killings," Rebecca said,

"this horrendous assault mimics that of a wild animal, in particular a wildcat. Are we certain it was not an actual animal attack?"

"Though the wounds do mimic an animal, there are discrepancies that prove it could only have been done by the hand of a human."

"Can you describe those discrepancies?"

"I'm afraid not at this time, no."

Suddenly we heard yelling, and the sergeant glanced offscreen. The camera swung around to catch a policeman rushing through the back gate, waving wildly.

Sargent Hooper bid Rebecca Russ a hasty farewell. On air, she didn't miss a beat: "That was Sargent Louis Hooper of the Portland Police. It looks like there may have been a new development."

"Do you know the nature of this development, Rebecca?" asked the voice from the studio.

"I do not, John. Only what the officer who came to get the sergeant was saying as he ran up."

"And what was that?"

"Well, I didn't catch the whole thing, but it sounded like they may have found a clue. Or a claw."

* * *

Toward midday, it began to drizzle, one of the most common of the twenty-seven different types of precipitation we have here in the northwest. Drizzle is especially miserable: an insidious little rain that gets in everywhere and can soak through just about anything before you know it. There had been no news since the discovery of the claw clue. In fact, the newswoman had never been able to confirm or deny what she thought she had heard. She'd been treading water for some time now, rehashing the same old stories and interviewing petty functionaries who knew even less than she did. The television station had long since gone back to regular programming.

We'd lost a few of our group when the rain started, and Frannie and I decided we'd had enough as well. Maryell, who aspired to be an actor and couldn't pass up an opportunity for air time, even if it was just the morning news, had gone to see if she could get an interview. Judging from Rebecca Russ's nods, smiles, and desperation, she was successful.

Instead of going home, we headed for the English Tea Shoppe nearby. That's the great thing about being retired: the spontaneity returns to one's life. It can also be the bad thing if a person doesn't have many interests, but neither Frannie nor I had any such problem.

Once inside the warm, heavenly-scented atmosphere of the bakery, we shed our wet things and freshened up in the ladies' room. What a relief to get out of those cold, clammy coats! For a few minutes, we merely basked, letting the feeling creep back into half-frozen fingers and toes.

We decided on a pot of gen-mi cha, not exactly a British favorite but certainly one of ours, and the little waitress had it steeping on the table in no time. The pot was round and cobalt blue; the tea cups, complete with saucers, were mismatched Royal Doulton. That was part of the fun of the place; no two pieces of China were alike.

"It feels strange not to be at the shelter," said Frannie as she sipped her steaming beverage.

"The only time we ever come here is after a shift," I agreed.

"I wonder how long it will be closed?"

I shrugged. "Hopefully not too long. I don't know

who's going to be taking care of the cats, but that's a big job."

"I'm sure they'll just be given the basics: food, water, clean litter. Probably not much play time or socializing."

"Probably not any."

"It's too bad," Frannie said. "I've been working with Mona, you know, the one they said was feral when they brought her in?"

I nodded. "I don't think she's feral at all, just scared."

"More like traumatized. I've been trying to find out what happened to her so we can tackle her PTSD."

"She was a stray. They don't have any information, do they? Oh. You mean with *communication*?"

"That's right." Frannie gave a big smile. "And it seems to be working. So far, I'm just concentrating on letting her know she's safe, sending the meditation we learned. But she comes out from under her blanket whenever I speak to her now. And she's beginning to show interest when I wiggle a ribbon toy outside her kennel. She still hisses and hides if I put it through the bars, but it's a start."

"That's great, Frannie. The class really worked for you, didn't it?"

"Well, yes, I think so. Or maybe it just helps me clear away my own thoughts so I can be more empathic with the cats. I don't know." She paused. "But I've been working with Mona every day—if I don't continue, there may be a setback. This murder really is a complication."

"I bet the dead guy thinks so too," I commented with a grin.

Frannie gasped. "Oh, I didn't mean..."

"I know. Just kidding. I wonder if they've released his identification yet?"

"My kingdom for a smartphone," Frannie said.

I sat up in my chair. "And I have one! Let's see if I can figure out how to make it work." I pulled the little instrument out of my purse and clicked it on. For a few moments, I just stared at the brilliant and complex face, then chose a tiny world icon and poked it with my finger. When nothing happened, I poked it again. This time it produced a neon rainbow of flashing, pulsing colors. I waited while it finished its vibrant thinking.

"When did you get that?" Frannie asked, watching the tiny dynamo go through its motions.

"When mine was stolen back in January. I haven't showed it to you before?"

"No, but then we don't use them during shelter shifts, do we? The ringtones distract the patrons and bother the cats. I leave mine in my locker."

"Me, too. I've had it for three months but still don't really know how to do anything besides make phone calls and play games."

"I'm planning on getting one at my next upgrade. I'm looking forward to it, but confidentially I'm a little afraid at the same time. They seem so complicated."

"There is a learning curve, for sure. Oh!" I exclaimed as the small screen asked me which of several locked Wi-Fi networks I wanted, then informed me there was no internet connection. I knew it was lying—I could see the familiar Wi-Fi symbol on a sticker beside the cash register—but I didn't feel like arguing with a technological wonder; I'd sunk many a good hour following its path of links that led nowhere, at least nowhere I wanted to go, and wasn't in the mood right now. I shut it off and put it on the table. "I give up. We'll just have to wait till we get home."

Frannie laughed, and we both took a nip off our tea, hot, pungent and reviving.

"Why do you suppose someone would try to make their murders look like a cat attack? It really seems like a grisly way to kill someone."

"Yes, very tactile," I replied. "The killer must be covered with blood by the time he's done."

"And it seems like it would take some amount of strength. Is that why they assume it's a man?" Frannie picked up a small brown menu that lay on the table, perused it distractedly, then put it down again. "Or could someone have a wild cat for a pet? You know, like an attack tiger that he lets loose on his enemies?"

"They seem sure it wasn't a real animal. And I think I know why." I paused, collecting thoughts. "If it were a real cat, there would be bite wounds as well as claw marks. Cats like to rip out the throats of their prey."

"Good point, if a little on the graphic side."

We both laughed. "What? You think it's out of place to be discussing the morbid points of murder over a cup of tea?"

"We are a couple of Miss Marples sometimes, I must confess."

I heard a soft squeak coming up behind me and turned to see our waitress wheeling up a pastry cart. "Time for a goodie?" she asked in her lilting British accent.

Looking over the pretty plates of chocolate éclairs, cream puffs, glazed Napoleons, pastel-tinted *petits fours*, and various other pies, cakes and fancies, Frannie and I nodded a synchronous yes.

I gave a short prayer of thanks that I was alive and about to eat a wonderful pastry instead of dead and mangled down by the lake in the Wilds.

Chapter 16

Thirty percent of the average cat's waking time is spent grooming.

After tea, Frannie and I went shopping, then to a movie, one of the new action hero flicks based on a comic book character. Lots of smash 'em, crash 'em, brilliant special effects in 3D. We both enjoyed it tremendously and laughed because the hero who was exciting all the young fans had come straight out of a comic Frannie and I had read as children. We won't go into how long ago that was but suffice it to say, this hunky fellow in the red tights, if judged by years alone, would be a senior citizen by now.

It was six o'clock when I finally got home. After a hello to the kitties, I went straight to the TV to see if I could catch some news about the murder at FOF. As I stripped off coat, hat, scarf, gloves, and soggy shoes, I heard the announcement that they would be back with more on the murder after this brief message. I plopped down on the couch and muted the commercial. Four minutes later, I was still waiting for the furniture ads, insurance ads, fast food ads to end; no one in their right mind could call that brief!

Little had instantly claimed her spot on my lap. Violet was insisting it was dinner time, which it was. Solo, my shy white girl, poked her nose out from under the couch to agree with Violet. Tinkerbelle lay curled by the window, but one eye was wide open so as not to miss any important action. Big Red had got the jump on the others; I could hear him munching leftover kibble in the kitchen, not bothering to wait for more savory fare.

Harry wanted to go outside even though it was cold and I knew he wouldn't like it. I ignored them all. They could wait a few minutes longer.

Then the phone rang.

Oh, brother, I said to myself. The news was back on, and I considered not answering, but after the fourth ring, I couldn't stand it any longer. I heard my mother in my head saying, *it might be something important;* why, it might even be my mother, though she usually calls on my cell. Launching myself toward the kitchen with a few colorful expletives, I grabbed the cordless receiver and stepped back into the doorway where I could at least see the TV.

"Yes?"

There was a pause on the line, and I figured it was one of those spam calls that the no-call registry was supposed to opt me out of. I was about to hang up when I heard a faint "Hello?" on the other end.

"Yes?" I repeated. "Who is this?"

"Lynley Cannon? This is Lenore Todd, your hospice patient?"

I ducked back into the kitchen, beyond the noise of the news. "Lenore! Yes, this is Lynley. I'm sorry, I didn't recognize your voice on the telephone."

"Oh, I understand completely. A woman alone can't be too careful these days. And I really am sorry to bother you. But I didn't know who else to call."

I caught the worry in her tone. "It's fine, Lenore. What can I do for you?"

"Well, it's my nephew's cat, you see."

"The new one? Zoom?"

"No, actually it's Bonnie, the one he had before."

"What's up with Bonnie?" I was expecting some

behavioral question. I get that a lot, being the local cat lady: *Fluffy's clawing the furniture; Max and Miss Kitty don't get along;* and let's not forget the oh-too-familiar *Toby or Muffy or Baby isn't using the litter box—whatever shall I do?*

I was caught completely by surprise when Lenore said in her most succinct voice, "Bonnie's been stolen. I want you to find her and bring her home to us."

* * *

"I'm willing to pay you, Lynley," Lenore continued when I didn't reply. "Of course I would never expect you to do it without compensation."

"Well, I...," I began but I really didn't know what to say. "Why do you think she's been stolen? People don't usually steal cats, even expensive ones."

"Oh, she was stolen alright!" Lenore exclaimed, barely controlling her octogenarian rage. "Someone broke right into Bill's condo when he wasn't there and seized her!"

"Isn't it more likely that the thief was after something of value, something easy to sell? What did the police say?"

"They weren't much help. You see, nothing else was taken. Only Bonnie, bless her little soul."

"Maybe the thief was interrupted before he could get what he was after and then left the door open. Bonnie got out and got lost. Has your nephew contacted the local shelters? Maybe Bonnie's been turned over to one of them."

"No, sweetie," Lenore said with the patient voice one uses with a wayward child. "Someone took her. She was stolen, snatched right out from under his eyes. There's no doubt about it. Filched, that cat was. Pilfered, nabbed, grabbed..."

"Okay, okay, I'm convinced. But why call me? There are people who do that sort of thing professionally, aren't there? Pet detectives?"

Lenore gave a snort. "Yes, and Bill's already got one of them working on it. *Best in town,* according to their own advertising."

"Well, there you go. I know this is a hard thing to deal with, but I'm sure they'll do everything they can..."

"No, Lynley," Lenore broke in. Her voice was raspy, and I knew she was becoming fatigued. "You! I want you. Please will you come?"

"Yes, of course I'll come," I agreed quickly, just to get her to relax. "I'll stop over tomorrow morning. But I don't know what I..."

"Hello?" a man's deep voice came on the line.

"Hello?"

"This is Evan, the night nurse. I'm afraid Lenore's too tired to talk any more right now."

"I understand." I could hear Lenore clamoring in the background. "Just tell her I'll see her in the morning, I promise. And not to worry."

The nurse conveyed the message and the rampage quit.

"Thanks," I was saying when I heard a click on the other end. "Goodbye," I said sarcastically to the terminated line and replaced the handset in its cradle.

As I walked slowly back into the living room, I saw the weather report was on, dubious warnings of showers, sprinkles, and drizzle spots, three more types of Portland rain. I had missed the update on the murder; now I'd have to wait until ten o'clock if I wanted to find out the news.

I wasn't really thinking about the murder anymore, however. I was thinking about Lenore and her nephew's missing cat. I still didn't understand what I could do that a professional investigator couldn't, but I didn't want to upset her in her fragile state of health. I would go and talk to her face to face, see what she was thinking and take it from there. And maybe she would have forgotten all about it by morning. Though from what I knew of Lenore, that would not be the case.

Something was nagging at the back of my mind. Something dark and musty, like an old, abandoned mill. Then it came to me: here I was again, in the middle of another Siamese mystery.

And why, if they took the trouble to break in, did they only take the one cat? Why did they leave Zoom behind?

Before I could answer the unanswerable, the phone rang again. This time it was my cell, Kerry from foster.

"Hi, Lynley. How's it going?" Kerry said cheerfully.

"Fine. How's it going with you? Are you at the shelter? Do you know what's happening there?"

"I'm at the shelter. It's really calmed down a lot here since they took the, um, body away. They've got big halogen lights set up by the lake and a few police are still hanging around. There's one lone news truck and it's really more of a news minivan. We felt sorry for them and invited them in for coffee. But that's about it."

"Will the shelter be open tomorrow?"

"I think so. We're treating it as if. Won't get the final word until someone calls to confirm, but I can't see why not. Business at the shelter doesn't have any effect on the Wilds."

"Well, let me know so I can come in for my shift. Or is that what you're calling about?"

There was a pause on the line, then Kerry said, "There's been a development in the kitty counterfeiting case." Her tone was different, the lighthearted banter gone. "Special Agent Paris was wondering if he could consult with you?"

I was taken completely by surprise. "Denny wants to

consult with me? Whatever for? I mean, I'd be honored," I added quickly, "but I can't imagine how I could help."

"He thinks very highly of you, Lynley. As we all do."

"Well, thanks...," I muttered self-consciously.

"So you'll do it?"

"Well, sure. But really?"

"Can you be here tomorrow morning?"

I thought about my promise to visit Lenore; she didn't get up until ten or so. "Can it be early?"

"As early as you like."

"Eight-thirty?"

"Great. We'll see you then."

"Okeydokey," I said, flustered into using the archaic term from my childhood days.

Kerry laughed and hung up the phone. I stood for a few moments, considering the ramifications.

Suddenly I was in great demand, but not for my poetry writing, my afghan crocheting, or my intimate knowledge of what really went on during the hippie era. Not even for my wealth of experience with cats, at least not directly. I was wanted for my powers of detection, an aspect of myself I really didn't know I had. I could use some extra income: if these two cases panned out, maybe I'd start a business as a private Jane.

I felt a soft head nudge my leg, gentle but insistent. I looked around and saw a sea of small faces, six pairs of cat eyes all staring at me. Fraulein Fluffs, the head-butter, opened her mouth and let go a wail of discontent.

"Alright, guys," I appeased. "Dinner's on the way."

* * *

I went to bed after nodding off in front of the television and missing the wrap-up of the cop show I was watching, but when my head finally hit the pillow, I couldn't sleep. I'd had a disturbing dream during my few minutes of TV slumber, something about Lenore's nephew's stolen cat ganging up with the counterfeit Siamese and solving the Panther murders. I'm not sure how they accomplished it; the only part I remember clearly was what they did to the killer once they found him. Suffice it to say, a panther had nothing on the damage those little cats inflicted on that depraved human being.

I couldn't get the dream out of my mind, but it wasn't the image of the mutilated corpse that bothered me; it was the premise that the theft of Bonnie and the Siamese counterfeiting were related. Maybe I'd been watching too many police dramas where everything presented to the viewer is in some way linked, and at the end of the hour, all wrapped up in a neat little package and tied with a bow. Life wasn't like that. Or was it? Could there be a connection between the two off-beat crimes? Both had a similar timbre; both were unusual, unheard-of offenses with no real monetary or psychological gain. In other words, both were a bit weird.

I reminded myself that I couldn't be sure there had even been a theft until I talked with Lenore in the morning. So far, she had exhibited no dementia, but she was on various medications to control her ever-increasing pain; there was always a possibility the cat-theft was partially—or completely—a figment of her imagination. In which case all my speculation was for naught.

I checked the clock by my bedside; it was one-fifty-two. I rolled over, displacing Little who was sleeping by my side, and using a meditative technique I'd learned from a handsome guru-wannabe back in the peace-love sixties, Om-ed all thoughts of cat-crimes out of my mind.

Chapter 17

Millions of cats are lost each year; less than 2% are ever returned to their families. Of those, most have tags or a microchip.

The next morning I got to the shelter early so I could visit all my friends—feline, that is. There was an air of wild abandon in the cattery; I didn't know if it was the result of having a whole day by themselves—even on holidays, staff and volunteers are in and out—or something more intuitive. Did the cats know there had been a murder nearby? Did they sense that the killer had used a cat-like technique to dispatch the stranger? Could they pinpoint the slayer like they had in my dream? The possibilities—or should I say, impossibilities—were endless.

I had no idea what to expect from my consultation with Special Agent Paris. Kerry mentioned a development in the case, but to speculate on what that might be was as futile as fixating on the telepathic power of cats.

Steeling myself with a cup of coffee from the volunteer break room, I went to check in. The foster room was scattered with cat carriers implying that it was yet another spay day. There were about a dozen assorted plastic boxes—empty, meaning the cats were already being prepped for surgery. Kerry and Denny weren't there either. I seated myself on one of the plastic chairs and waited.

I sipped my coffee; it was getting cold. I got up and tossed it in the trash.

I walked around checking out the foster orders lying in

Kerry's inbox, the animal jokes on the bulletin board, the candy dish.

Taking a butterscotch, I sat back down and began to unwrap it but thought better; it would be just my luck for Denny to pick that moment to arrive, and there I'd be with my mouth full of rock-hard sugar.

It was a good call, because a mere few seconds later, Kerry burst through the door, talking fast to one of the vet techs. She gave me a smile and a hand-signal that I assumed meant she'd be with me in a moment. I nodded back and settled down for another round of waiting.

"Oh, Lynley," she said when the tech went on her way. "I'm so sorry to have got you down here for nothing. The investigations team was called away. Special Agent Paris still wants to talk with you but he's going to have to reschedule."

"Oh, that's okay. I wanted to come visit the kitties anyway. Give everyone some extra care after yesterday's fiasco." I paused. "What's the big investigations emergency? Does it have to do with the breed simulation case?"

"I don't really know," she said in a tone that led me to believe she knew but wasn't telling.

"You mentioned some news. What's that all about?"

Kerry tensed but didn't answer.

"Hey, it was you who called me, remember? You said Special Agent Paris wanted me to consult with him." I was putting her on the spot, but I had no intention of leaving until I knew what had happened that had got her so riled.

Kerry must have sensed my determination because she sighed, then sat down hard in her office chair.

"I really don't know where the team is going this morning, but I know a little of what it's about. They're pretty closed-mouthed, but Denny was here in the office when he got the call."

I dragged over the plastic chair so we wouldn't have to talk across the room and reseated myself. "Go on."

She was quiet and this time I let her gather her thoughts. "It did have something to do with the counterfeiting. They've been working on that all along, but I don't think there has been much progress until recently. Then suddenly they got an anonymous call."

"Call? What kind of call?"

"An untraceable phone call. Well, not exactly untraceable—it was made at a phone booth so no telling who may have placed it. It was from someone who referred to herself as a *concerned citizen*. I don't know where she got her information, and granted it was a little scattered, but it panned out. The team found evidence of the counterfeiters' dye in a sink in a public men's room downtown. The CC said she'd seen a man taking a cat carrier into the bathroom and the cat was crying something awful. When he came out, the carrier was silent. The woman was worried he might have done something to the cat, left it in the bathroom, or worse. Being female, she declined to go in and see for herself. Denny and Frank went to check it out."

"There was no sign of the cat?"

"No cat. Just that stinky, gooey substance in the sink. They took samples and it came back as a match to the dye the counterfeiters are using."

"Did she give a description of the man?"

Kerry shuffled some papers on her desk. "White male, short, about five-foot-four, lean build."

"Anything else?"

"Not really. He was all bundled up in a coat with a hood. She didn't leave a number where to reach her, and like I said, her call originated at a phone booth near the public facility so there was no way to interview her after they realized what they had."

"And now she's called again?"

"Yeah. Denny grabbed Frank and they went racing out of here like a cheetah after its lunch."

There was a short ping on the foster line, and a red button lit up and began to blink. I looked at the clock; it was almost nine-thirty.

"Well, I guess it's back to business as usual?" I said, nodding to the strobing phone.

"Always," Kerry signed. "We have a group of cats coming in from a quasi-hoarder. He's got at least thirty in a two-bedroom apartment, but the conditions are passable, not bad enough to take the cats into custody."

"He?" I commented. "One usually thinks of cat hoarders as female."

Kerry laughed. "Sexist misconception. Connie Lee managed to convince him to relinquish a number of the cats on his own. But now we're arranging transportation before he changes his mind."

"Well, good luck with that. I need to be going anyway."

I rose and moved my chair back where it belonged. There was a knock on the door, and a young man stuck his head in. "Kerry, sorry to interrupt but are you ready for some more Spay & Save kitties? We've got the nine o'clocks checked in."

Kerry looked at me.

"I was just leaving."

Kerry nodded to the man, and he ducked back out again. She went to the door and propped it open for the onslaught.

"Can I have Denny call you when he gets back?"

"That's fine." I shrugged on my hooded coat and gathered my purse and bag. "You sure you don't know why he wanted me?"

"I really don't." She smiled innocently.

I bet you don't! I thought to myself, but whatever I might suspect about Kerry's veracity would have to wait. I squeezed out of the office between a parade of carrier-bearing volunteers and headed for my next case.

* * *

I pulled into the parking lot at Lenore's facility on the dot of ten. It felt strange to be there without Tinkerbelle. I walked quickly past the front desk nodding to the receptionist and made my way down the hall. Things were quiet, only a few residents out wheeling themselves around. Later in the day, activity would accelerate into a controlled pandemonium: the clatter of meal trays, the whine of the vacuum, the shouts or laughter of the varied clientele.

As I made my way toward Lenore's room, I heard someone call my name. I turned and saw Evan trotting over. The white scrubs shone radiant against the big man's dark skin, but his usually cheerful face held a worried look.

"Lynley, glad to see you."

"Hi, Evan. You're still here?"

He looked at me quizzically, then smiled. "Oh, yeah. I talked to you last night on the phone, didn't I? They got me on twelve-hour shifts. I should have gone off at nine-thirty, but I stuck around to make sure Lenore was okay. Now that you're here, I'll clock out. But I wanted to talk to you first, if you don't mind."

"Of course not. What's going on with Lenore? Is this cat theft a real thing, or...?"

"No, it's real alright. Don't worry about dementia, at least not yet. She's sharp as a needle, that one. But this has got her really ruffled. I don't know why. It's not even her cat."

He held up his hands palms out. "Not that I have anything against cats," he added quickly. "Got one of my own, and I'd be off the wall if he ever went missing. But Lenore's got it into her head that this cat was stolen for nefarious purposes."

I frowned. "What sort of purposes?"

"Oh, she'll tell you all about it. I just wanted to give you a heads-up."

"Heads-up duly noted." I touched the big man's arm. "I'll talk to her, Evan. But I don't know what I can do besides that."

"Find it," he said bluntly. Then with a smile that could light all Portland, he turned. "See you next time, Lynley."

I watched him saunter down the hallway, greeting everyone he met with the same heartfelt enthusiasm. *When I go into a home*, I thought to myself, *I want a caregiver just like him!*

Lenore's door was ajar, but I gave a little knock. "Hi, Lenore," I said through the space. "It's me, Lynley."

"Oh, come in, Lynley. Finally! I feel as if I've been waiting forever!"

I walked into the spacious room and put my purse on the side table. "I know you usually sleep late; I didn't want to wake you."

She turned to me, and I noticed dark circles under her eyes. "I couldn't sleep. Not with this going on." She held out her hand. "Come sit down and I'll tell you."

I came over and sank into the easy chair beside her bed. I took her hand, noting how thin it was, fingers like twigs but thankfully warm. "Okay, now what's all this about Bonnie being stolen?"

Lenore stuck with the story she had told me on the phone: that someone broke in to Bill's place for the sole purpose of taking Bonnie; that they had not bothered with Zoom, for no reason she could think of; that there was no one on this Earth who could find said lost cat except for me.

I had gone in there with the intention of listening to the elderly woman, appeasing her fears as best I could, then continuing on about my business, but things hadn't happened quite as planned. As I got into my car an hour later, I realized I had not only accepted the commission of finding the stolen Bonnie; I had given Lenore my solemn promise that Bonnie would be back home soon. What had I been thinking? At fifty-nine, (sixty next month, but we won't talk about that) I knew better than to make promises I couldn't keep. Yet I had done just that.

Rats.

I didn't have a clue where to start. How does someone go about finding a cat in a city of millions?

I started the car, cursing my stupidity a few more times with each rev of the motor. But it was too late to take it back. I had to at least give it a try. Who knew? Maybe the real pet detective would find Bonnie, had found her already and I'd be off the hook. Wouldn't that be nice? I sighed. Somehow I doubted fate would let me go that easily.

I had taken Lenore's nephew's phone number and address and decided to give him a call. If nothing else, I could do an interview before I threw up my hands in blind and utter defeat. Lenore had supplied me with a small notebook to write down my findings and a very old pen, the clicker kind with the clip that fits in your pocket right before it squirts indelible ink onto your shirt. She had also given me five hundred dollars in cash for expenditures. I tried to refuse the money but could only get as far as giving her a signed receipt and a promise that I would return what I didn't spend, which would probably be all of it. Minus gas. I figured if I was going to be driving around in search of Bonnie, I might as well fill my tank.

Chapter 18

The HSUS and many cat experts recommend cats live indoors. Indoor cats live longer and have better health because they are not exposed to disease or risk from cars and predators.

Bill Todd lived in a relatively new downtown luxury condo with a view of the Willamette River and the southeast side of the city beyond. On a clear day, he would see Mt. Hood, but this was not such a day. Inky cumulus clouds hung like dead weights on the horizon, effectively obscuring everything beyond Mt. Tabor, the infamous inner city cinder cone just east of my house. It looked like the weather person might be right about an impending spring storm. Wondering if I should be home battening down the hatches, I gazed out the wall of windows while Bill played the perfect host, something he probably learned from his aunt, and fetched coffee. He must have had one of those Keurig machines because he gave me a list of beverage options that rivaled any Starbucks.

"I'm really sorry you came all this way for nothing," he apologized, crossing the plush carpet with two steaming mugs in hand. "I told Lenore I had already hired someone to search for Bonnie, but you know Lenore when she gets an idea into her head." Handing me one of the mugs, he smiled sheepishly and motioned for me to be seated on a deep red leather couch. I opted for a slim but comfortable easy chair instead, disliking the feel of defunct cow skin anywhere near my body.

"I know," I agreed politically, "and that's partially why I came, if you know what I mean."

He sighed. "You're probably right. She'd never let either of us rest if you didn't at least pretend to do as she asked."

William Todd was a large man in his mid-fifties, probably not much younger than I was. He must have been formidable in his salad days—tall, brawny, and muscular—but retirement had softened him. He was still ruggedly tanned and handsomely weather-beaten, rather like a citified Dennis Quaid, but the beginning of a paunch had replaced the six-pack, and a hint of a slouch marred the military posture that he must have adopted for his career as an airline pilot.

He reclined onto the couch, then sat forward, elbows on his knees. "But aren't you her hospice volunteer, Mrs. Cannon? The one who visits with your cat? That's a wonderful thing to do and all—don't get me wrong—but detective work is a far cry from kitty visits. Is this something you did before you retired?"

"Please, call me Lynley. I have some experience with investigations," I explained ambiguously, figuring he was the sort of man who would give me more credence if he didn't see me as a Murder-She-Wrote wannabe. "Currently I'm helping the Northwest Humane Society with a very complex animal abuse case." Not a lie, at least not quite.

Bill seemed appeased.

"I know it's probably a bit tedious for you, but if you could just go through Bonnie's disappearance for me; at best, I might have something to add to the ongoing case, and at the very least, I can report back to your aunt that I tried."

Bill nodded conspiratorially. "I get it. Besides, what

better do I have to do?" That last sounded just a trace flat.

I took out the little notebook Lenore had given me and clicked the ancient pen. "First let's talk about Bonnie herself—Lenore told me she is Siamese. Is she pedigreed?"

"Oh, Bonnie has a certified pedigree, full show-quality. The best of the best, that one. You may not believe it but I'd never had a cat before."

"Lenore mentioned that."

"I really didn't know what I was doing. I found her for sale at a cat show, and after chatting to some of the owners, I was all excited about taking up the show circuit myself. My impression was one of glamour and glory—all the travel, bright lights, and pretty, decorated cages. The people seemed like a nice group, and according to my aunt, cats were the best of company. I thought it would be a good hobby for a retired person like myself. I'd probably been to all of three cat shows in my life and that's being generous." He laughed. "When I got home and started studying about showing cats and all it entailed, I realized it was a business like anything else. From then on, Bonnie became an incredibly expensive pet." Bill sat back. Locking his fingers behind his head in the expansive gesture that always makes me think of birds in flight.

"Actually to the credit of the seller, she did try to convince me to start with a less expensive animal and see how I liked being kitty-dad before I moved on to higher aspirations, but I didn't listen. Not that I regret getting Bonnie—I love her dearly and could well afford the cost."

"Being show quality, she must have papers."

"Oh, yes! Papers and certificates and guarantees from the breeder."

"Where did you keep them?"

His face reddened. "I had them framed and hung on

the wall of Bonnie's room. So stupid!" Bill chided himself. "I should have kept them in the safe, like the seller suggested. The thief took them all when he took Bonnie. I just never thought..."

"It's totally understandable. You're proud of her and want to show off her credentials. Who could imagine someone would steal her?"

He shrugged, appreciative of the absolution.

"Can you give me the facts about her disappearance, Bill—when, what happened, that sort of thing?"

Bill Todd went over the theft, almost word for word what Lenore had told me already. I wrote it all down in my book: Bill had been out for the evening; when he came back the door was closed but not locked; nothing was missing that he could see, and at first, he thought maybe he had left it that way himself; he then discovered with great agony that Bonnie was gone. He called the police, reported the theft, then went online and found a local pet detective with a four-star reputation.

"It must be pretty hard to break into this place. There's the lock box at the front door and even a guard in the entrance hall. I see you have a security system here in your condo." I gestured toward the little blinking keypad in the entryway. "How do you think someone could bypass all that?"

"I did not leave the door unlocked!" he blustered.

"No, I believe you. I'm just wondering if you have any idea how they pulled it off."

"Um, sorry. No. None at all."

Once he finished his statement, Bill fell silent. I let him settle for a while, then said, "Is there anything else you can think of? It doesn't have to seem important."

Bill shifted his position on the couch, the leather giving

its characteristic squeak under his weight. "Like what?" he asked uncomfortably.

"Oh, I don't know. Something about the cat, any odd behavior lately? Or strangers hanging around, phone calls out of the ordinary? Don't think too hard; just whatever that comes to mind."

He thought for a minute while I drank my coffee. I'd opted for Sumatra, and it really was quite good.

"There was one thing."

I rejoiced inwardly—those cop shows I watched all too often really were on the mark.

"I don't know if it means anything, but when I came home that night, before I knew anything was wrong, I noticed an odd aroma in the air."

I frowned. This was not the *one thing* I had been hoping for. What would a smell have to do with a break-in after all? A neighbor boiling cauliflower? The exterminator in the next door flat?

"What sort of aroma?" I asked dutifully.

"I really can't say. It was like nothing I could place. Tangy." He paused and gazed up at the ceiling. "And astringent. Like turpentine or linseed oil—one of those painty smells, but old time, not like the acrylic paints we have today."

Suddenly I felt like someone had put my brain cells in a tin can and shook them around like marbles. "Was it a sort of chemical type smell? Like a dye?"

"Dye? I don't know. To my knowledge, I've never smelled dye. But certainly something chemical. Why? Do you know what it might have been?" He sat forward on the couch. "Is it connected with the disappearance of Bonnie?"

I hesitated to answer; the thoughts pinging around my synapses were far too wild to be given out as facts or even speculation. Just to be safe, I pushed a little farther. "What did you think it was?"

"No idea."

"Then what gave you the feeling it had to do with the missing cat?"

"You asked, Mrs. Cannon—Lynley. I have no thoughts on what it might have had to do with Bonnie, if anything. I just noticed it, that's all."

"I'm sorry," I said quickly. "I apologize if I sounded brusque. It may be important, it may not. Thank you for telling me though. In this business, we never know."

Bill stood. "Well, Lynley. I really must get busy now. I'm writing my memoirs, you see," he said with a smile. "The working title is *Fly Me to the Moon.* It's about my career in the sky. There were some great stories up there at thirty thousand feet," he chuckled.

"Sounds very interesting. Well, I'll let you get to it." I put my notebook away and was beginning to gather up my purse when a furry weight landed on my lap. "Oof," I commented, looking down into the near-purple eyes of a large Siamese who was settling himself as if he owned me.

Bill smiled. "That's Zoom. My other sweetheart." Bill reached over and plucked the big cat up in his arms. "Come on, Zoomy, let the nice lady get on with her day."

I went to stand but my knees were weak, and I dropped back down again.

Bill hastily put Zoom on the floor and took my arm. "Are you alright, Lynley?"

"Yes, I'm okay." This time, with the help of Bill's strong hand, I made it to my feet. "But would you mind if I took another look at Zoom?"

He swallowed his impatience and managed a polite, "No, of course not. He is magnificent, isn't he? Be careful though, he does seem to have his moods."

I nodded distractedly as I squatted to check out the seal-point boy. Running my fingers over his cheek and lower spine, I felt a remnant of the telltale coarseness of fur. His eyes were that deep, purply-blue. There was no doubt about it—this was Meow, my stolen foster. I had known it the moment Lenore had shown me his photograph, but it had seemed too much of a coincidence to be true. Now I realized I should have followed up right then and there.

Could that be why the thief took the genuine Siamese and left the counterfeit behind? Was he a cat expert who could instantly tell the difference? Or could it be that the cat-thief and the counterfeiter were one and the same?

I had to call Denny. He needed to come take a look at this cat, probably even remove him into custody. That would be hard on Bill Todd who had just lost his other cat, but maybe by bringing NHS on board, Bonnie would be found.

I looked up at the hefty man who was staring at me with a mixture of dread and exasperation. "I'm afraid there's something I have to tell you."

* * *

Within half an hour, the entire Northwest Humane Society Special Investigations Team was tramping through Bill Todd's pristine condo. To his credit, Bill didn't seem the least perturbed about the military-grade boots on his white wall-to-wall, concentrating only on his missing cat and the surprising news about the one left behind. He had called in his own hired gun, one Chester Perkins, private investigator specializing in animal cases. Turned out that Chester was a reputable private eye with a respected success record. He knew the NHS team, and for a few moments, it was old home week while they briefly—very briefly—caught up with each other's doings.

I hung out by the door feeling a little like an extra tail as Denny went over Chester's findings and Connie got the info—again—from Bill. I figured I might as well be on my way, but when I made to leave, Denny stopped me.

"Can you hold on, Lynley?" he asked, flashing those cat-green eyes and perfect, pearly smile.

"Sure, Special Agent Paris," I played back. "If you think you need me."

He grinned even wider. "Always, Lynley." Then more seriously, "Give me a few minutes with Chess, okay?"

I moved over to the bay window and stood fingering my long-empty coffee cup. What was the world coming to? People stealing beloved pets; people exposing animals to toxic products so they could sell them as something they weren't? Meow's fur had grown back where the FOF vets had shaved off the colorant, and the counterfeiters had reapplied the dark goo to create the perfect markings of a seal-point Siamese. I felt bad for the cat who was now confined to a carrier; his infant-like cries could be heard throughout the condo and probably the rest of the building as well. He'd have to go back to a kennel at FOF or possibly even a holding cell at Northwest Humane until the case was solved, which could be a long time. Maybe they would let me foster him again, though I doubted it after having a clowder stolen right out from under my nose, even though that was in no way my fault.

"Hey, Lynley."

I turned and saw Frank Dawson coming up beside me. "Oh, hi, Frank. How are you guys doing with the interviews?"

"Oh, good, good. Quite a coincidence, don't you think?

Good thing you spotted Mr. Meow there. This, combined with the other details we've been able to establish lately, may just give us an edge with this case."

"Really?"

"Yeah," Denny Paris said as he joined us. "Things are coming together. I wanted to ask you if you'd consider sitting in on a meeting with Detective Garrison."

I cringed, remembering my maltreatment from the rude and abrasive Montana cop. "Garrison? Whatever for?"

"Now I know he's not one of your favorite people," Denny went on quickly, "but he's a good detective and has a lot of background on this case. We need him," Paris added.

"I don't know how I could help," I managed.

"You've helped already." Denny gestured to the squalling carrier. "I don't know how you did it, but finding Meow's buyer so we can establish how this guy is selling the animals will be of great assistance."

"Do you think Bonnie's theft was carried out by the same people?"

Denny frowned. "That's a stretch, but it's not impossible. That smell Mr. Todd describes sounds like it could have come from the counterfeit dye. But then there's twenty other things it might have been as well, all of them with a more reasonable explanation. Todd's going to come into the office and do a sniff test, see if he can identify it for sure.

"Thing is," Frank mused, "the colorant only smells when it's wet. Once it dries on the cat, it's virtually undetectable. What the thief was doing with a liquid form of the dye is a question we have to answer in order to accept the premise that the smell has anything to do with the theft."

Denny looked around. Connie Lee was winding up her interview with Bill Todd, and Chester Perkins had apparently left.

"How about it, Lynley? Will you add your great cat expertise to our inquiry?"

I inhaled deeply. "I'd be happy to, Special Agent Paris. When do you want me?"

Chapter 19

First aid kits are as important for your cat as they are for you. When an accident happens, having the necessary information and supplies within easy reach may mean the difference between life and death.

Garrison wasn't due to arrive in Portland until the following day, so I had a good eighteen hours to dread or deny, whichever tactic I chose to employ. I chose denial for the time being. Since Bill Todd had promised to fill Lenore in on the news, I was off the hook and free as a lioness.

First thing I did was go home; second was to bolt the door behind me with no plans to leave again anytime soon. It wasn't that I was hiding, exactly, though all this hands-on with theft and crime did have me feeling a little paranoid. You never knew what you were getting into when you tangled with criminals. Of course there was really no reason for me to worry; whoever was committing these crimes—be it single or multiple perpetrators—didn't know where I lived or that I was even involved.

Did they?

For a moment, I stared out of the window, watching the wind whip at the new leaves on the maple tree across the street. It really was getting quite stormy as the low moan of the telephone wires could attest. I realized I was shivering, and it wasn't from the cold.

I wasn't that involved, I told myself sternly, certainly not enough to be a threat to anyone. Denial, I reminded myself. Denial was going to allow me a blissful and productive afternoon, whatever the 'morrow might bring.

After playing with the cats and giving them treats, I decided it was time to catch up on some projects I'd been shining on for far too long. I slipped into my office-slash-workroom-slash-extra bedroom. Retrieving a carton from under the desk, I began to unpack the contents and lay them on the work table: tweezers, rectal thermometer, blunt-end scissors, sterile gauze pads, surgical tape, cotton swabs, cold pack, antiseptic wipes, eye droppers, and a phone list, laminated in plastic, with the number of my vet in red at the top. I pulled a three-ring binder out from beneath a pile of papers and turned to the page headed Animal First Aid. I had taken the class months ago but had not yet got around to the one thing they taught us we should do immediately: put together a first aid kit for our pets.

I read down my notes. There were several different kinds of kits: ones for general emergencies, ones for disasters, ones to keep in the car, and so on. I'd got as far as buying the components at the drug store and had even had great fun picking out a colorful assortment of waterproof makeup bags to put the things in, but there it had stalled.

Everything in its time, I told myself, and today was the day. For the next hour, I sorted, organized, and loaded the bags. When I was finished, I proudly surveyed my work: six fat little cases filled with notes, equipment, and supplies I hoped I would never have to use. That's what first aid is all about, and no amount of denial is going to replace a good first aid kit when you need one.

I was putting on the final finishing touches and labeling the bags with content and date so I wouldn't end up in ten years with expired antibiotic and tape that had lost its stick or glued itself into a solid rock ball, when the doorbell rang. I glanced at the clock: a little after seven. I wasn't expecting anyone, but friends did drop by from time to time. Wiping my hands, I headed for the front door. I clicked on the porch light and peered through the window, expecting to see Frannie or Halle or one of the multitudes of ecological canvassers that ran rampant in my neighborhood, but it was none of them. To my surprise—shock was more like it—I found myself confronted with Carol, Seleia, and Lisa: my family in three generations. They looked cold, huddled against a rampaging wind, and I knew, despite an urge to run and hide, I had no choice but to let them in.

I may be bearing down on my sixtieth birthday, but there are still some things that make me feel like a child, and not in a good way. One of those is my only child Lisa Voxx. Don't get me wrong—Lisa and I love each other, but we have very little in common. Her typical day begins at ten-thirty with a mimosa and ends around three in the morning at some exclusive club; mine starts closer to six with feeding cats and cleaning litter boxes, then peters out sometime after dinner in a warm pile of fur. She and her husband, the renowned architect Gene Voxx, have a second home in Los Angeles; I can't afford a second home but if I could, it would be at the beach, as far away from the city as I could drive in a two-hour time-frame. They have no pets; I have... well, you know that part.

On the whole, I don't understand people who choose by their own free will not to have a pet. It doesn't need to be a cat; dogs are perfect for many people, as are birds, hamsters, rats, horses, and snakes. Some animals are more people-friendly than others, but if someone chooses to love a scaly, legless being, that's totally up to them. It's better than living petless; in my opinion, people without an animal in their lives tend to give their own species far more importance than it's due.

Lisa is an artist, and a good one. I do appreciate her work, huge canvases in oils of dark, impressionistic inner-city scenes. I even own one, a very early, very small one that hangs in my office room. Sometimes I stare at it, lost in its swirling reds and grays and sepias, wondering about the fate of the modern world.

Why seeing my daughter puts me on edge, I'm not certain. We recently celebrated the Thanksgiving holiday on a cruise that she and her husband arranged for the family, and it was actually lots of fun though I spent more time with Seleia and Carol and probably the ship's masseuse than with the notable Voxxes.

I checked my look in the mirror, something I wouldn't have done for anyone but Lisa, put on a smile, and opened the door. The three tumbled in along with a nasty splutter of sideways rain, and we exchanged a gush of hugs, hellos, and how-are-yous. I dutifully declared it was *oh, such a wonderful surprise.* Coats were taken, purses laid aside, and remarks about the nasty weather were bandied about before anyone slowed down enough to stop speaking at once.

"Please, come in, come in," I said in a tone of politeness I reserved for Lisa and possibly her majesty, the Queen of England, should she ever arrive on my doorstep. "Would anyone like some tea?"

There were nods all around, and we headed for the kitchen in a somber little parade.

"Ack," Lisa grunted as she stumbled over a soft green tube on the living room floor. "What is that thing?" she demanded, staring back at the offending item.

"Play tunnel," I said without missing a beat. "For the

cats."

"Of course it is," she muttered, but her look had softened, and I caught the hint of a smile at the corners of her perfectly painted lips.

The trio seated themselves around my big kitchen table. Seeing them all together I could pick out the family resemblance though the years between youngest and oldest spanned nearly six decades.

Carol Mackey, my mother, was eighty-three but didn't look her age. Though her hair was gray and pulled back in a no-nonsense ponytail, her eyes were bright and sparkled with enthusiasm at the least little thing.

My daughter's eyes, though the same shape and color, never looked like that, though maybe when she was doing her artwork, they lit up more. Her hair—sometimes red, sometimes black, and sometimes turquoise blue—was always cut expensively and to perfection. Currently she sported a deep auburn bob with long, soft wings to each side of her face. On Lisa, who tended to be Botticelli overweight, the cut gave her a Kewpie doll look that was attractive and ridiculous at the same time.

Then there was Seleia. Again the familial eyes, but young and without even the promise of a wrinkle. She was a princess, an angel, a vision of teenage loveliness no matter what she did with hair or dress. If I didn't think it was the road to madness and debauchery, I would have suggested she take up modeling, she was that beautiful.

Lisa cleared her throat with a tiny "ahem," and I realized I was staring.

"Excuse the mess," I said lamely.

"Oh, no worries, mother," Lisa replied as she pointedly plucked up a stack of notes off the table in front of her and held them aloft. "Should I put these somewhere in particular?"

"Anywhere, dear," I said, busying myself with the tea things while working to get a grip on my irritation. She had been here less than five minutes, and I was already feeling as edgy as a cornered cat.

"Where are the kitties?" Seleia asked with a smile. My clever little granddaughter was wise beyond her years and knew instinctively that some cat-talk would help break the ice.

"Oh, they're around. Little and Harry are probably on the bed in my office. Violet might be there too. I think Fluffs is on the chair next to you." Seleia looked down under the table and nodded, smoothing her hand gently across the silver fur. Fraulein Fluffs opened an eye and gave a small purr.

I tossed Seleia a bag of cat treats. "You can give them their goodies if you like."

The young girl jumped up enthusiastically. Placing three fish-shaped morsels on Fluff's pillow, she skipped out of the room. I smiled after her. "Don't forget Solo under the couch."

"I won't."

I poured the boiling water into the teapot and placed it along with four mugs on a red lacquer tray. Since I was serving Japanese tea, I skipped the milk, sugar, and lemon. Taking the tray over to the table, I scooched down beside Fluffs; she was so tiny the both of us could easily share. "Give it a moment to steep. I don't have any cookies, I'm afraid."

My mother gave a start. "Cookies!" She exclaimed as she rose and scuttled into the living room where she had left her bag. She returned a moment later with a white box that read Cupcake City on the lid.

"Oh, grandmother, did you forget again?" Lisa accused, as if the octogenarian had somehow failed a test.

I began to bristle—Carol was sharper than most people half her age—but the older woman just smiled and played into her granddaughter's hands. "I'd forget my head if it wasn't attached. Don't worry. I remember where the plates are."

Carol went to the cupboard and selected a large chartreuse platter on which she arranged a delicious assortment of bakery cookies. Setting them on the table, she reclaimed her seat; I poured the tea. No more delaying the inevitable: it was time for the dreaded chit-chat.

I took a deep breath, knowing that anything I said would be open to ridicule. I patted my daughter's hand. "What have you been up to, dear?" I said blithely. I mean, how much more innocuous could I get?

"Oh, nothing much. Gene and I just got back from LA. In February, I did an art tour through the eastern states—New England, New York, you know, the usual. Let's see, before that we were here for a little while. And for Christmas we flew to Belize with the Allens."

I ignored her unambiguous name-dropping. "And how's Gene coming with the Twin Tower work?"

Lisa gave me a dismayed look. "Oh, mother, he finished that ages ago. Don't you read the papers?"

"Well, no. As a matter of fact I don't."

Lisa heaved one of her patented sighs, the kind that began at high C and descended an octave or so. "You really should be more informed."

"I'm as informed as I need to be," I retorted.

"Another cookie, anyone?" said Carol, sticking the plate in my face before I could say anything I would regret later.

Diplomatically, I took a pink iced shortbread and bit down hard.

"Your mother's been doing some detective work," Carol said to Lisa. "Haven't you, dear?"

For a moment I wondered how she knew about the theft of Bonnie the Siamese but then realized she must be talking about the ride-along with Special Agent Dawson earlier in the season.

"You mean the trip to Sharon with Northwest Humane? That wasn't really detecting, per se," I rationalized.

"But you hit that old abandoned mill," Carol pointed out, "to dig up some dirt on those cat offenders. Why if you hadn't been there, that cop might have bit it."

I smiled at Carol's pulp fiction slang. *Hit the mill? Dig up some dirt?* She and her roommate, Candy, were keen on cop shows and practiced the vernacular whenever the conversation turned to crime.

As Lisa stared at her grandmother in utter horror, I gave a slight shake of my head and mouthed the word, no, but it was too late. Lisa's gaze slipped seamlessly to me. "You what?" she said aghast.

"Oh, it was really nothing," I giggled self-consciously. "Carol's exaggerating. As usual." I gave my mother a dirty look.

"I thought that business last summer would have dissuaded you from getting involved with criminals again. And whatever is a *cat offender*?"

Just then, Seleia came back from her excursion. "Ooh, cookies!" she exclaimed, diving on a big oatmeal-craisin with cream cheese frosting.

I was just about to utter a prayer of thanks to the gods of perfect timing when all of a sudden there came a wild yowl from the seat beside me. Fluffs, who had been sleeping through the conversation, sat bolt upright. She stared around, gave another loud meow, then leapt off the chair and dashed for the bathroom. We all watched in amazement, even Lisa.

"What was that about?" she asked.

Before I could reply, there was a deafening boom, and the house shook on its hundred-year-old foundations. For a moment, I couldn't place the origin.

"Thunder!" Seleia exclaimed with the delight of someone who had always lived where electrical storms were more entertaining than deadly.

"I didn't notice any lightning," Lisa commented.

"They were saying on the news that there might be a storm tonight." Carol grinned. "I love storms."

"I know you do." I remembered when I was a little girl that Carol, instead of cowering in the bedroom like other mothers, would be out on the front porch, howling with the wind. Sometimes she wouldn't come in until she was soaked through. She always said the lightning recharged her battery. "You're not going to go outside now, are you, mum?"

Carol shrugged. "I gave that up awhile back. My batteries are too old to recharge anymore."

There was another clap, even louder this time, and we all flinched. "I better make sure all the storm windows are shut," I said. "Will you excuse me for a minute?"

I got up and headed for the stairs. I was relatively sure everything was already as stormproof as it could be considering the age of the house, but I knew I would feel better after checking.

Once I got upstairs, I could hear the full force of the gale. The moan in the wires had heightened to banshee howling; rain pelted the windows like hail. As I moved through the bedrooms, there was not a cat in sight; even bashful Red, who retires to my bed when I had company, was not in his usual spot.

Thunder erupted again, and suddenly the room was pitched into darkness. I peered out the window and saw that the whole neighborhood had blacked out. Several blocks away on Hawthorne, the streetlights still glimmered feebly against the gloom, and to the west, downtown remained lit up like an electric festival, but from what I could tell, power was out both north and east. This time, when the lightning zagged across the burnt, ashen sky, there was no missing it.

I counted the seconds until the thunder: One-thousand, two-thousand—bang! At the moment, I couldn't remember the exact ratio of time to distance, but the storm was close.

I knew there was a set of decorative candles on my dresser—if I could find my dresser. I felt my way along the wall, marveling at just how dark it was without the perpetual glow of the ambient light. Once I made it to the candles, I was relieved to find I had left a few packs of matches in the dresser drawer. I was about to strike one when the lightning came again. Instinctively my head swiveled toward the window; in a flash that was incandescent yet monotone, I could see every detail of the street below me in stark black and white.

It was like a scene from a graphic novel; then it was gone, back to black, but the bizarre image had imprinted itself on my retinas. I stumbled; catching myself on the bedstead, I sank down.

My heart was racing, adrenaline pumping through my blood. I had seen it, I was certain, yet how could it be? It didn't make any sense. And even if it were real, logically there was no reason why it should scare me so much. But it had.

Burned into the inside of my eyelids was the figure of a man in a tight black hoodie. He stood, arms wide, in the deserted, rain-swept avenue, staring up at my window.

* * *

"Lynley dear," came my mother's voice up the stairs. "Are you alright? You've been up there quite a long time. The lights are out, you know."

With a start, I recalled that I had visitors and that, as hostess to this impromptu out-of-season Halloween party, I should be the one asking them how they were doing.

"I'm fine," I called back, hoping she could hear me over the noise of the storm. "I'm just getting candles. Stay where you are; I'll be right down. I don't want anyone falling in the dark."

I lit one of the votives, then grabbed up the rest and headed for the stairs. As I neared, my little flickering glow coalesced with a stronger illumination, steady and bright. At the top of the staircase, I paused and looked down toward the glare of a tiny but powerful halogen flashlight.

"I guess you came prepared," I said to my mother as I descended.

"Always, dear. You never know when you might need to see."

The two of us went back to the kitchen where Seleia and Lisa were sitting in the homey glimmer of my kerosene lamp.

"I hope you don't mind," said Lisa, nodding to the antique. "Grandmother figured it wasn't just for show."

Actually it was, but at one time in its life it had been functional, and I'd never got around to cleaning it. Now I was thankful for my procrastination.

"May I borrow the flashlight?" I asked Carol when she got herself safely seated. "I need to make sure the cats are okay." She handed over the small chrome object. "I won't be long."

There really wasn't anything I could do for the cats: Fluffs, Red, Little, and Solo would be in complete and utter terror until the storm had passed; Harry and Tinkerbelle could care less; Violet could go either way depending on her mood and the state of her stomach. I just needed to see them and extend a modicum of psychic calm. The search was simple, and the whole thing took less than five minutes.

When I returned to the kitchen table, Seleia, Lisa, and Carol were quietly talking about nothing in particular, everyday matters: Seleia's classes; Lisa's art; Carol and her roommate, Candy's, latest favorite mystery story. I felt better now that I was with the group. As I thought back, the man in the street seemed more pathetic than threatening. Cold and alone, he was probably just one of the local homeless. It crossed my mind that I should offer him a hot cup of tea and let him wait out the storm on my front porch, but the little sliver of fear that remained embedded in the back of my mind like a microscopic splinter of glass, invisible but hurting, stopped me from acting on my goodwill.

"Maybe we should go," said Lisa.

"Oh, I don't think so, dear. All that lightning? It would be better to stay right where we are until this blows over."

"Carol's right," I admitted. "It probably won't last much longer. They usually don't in this area."

"But they've been having strange weather patterns all over the world this year," Seleia commented. "Hurricanes on the eastern seaboard; heat waves, droughts, fires, and flooding. Snow in summer. Maybe this will be an anomaly!" The young teen seemed enervated by the thought.

Carol was back rummaging in her bag again; I wondered what she would pull out this time and was not surprised when she retrieved a pink transistor radio that looked like something she'd had since the sixties, which it probably was. She clicked it on and moved the dial, searching for some weather news.

"Can I go watch from the living room?" asked Seleia.

"Whatever for...?" her mother began.

"Go ahead," I injected—for goodness' sake, Lisa, let the little girl indulge her scientific interest; she may be the one to invent a way of harnessing the energy from lightning storms to run our future generation of electric cars—"but not too close to the windows. They can blow out during a storm like this."

"I'll be careful." She scampered from the room, taking one of the lit candles with her. She placed it carefully on the coffee table, then sat on the floor in the center of the room where she could get a good view of the sky without being too close to flying glass.

The conversation stalled. I guess the family dynamics that had allowed for the homey chatter had shifted with my presence. Carol fiddled with the radio; Lisa and I both listened as if our life depended on it. The static with its intermittent bursts of music and advertising jingles was punctuated by the thunder, at which time we would all look toward the window, waiting for the next flash.

"Radio isn't what it used to be," Carol said in exasperation. "You would think at least one local station would interrupt their regular broadcasting for news of a storm like this."

"They can't cut their ads. They'll lose their capital," I told her.

"Are you always so cynical, mother?" Lisa scathed.

"I wasn't meaning to be cynical," I began but didn't bother to finish. Lisa saw what she wanted to see, and granted, I had been the queen of cynicism while she was growing up. The fact that I'd had an epiphany along the way had yet to sink in.

We lapsed into silence and the static of the antiquated device when a bloodcurdling scream rang out from the living room. All complacency shattered, we rushed in to see what was wrong. Seleia was no longer sitting on the carpet but crouched on the couch in the bay window staring into the street. She screamed again. "It's killing him!" she cried in absolute terror.

Instantly Carol and I were at her side, Lisa only a millisecond behind.

"What?" Carol blurted. "What is it, dear?"

Seleia pointed a trembling finger at the blackness outside but all we could was her own frightened reflection.

Then the sky lit up once more and there he was. Seleia turned away and buried her head in my sweater. Lisa gave a little scream of her own. I stood, dumb as a post, staring at the man I had seen from my bedroom window.

He was still in the street, but this time he wasn't looking at the house. This time he was crouching low to the ground. Something bulky was stretched out underneath him.

As I watched in horror, I saw his arm rise as if to strike. His hand was huge, like a paw. At the end of his fingers, the lightning glinted off a set of razor-sharp claws.

Chapter 20

It is common for cats to be afraid of loud noises, especially thunder. Make sure they're inside, then leave them alone; they will find the place where they feel safest, often under a bed or couch where the sound is muffled.

The scene went black again, leaving me wondering if I'd hallucinated the whole macabre scenario. This time the thunder was several seconds behind; the storm was receding. I held my granddaughter while she sobbed in fear. I didn't know what else to do.

"Call nine-one-one!" I finally croaked. Lisa, who had been as stunned as I was, fumbled in her pocket for her phone. She got it, dropped it, and sank to her knees, feeling around the floor for the slim instrument.

"I can't find the damned thing!" she sobbed.

I crouched down beside her, Seleia clinging to my side. Together we corralled the wayward phone that had slipped underneath the couch. Lisa, remaining on the floor, dialed frantically.

"It's busy!" she panicked. "Oh, no, what are we going to do?"

"Keep trying! We should get back from the window," I added as I pulled Seleia with me. "The man might have a gun."

I don't know where that came from, but it did the trick. Lisa scrambled to the back of the room. "Oh, no!" she cried a second time as she knocked over the candle on her way.

"It's okay, Lisa," I commanded, noting the little flame had harmlessly fizzled out. "Better to be in the dark anyway so he can't tell that we're watching him."

"You sound like a television show," she said, but only softly and more in thanks than derision.

"Carol?" I called. In the dark, I couldn't see if she was still at the window or right next to me.

There was no answer.

"Carol? Mum, where are you?"

Then I heard the front door close.

"Good grief, what has she done now?" Lisa raved.

"Keep trying nine-one-one. I'll get Carol."

"That woman has no fear. You don't know what she's capable of."

Oh, yes I do, I thought to myself as I disentangled from my granddaughter and headed after my mother, all sorts of crazy memories rampaging through my head.

I felt my way across the room, tripping only once on someone's purse that had been left in the hallway when the visitors arrived what seemed like a lifetime ago. When I reached the front door, I paused. Did I really want to do this? There was a dangerous man out there, and by opening the door, I would be calling all sorts of unnecessary attention to myself and my family inside.

But part of my family was outside.

I cursed my impetuous mother and cautiously turned the knob. It was then that I heard a gunshot.

Throwing the door wide, I cast all fear and most of my sanity to the four winds and ran out onto the porch, turning only long enough to shut the security door so the cats couldn't get out.

"Mum?" I hissed, sinking into a crouch. "Where are you? Are you okay?"

Without the lightning, I couldn't see a thing, but as my eyes adjusted, lighter patches and then discernable shapes began to stand out through the rain. The man in the street was gone, though the lump that had been beneath him remained: a black, human-sized bundle of sodden rags.

I looked feverishly around for Carol and found her slumped by the porch rail. In one long step, I was beside her. "Are you alright? Did he shoot at you?"

Carol turned and even in the strange dim, I could see she was smiling.

"I think I winged him," she said with a satisfied nod.

"What are you...?" I looked down and saw in her hand she was holding a gun. She slipped the small pistol into a slim leather purse and slung it over her shoulder.

"Mum! Wha... what is that?" I stammered.

"Why, it's a baby Glock, dear. You should know that."

"But since when do you carry a gun? Do you have a license? Do you know how to use it?"

"Yes and of course to all that," she said, infuriatingly calm, "but now don't you think we should see how that man in the street is doing?"

I gazed through the torrent at the dark mound. "Man?"

"Well yes, unless it's a woman." She pulled herself up with the help of the railing and walked boldly down the steps.

"Wait! Mum! What about the attacker?"

"Oh, he's long gone. As I told you, I hit him, I'm sure of it. It must not have been too bad since he managed to run away—I need to go to the shooting range more often," she chided herself. "But the police may be able to track him by the blood, if there's anything not washed away in this dreadful weather."

The red and blue strobe of the police car accompanied

the welcome siren screech, rising in pitch as it neared. Lisa must have finally gotten through to Emergency.

Carol stopped when she heard the police. I came up to her, trying to ignore the flail of the rain. She put her hand on my arm. "We can go back inside now and wait for the interview. The ambulance will take care of the victim, and we wouldn't want to contaminate the scene of the crime.

* * *

The police had hung around for the next few hours, securing the crime scene, bringing in dazzling lights and putting up tarps and shelters for the forensics unit. The man had been taken away in an ambulance, and we learned sometime later that he was alive, thanks to Carol's quick shooting for which she was both admonished and extolled by members of the force. I was surprised by an old acquaintance, Detective Marsha Croft of the Portland PD, whom I'd met the previous summer, but it was no time for old home week so aside from a curt nod of recognition and a short comment along the lines of "here we are again," her interview had been all business.

I gauged Croft to be in her mid-thirties, a big girl, tall and substantial under her trademark business suit. Her smoky eyes could bore a hole right through you if she had a mind to, and in all the time I'd spent in her presence, I had rarely seen those bright red lips softened with a smile. She had cut her hair since last I'd seen her, the tight black bun giving way to a shoulder-length blunt cut—not stylish but silky and charming, though I doubt charm had been her intention. On first impression, the word that came to mind was formidable. Luckily, I was privy to the little known secret that she had a gentler side.

Tonight that side was not in evidence, however. I tried

to get some information out of her: the identity of the victim; the identity of the attacker; why he had chosen my street for his midnight foray. Detective Croft just gave me her enigmatic stare and went on with her questioning.

Lisa and Carol had finally driven home around midnight with the promise that Carol would drop by the police station the next day to fill out some papers concerning her shoot. The lights were back on and the storm had settled into a straightforward deluge. Seleia had long since passed out with the cats on my spare bed, and it was unanimously decided not to disturb her. She only had a few classes the next day and would have plenty of time to bus it home to get her books.

And I had the exciting and wonderful consult with Detective Garrison in the morning. Oh, yay. I was looking forward to it about as much as a cat visiting the vet.

After a short, dreamless fit of sleep, I rose unrested but resigned to my fate. I took special care with my dress: black slacks instead of my usual jeans; a tan blouse that I deemed neither too dressy nor too casual. I added a soft brown fleece vest with my lucky gray and black silk scarf and called it good.

Seleia and I had a nice breakfast before she headed out. She fixed boiled eggs, and I concocted a fruit and yogurt bowl. We talked briefly and superficially about the night before, but I didn't press it. She needed time to process the real-life drama. I thanked God that no one was killed; instead of a tragedy, her young mind could probably turn the experience into an adventure that she could talk about among *oohs!* and *aahs!* from envious friends.

Then Seleia left for the bus stop, and it was time for me to get on my way. I packed a notebook into my bag, the old-fashioned kind made of paper, not pixels, and a few pens for taking notes. I checked my phone, hoping for a message that the meeting had been canceled but no such luck. Setting it on vibrate, I dropped it into my purse.

Outside the sky was streaked with blue the color of a Mediterranean ocean, and what clouds were left from the last night's rampage were washed clean and bleached cotton white. Having lived in Portland for most of my life, I knew better. I shrugged on a wool coat and shoved a rain hat in beside the notebook.

The air smelled fresh. I took deep, thankful breaths as I locked up and trotted down the steps to my car. Once on the sidewalk, though, I hesitated. I gazed around me: cars were passing; people were walking, enjoying the weather's reprieve, completely oblivious to what had transpired only hours before. I stared at the spot in the street where the assault had taken place. There was not a trace of it left. Not a hint that someone had been savagely attacked and made to fight for their very life.

Had they been successful? Or had they become the sixth victim of the serial killer known as the Panther? Because that's who it was, I was as sure of it as anything. I'd seen the giant hand with which he struck those gashing blows. I'd seen the savage look in his madman's eyes.

With a shrug and a shudder, I got into my vehicle and started the motor. I pulled away from the curb, a little faster than necessary.

* * *

At ten minutes to ten, I walked into the Northwest Humane Society conference room. Gazing around the large oval table, I saw I was the only person there. I had a paranoid flash that I was in the wrong place but then remembered Denny specifically giving me the directions. I was early, that was all. I figured it was better than the alternative. With meetings, there is no such thing as being fashionably late.

I seated myself across from the door in the middle of the long side of the table which I gauged to be the most innocuous placement, got out my notebook and pen, then sat feeling self-conscious as I waited for the others to arrive.

I didn't have to wait long. The three special agents came in at once, loud, happy, and full of coffee.

"Lynley," Denny exclaimed. "Glad you could make it."

I smiled as best I could and kept my misgivings to myself.

Connie Lee and Frank Dawson plunked themselves down opposite me, and Denny sank into the big chair at the head of the table. He had a laptop and a pile of file folders and documents which he spread out in front of himself. Connie and Frank were talking about another case they were working on concerning a trailer full of cats.

"We can't really tell how bad it is until we get inside," Connie was saying. "But we don't have enough evidence to get a search warrant and her son still won't let us in."

Frank leaned back in his chair, resting his head on the high fabric back. "If you ask me, it's borderline at best. The nose knows." He tapped his nose with a forefinger.

Connie nodded. "Well, you got it right there. They may have a lot of cats, but it certainly didn't smell like a neglect situation. And there's no way she's abusing them. From what I saw through the doorway, she loves those cats. I caught a glimpse of her in her recliner. She had one on her lap that she was brushing; two others were perched on either arm of the chair, and one was curled up on the back. I could almost hear the purrs," she snickered.

"It's just the one neighbor who's registering the

complaints. Maybe we should talk to her again."

"And drop off some information about low-cost spay and neuter clinics with the trailer, though her son says the cats are already altered."

Denny tamped a sheaf of papers on the table, and everyone looked his way. "I think we can get started before Detective Garrison arrives. Go over what we know. With the possible lead from our *concerned citizen* plus the information Lynley turned us on to yesterday, we may be able to open a new line of inquiry, hopefully be able to find these guys and put an end to the mutilation of these beautiful cats."

"Kerry mentioned you had an informer," I said, curiosity momentarily trumping my unease. "So who is this concerned citizen that had you running out on our meeting yesterday?"

"I'm sorry about that, Lynley," Denny said. "We have no idea who she is."

"Did you get anything?"

"Yesterday's tip turned out to be a bust, but the previous call gave us some real evidence."

"The counterfeiter's dye in the public bathroom?"

Denny nodded, then got busy passing out a stapled brief to the three of us and skidded one across the table to the empty space at the other end. I glanced at mine: it was a compilation of facts and legalities concerning the breed simulation case in type as tiny as the bottom line on an optometrist's eye chart. I feared what would happen if I actually needed to read any of it.

"So here we have one of the strangest cases I've ever come across," Denny began, running a hand through his curly brown hair. "Part of the problem is that our information is so scattered, bits and pieces only. I'm hoping that Detective Garrison can fill in some of the blanks when he gets here, but until then, let's recap.

"The perps are taking flawed breed cats, primarily Siamese, and touching them up to look like the genuine article. Cases have been reported in several states, but it looks like they've made the Portland area their home for the duration.

"They are breaking laws here—committing fraud, for one. And some of their cats are stolen, so that brings in theft. The NHS focus is, of course, on any animal abuse that may be involved."

"The colorant they use is highly toxic and can be absorbed through the tender skin of the cat," Connie Lee put in. "The exposure can make them sick or crazy or both, so that's one count of abuse right there."

"Sometimes they fit the cat with colored contact lenses," said Frank. "Not the good ones either. Really unhealthy for the cat's eyes."

Denny nodded. "Once the cat is properly dyed, the perps, using forged papers, convince customers that they are reputable breeders with a high-end product. It looks like they target wealthy but naive buyers who don't mingle with the experts. Bill Todd is a perfect example. After purchasing one show-quality Siamese from an honest source, he bought a counterfeit from our perps. He personally couldn't tell the difference, either in the cat or the papers that came with it. And in spite of his having decided he didn't want to be part of the show circuit, they managed to convince him to buy this supposed show cat for show prices. Coincidently someone chose to steal the real Siamese, and through that case, the simulation was revealed. We were able to go back and trace Todd's transaction from the beginning."

"Did it lead anywhere?" I asked. "The phone numbers he gave you?"

"Burn phones. No longer in service. I'm afraid what we got from Mr. Todd was more on the informational side and less, the actual data. But now we know their process. It all adds up. Good stuff."

"What about the theft of Bonnie, the real Siamese? Have you thought about the possibility that the two crimes could have been related?"

Denny smiled. "Sure, I thought about it, but there's nothing to go on there."

"Maybe they saw her or heard about her while they were doing the sale of Meow. Maybe Bill Todd was bragging—he's very proud of her. Evidently she's one very expensive kitty."

"Yeah, but how do you vend a stolen cat?" asked Connie. "There must be some animal all-points bulletin out about the theft. No one would dare try to sell her, knowing they'd be turned in the minute she surfaced."

"I don't know," I sighed. "I'm not sure cat-theft has the same networking that crimes against humans have. I've never heard of a kitty Amber Alert. I bet you could find lots of buyers who would never know the difference until it was too late."

"That's something to ask Garrison when he gets here."

As if summoned up by the mention of his name, the grim detective strode into the room. His dark suit jacket was rumpled from traveling, and his perpetual frown was even more deep-set than I remembered. He moved to the end of the table and pulled out the chair, then stopped dead. His mousy eyes hit mine and squinted nearly shut. Looming in my direction, he eyed Denny. "What's she doing here, Paris?"

Denny wasn't fazed by the detective's abruptness. "You remember Lynley Cannon, don't you, sir?" He said lightly.

"I remember her. The busybody that stuck herself in the middle of my business last time I was here."

"Nice to see you again, detective," I said with a composure I didn't feel.

He glared at me.

"Yesterday Mrs. Cannon discovered one of our counterfeit cats which had been sold to a friend. Considering that and the other experiences she's had with this case, I thought she might like to sit in on our meeting."

"I disagree," Garrison barked. "There is no place for an amateur sleuth in this investigation. If we need her deposition, we can get it in an interview. Until then, Mrs. Cannon goes."

A new figure appeared in the doorway of the conference room. With surprise, I recognized the dark-haired dark-eyed Detective Marsha Croft. She took an assertive step forward, giving me the briefest of smiles. To Garrison, she announced, "Mrs. Cannon stays."

Chapter 21

Hydration is a key element of cat health. Have water bowls in multiple places throughout the house instead of only at the feeding station. Cats may be distracted by the food and neglect the water.

No one was more surprised to see the attractive detective than I, except for maybe Garrison. His face had turned an ugly shade of mauve, and his hands had clenched into fists. He turned to Denny. "Is this another one of your Miss Marple knitting circle?"

Denny rose. "May I introduce Detective Marsha Croft of the Portland Police Department?"

Croft nodded politely and flipped her dark, nondescript jacket back just enough to show the shiny badge clipped at her waistline.

"Detective Croft, this is Detective Robert Garrison from the Missoula PD."

"Montana?" Croft asked with that slight accent that I never had been able to place. "You are out of your jurisdiction, are you not, Detective?"

"Bob's here unofficially," Denny said. "He's consulting on a mutual case."

"I see." Croft's eyes swiveled to me. "And you, Lynley. I did not expect to see you here. Are you also consulting?"

"Well, I'm more just sitting in, I think."

"Good. I, for one, am glad of any input you may have to give." She turned to Garrison. "Mrs. Cannon has a genuine gift for observation and logic. I would not be so fast to pass her off as... what did you call it? One of Miss Marple's knitting circle?"

Garrison turned a deeper shade of red but said nothing.

"I apologize for interrupting your meeting, Special Agent Paris," Croft said to Denny. "I was actually coming to see you."

"Oh? Alright," Paris said, nearly successful at covering his astonishment. "We can talk in my office. I'm sure everyone will excuse me for a few minutes."

Paris started for the door, but Croft stepped around the table and took the empty seat beside me. "Do not disturb yourself, Special Agent. I think I will attend as well, if you do not mind."

"Well, no, of course not. You're certainly welcome, Detective Croft."

"Then please, gentlemen, sit down and let us begin."

She waited for the two men to take their seats. Denny sat first; Garrison took a few purposeful glares from his female counterpart before he slung his rain-soaked coat over the back of the chair and seated himself as well. Obstinately he began pulling files and papers out of his briefcase.

"That is better. You are discussing the case of the faux Siamese, are you not?"

"Yes. It's had us baffled for several months, but we think we might be finally getting somewhere."

"Excellent. An interesting case."

"You're familiar with it? I assumed you were here about the murder at the Friends of Felines shelter."

"That is true."

"I don't understand."

Croft leveled her smoky gaze at the humane investigator. "It has come to our attention that the two cases may have some aspects in common."

I stared at the detective in absolute horror. She was serene as a sphinx. Not so, the faces around the table which ran from surprise to shock. The only person who didn't seem caught off guard was Detective Garrison. He sat as glum as ever, glaring at Croft as if she were a rival tomcat.

"You're kidding!" Connie Lee exclaimed. The husky detective slapped her palm on the table and laughed. "This I gotta hear."

Croft smiled briefly at the impulsive young woman. "I cannot reveal many facts about the murder investigation, but suffice it to say, our suspect may indeed have some involvement with cats. He may even be the simulator himself."

"The claw murderer?" I gasped. "The man outside my house last night?"

"Wait a minute," Denny cut in. "You actually saw the Panther? Why didn't you tell me? Are you alright?"

"I'm fine. My mother shot at him and he ran away." This explanation, far from clearing things up, began another round of questions from the special agents.

"Ask Detective Croft," I finally deferred. "And yes, my mother has a license to carry, I found out somewhat after the fact."

All eyes turned to Croft. "There was an incident last night that was likely committed by the suspect whom the media have dubbed the *Panther*. This time the victim was fortunate enough to have Mrs. Mackey there to defend him. He was taken to a hospital, where he remains in intensive care from the claw slashes which carry a natural bacterial poison similar to *Bartonella henselae*, also known as Cat Scratch Disease. Though this strain is much more potent than normal, he is expected to fully recover. The police have not yet been able to interview him however because he is currently comatose."

"Did Lynley's mom really shoot the guy?" Connie snickered.

"So she claims, and it is possible. The precipitation was so intense there were no obvious signs of blood left on the street by the time the police arrived, but we have taken some suspicious samples from the clothing of the victim. We should have some results later this afternoon."

Garrison, who had been quietly smoldering throughout the exchange, suddenly stood up. "You shot him?" he roared.

Croft turned and frowned. "*I* did not shoot him, Detective; in fact, as I explained, we do not know for certain that he was hit at all. We have been monitoring hospitals and urgent care units for possible gunshot wounds, but so far nothing."

Croft stood and faced Garrison. "But whether or not he was hit by Mrs. Mackey's bullet," she continued, "what was surely to be this killer's sixth victim is still alive. We have no mercy for this man, Detective Garrison. I do not know how you do it in Montana, but here in Portland, when someone is caught in the act of murder—someone who has killed five times before—we feel no remorse for using deadly force. If that had been one of us and not an eighty-year-old civilian, the man would not be wounded but dead."

Garrison was silent, a forbidding statue of complete and utter rage. Then he slammed his fist on the table. "I've had enough of this! I came here in good faith to discuss an animal abuse case. A case about cats." He glared at Denny Paris. "And all I've seen so far is a circus. Claw killers and little old ladies!" he harrumphed. "Nonsense!" He stuffed his files back in his briefcase and clicked the latch shut. Grabbing his overcoat, he made for the door.

The group around the table was speechless. "Bob, wait," Denny managed.

Garrison turned back to the special agent. "Phone me if you want to talk. Just you." He spun on his heel and stomped out of the room, leaving a stunned audience behind him.

"What was that about?" Detective Croft asked.

Frank Dawson, who had been quiet throughout the entire exchange, misquoted softly, *"Methinks he doth protest too much."*

* * *

For the next hour and a half, the five of us discussed the breed simulation case and the claw murder case which had suddenly morphed into one. Unfortunately Detective Croft was limited on what she could share so we never really learned how the cases intertwined. After an initial attempt at putting things together, Denny had gone nearly silent which I knew meant he was thinking. Why not? He had a lot to think about.

Detective Garrison, for one. The man had come all the way from Montana, not once but twice, on his own time to consult about a case involving the alleged abuse of cats. Either the burly detective was extremely dedicated to animal rights, which seemed doubtful since he never said anything caring about the kitty casualties themselves, or he had his own agenda. What that might be was surely something to consider.

And then there was always the new development of the crossover. Had Denny suspected the breed simulator could also be the killer Claw? He'd claimed the negative. Maybe he would be more forthcoming later when he and Detective Croft were alone. As for Croft, her doublespeak was more aggravation than enlightenment.

Denny was quiet; Marsha Croft, enigmatic. Frank and Connie were trying their best to collate the new information, taking notes and shuffling papers, but they both looked as confused as kittens. For all the logic and input with which Croft had flattered me, she didn't ask me anything and I didn't volunteer.

I rose. "You'll excuse me but I have to go." I didn't expect anyone to object, but I hesitated for a moment in case they did.

My instincts were correct: Denny looked up at me as if woken from sleep and gave a perfunctory thank you; Croft just said goodbye. I turned to Frank and Connie. Connie shrugged and raised her eyebrows in a gesture I took to mean *What a mess,* and Frank looked as if he wished he could come along. I smiled and ran.

* * *

I got in my car, started the engine, and sat. I wasn't sure what had transpired in that conference room, but I knew it was something important. I needed to rethink the exchange, concentrate on some of the nuances, and try to figure out what was going on underneath the surface of confusion and subtlety, but now was not the time. With no destination in mind, I pulled out of the parking lot. I wasn't ready to go home and be reminded of the serial killer who had invaded my neighborhood and my nightmares. For some reason, the idea that the killer was pulling the breed scam made things even worse. To think of those innocent cats at the mercy of a psychopath was cruel beyond imagination. The only good thing about it was that now the entire Portland Police Force would be out looking for him, where only a small though dedicated team of humane investigators had been available to follow up on the faux breeders. Maybe the jerk would be caught soon, then both the killings and the cat abuse would stop.

I realized I had been heading automatically for Friends of Felines. If anything could distract me from my dark and crazy thinking, it was a shift at the shelter. I hadn't signed up, but I knew no one would object to a drop-in volunteer. Blanking my mind from everything else, I went to play with the cats.

Chapter 22

Cats have been the subject of proverbs from around the world and going back many centuries. I especially like the English proverb, "In a cat's eye, all things belong to cats."

I really hadn't meant to, but before I knew it, I was pouring my heart out to Frannie, telling her all that had befallen me over the last forty-eight hours. I should probably have been keeping the information about the murder to myself, but then again, no one had specifically told me they would have to kill me if I blabbed. And besides, all Frannie's best friends were feline, and I'm pretty sure that even if she did spill to them, they would hardly care enough to pass it on.

We were sitting on the floor in one of the colony rooms, surrounded by fur. I had a gray male on my lap and a tiny tabby female slumped across my legs; Frannie was brushing a long-haired dilute calico who was purring her little heart out. A midnight-black female watched from an upper shelf; a few others slept, curled up in round beds, pointedly disinterested in our tete-a-tete.

"So I guess I'm off the hook about finding Bill Todd's missing Siamese. Since in my opinion, it's pretty much certain it was the breed simulator..."

"...and serial killer," Frannie put in.

I nodded. "...who stole her." I frowned thoughtfully. "Do you suppose he sells authentic breed cats as well as the faux ones? That might make it harder to trace him if some of the cats were genuine. He stole Bonnie's papers too, you know."

"Yes, but they won't do him any good." Frannie paused to pull a snarl of multicolored fur out of the brush tines. "She's been reported stolen. He'd be found out in a heartbeat if her name came up in any of the show or breeding circles."

"Not if he sells her to someone who doesn't care that she's stolen. You know, like famous art work or priceless jewels—some buyers want the things so badly they don't care where they come from." I smiled, smoothing my hand down the velvet gray back of my lap-sitter. "Or at least that's the way it happens in the movies."

Frannie laughed. "And we all know that everything you see in the movies is the absolute truth," she quipped sarcastically.

"You're probably right. No one would sell her as her true self; he'd have to forge new papers, and even if he did that, she's microchipped."

Frannie sat up suddenly, nearly displacing her charge. "You don't suppose he'd cut it out, do you?"

I shivered. "Yuck! I would hope not. Though the simulators are known to do minor surgery so I guess it's possible."

"That's horrible! And she still could be identified by a pro."

"Yes, but it wouldn't be the first element in this case that doesn't make sense."

"So why do you think he did it? Ransom?"

"No one's called Bill, at least not that I know of. But it's something to look into."

"I thought you were off the case now that Denny and the police will be taking over."

"I am, but, well..."

"I know, Lynley. You're like the proverbial curious cat. You won't be happy until your curiosity is satisfied or it kills you. Oh! I didn't mean that!" she exclaimed.

I looked up at her. Her eyes were round with embarrassment.

"I know you didn't, Frannie," I offered. "And there is a grain of truth in that whole 'curiosity killed the cat' thing. Believe me, I'm going to keep my distance from this one, now that I know the thief-slash-breed simulator might be a psychotic murderer as well."

We both fell silent, lost in softness and thoughts.

"Do you think the Claw Killer hurts the cats the way he does his human victims?" Frannie murmured.

"Of course not!" I said far too quickly. That was, after all, the burning question to anyone who cares for animals.

Frannie looked at me, one perfect eyebrow raised. Then she gently turned the purring calico on her side and continued brushing. "You're probably right. The cats are his livelihood; he wouldn't want to mess with that. But," she added, "why does he kill in the first place? And why in such a gruesome manner?"

"Who knows the minds of serial killers."

I shifted my legs which were falling asleep under the tabby's weight. Insulted by the movement, she sprang away and went for a drink of water. As I watched her crouch by the shiny stainless steel bowl and dip her tongue in the crystal liquid, I noticed the black female slinking closer. In a second, she pounced, the two rolling on the floor in a mock fight. The tabby was on her back, defending herself with her strong back legs as cats do; the black was on top, arm raised to strike. Then she hit, three swipes in quick succession. The tabby rolled aside; the black stood and shook herself; the two went their separate ways.

I had a flash: In my mind, I saw the killer outside my window in the cold, rainy night. His blows to his victim had been savage, inhuman, almost as if...

"Do you suppose he could think he's a cat, himself? I mean, look at the weapon he uses. From what I can tell, it's some sort of glove with claws attached. He uses it as a wild cat would, to catch its prey or defend against an attacker."

"Cats don't kill without reason."

"Maybe he has a reason. If we could figure out what that was, maybe we'd have some insight about where it might happen again."

"Again?" Frannie gasped.

"We have no basis for thinking he'll stop on his own."

"Oh, I never thought of that."

Just then, Frannie and I heard a key in the lock and we both looked up. Through the big glass door I could see one of the volunteers, a young girl I didn't know. She pulled the door open just wide enough to slip inside without letting out a wayward cat and shut it fast behind her.

She smiled shyly. "I hate to bother you but I have someone who wants to meet Sparks." She gestured to Frannie's calico.

"Really?" Frannie said with a smile. She lifted the calico up to the waiting woman. "Well, she's all beautiful for them."

The girl gave Sparks a cuddle and a pet before scruffing her securely for the trip down the public corridor to the visiting room.

Frannie and I watched her go, then Frannie hoisted herself up with the aid of a convenient shelf. "Oof, getting up gets harder every year."

"I know what you mean."

"I think I'll sit in on Sparks' visit," Frannie said. "She's one of my favorites, and I can probably tell the people a little more about her than Kendra. She's still pretty new here."

"I need to get going anyway. I hadn't meant to come in today at all, but after the fiasco with Garrison and Croft, I couldn't think of a better place to relax."

I faltered. "And to tell you the truth, I think I'm a little nervous about going home."

"Aw, sweetie. I'm sorry you had to go through that. Do the police have anyone watching your neighborhood?"

"I don't know. I don't think so, but maybe. It's okay," I added. "I'm sure he's long gone."

"Do you want me to drop by later on?"

I glanced at the floor, noting the spilled kibble around the feeding station and thinking I should clean that up before I left, anything to keep me busy. "Thanks but I'm sure I'll be fine."

"I think I said that wrong," Frannie amended. "What I meant was that I *will* be dropping by later on. If you think you're going to be home."

"Yeah, I'll be home. You don't have to, you know," I wavered. "But I wouldn't mind if you did. We can have tea. I have cookies."

"From Cupcake City?"

I nodded. "My mum brought them over last night. I think she buys them by the case."

"Any of the ones with the funny German name and the powdered sugar toppings? Or the maple nut ones?"

"Both, and more."

"Then I'll be there for sure." She smiled and touched my hand. "See you later."

Frannie slipped out into the hallway and disappeared among the folks come to look at or adopt a kitty. I watched her go, thankful I had friends like her and wishing the violence and intrigue that had plagued my life in recent months would come to an end.

* * *

A few weeks later, it looked as if I had got my wish. There had been no more reports of simulated breed cats; no one had been murdered in front of my house or anywhere else in the city; I hadn't been called back for any investigative consults, personal, official, or otherwise. All that was newsworthy was happily going on without me.

Things weren't perfect, of course. There was still a murderer at large who had no compunctions about torturing cats or people alike, but that was blissfully not my problem. I was an observer, nothing more, and as I cruised down the road past a kaleidoscope of azaleas, daffodils, and early dogwood, hip-hop pulsing from my car radio, window open to the fresh April air, I had the distinct feeling that things might turn out okay.

I had got Meow-slash-Zoom back in foster pending the result of his investigation. Hopefully he would then be returned to Bill Todd who was pining away without his cats whom he had come to love. Bill called me almost daily, and I sent many photos via my new smartphone, but he was still wrapped in gloom. I totally sympathized; no picture, no matter how cute, can replace the touch of fur, the warmth of your own sweet cat on your lap.

Meow was doing well. He was out of the kennel and mingling with my other kitties. I had no worries about leaving him alone anymore; he had completely mellowed now that he was safe and had the toxic colorant cleansed from his system. He looked a little odd with white splotches of skin at head and tail but seemed happy to be rid of that sticky, poisonous pigment. He had settled down to be quite an adorable cat. No more mood swings; Bill would be glad of that.

I glanced at the three large bakery boxes on my passenger seat and then in the back where flats of seedlings—strawberries, lettuce, and early veggies—were carefully stacked on newspaper. I felt a deep inner satisfaction with my purchases, especially the plants. The previous summer I'd had health problems, and my garden had suffered for it. I vowed to make up for it this year and had even got a neighbor with a roto-tiller come plow up another part of my lawn to make way for a pumpkin patch. From planting to canning, I was determined to do it all over the coming season.

I had been to the Hood River Humane Society Plant and Vegan Bake Sale which was a yearly event I was pleased to support. Hood River was quite a way from Portland, but on a nice day, it was a spectacular drive through the Columbia River Gorge, passing rivulets and waterfalls including the famous Multnomah Falls which descended six-hundred-some feet in a glimmering ribbon of light. Hood River itself was a gem with its turn of the century buildings and eclectic little shops. The plant sale coincided with the Apple Blossom Festival, and the many fruit orchards that flourished in the lush, green valley were in full bloom.

From the top of the hill where the sale took place, I'd looked out across a patchwork of spring green, white, and pink; what could be more beautiful? Once down, however, I connected with busy I-84 West, and the calm was instantly replaced by fast cars and exhaust smoke. Traffic was heavy as always on spring weekends, everybody going a million miles an hour to make the most of their short days off. An SUV honked past me—I guess he considered the speed limit a little slow—and I felt myself beginning to tense. If I had any hope of holding on to my serenity, I needed to find the road less traveled.

Fate seemed to be listening as I glimpsed a sign for the Historic Columbia River Highway turnoff up ahead. In a split-second, I decided to take the scenic route, a winding, forgotten byway with some of the most gorgeous views in the state. Slowing from sixty-five to thirty-five, I veered away from the fast pace into another world—one of ancient trees and silent forests. Dropping my speed another ten mph, I couldn't help but think how lucky I was. Or blessed, depending on one's philosophy. In that moment, I could see no problem that couldn't be overcome, no hardship too great to be lessened. No evil lurked in the primeval woodlands. I was awash with peace. I should have known right then that somehow, somewhere the axe was about to fall, but I guess my Murphy-sense was temporarily out of commission.

Humming along with a lively sonnet about good feelings, I glimpsed a sign tacked to a tree on the side of the road. It seemed strange that someone would put a sign there; most of the area along the old highway was state park where posting was uncommon if not forbidden. The red hand-painted letters could not have been more conspicuous had they been on a billboard.

In reality it wasn't the words that caught my eye since I hadn't really been able to make them out; it was the picture, a red circle with two triangles juxtaposed at the top, two spots for eyes, and a wavy line for a mouth—a cat as a child might draw it. Impulsively I slowed down. Pulling over as far as I could without going off into the muddy swale, I glanced both ways—not a car in sight. I was alone. For no good reason besides a compulsion I couldn't resist, I made a U-turn. Retracing my route, I stopped and clicked off the radio.

In the sudden silence, I could hear a multitude of birds and the far hum of the highway below but nothing more. I gazed across at the sign which read, "For Sale Siamese Kitten". It had originally said "kittens" but the "s" had been crossed out with a black X, leaving me to assume there was only the last of the litter remaining.

It was an innocent sign—only the four words, the cat face, and an arrow pointing up which I took to mean ahead, but there was something about the child-like execution that made my hair stand on end. That little placard had me anxious and afraid and compelled all at the same time. Just the thought of that one lonely kitten, his brothers and sisters wrenched from him, tugged at my heart.

Not many people lived out this way, but there were a few pockets of grandfathered homesteads: broken down shacks covered with moss and dark with rot from the constant barrage of rain and fog; properties peppered with moldering trailers and abandoned vehicles draped by threadbare blue tarps. It didn't seem like the place for a breeder with any reputation to uphold.

With a shock, all my anxiety coalesced into one bizarre thought: Could I have stumbled across the breed simulator, himself? This seemed the perfect environment, off in the wilderness, away from prying police eyes. Here he could do all his dirty deeds in private, as he had at the old mill before Northwest Humane came in and quashed that lair. He could be doing unspeakable things right now! He could...

The thought passed as quickly as it had come—after all, it would be a coincidence of extraordinary proportions.

Still, I couldn't quite shake the feeling that there was more to the little sign than met the eye.

I sat for a while longer, then swung out. Doing another turnabout, I resumed my trip toward town, but I kept a watch on the side of the road for another posting, another clue.

I had just about given up, turned the radio back on and was planning my garden in my head when I saw it. If I hadn't been taking the continuous rick-rack of curves at the suggested old-lady twenty-five miles per hour, I would surely have sped past the inconsequential red arrow partially concealed by the budding leaves of the maple it was tacked upon. Again the cat face, but this time, no words. I couldn't help but think it was not the best way to advertise one's wares. Still, this was the countryside, and besides, what did I know about how breeders operated? My image had always been of sparkling clean surroundings in upscale and convenient parts of the city, but truth be told, the only breeders I had met were at the few cat shows I'd attended. There, the cats were kenneled in little palaces with velvet cushions and rhinestone-encrusted food bowls; I didn't know where they went once the show was over.

Again I pulled to the side. This time the arrow pointed right, but for the life of me, I couldn't see any break in the forest cover. Creeping forward, I finally made out a small, dim gap in the trees. Sure enough, heading downward into obscurity was a deeply inclined drive. There wasn't much to it, only two muddy wheel ruts. This couldn't be the way, could it? Who in their right mind would drive a car down that perilous slope, risking getting stuck in the mire or having to back out of a dead end, just to look at a kitten?

Hoping for something that appeared more like a

driveway—anything would be preferable to that goat path—I continued on, but after another quarter mile, I was beginning to have my doubts. It was possible the signs were old and that some of them had blown down or fallen off their posts. As a garage-sale aficionado, I'd run into similar situations many times, where directions would take one on a magical mystery tour, only to leave one hanging and lost in the end.

Then I caught sight of a square of plywood on the opposite side of the road. I passed it and glanced back; it was the twin to the others, but this arrow pointed left. That could mean only one thing—I'd gone too far.

Without thought, I did another U-turn. I was beginning to feel odd. There were still no other vehicles. I hadn't seen a car since I'd entered the forest which added a surreal slant to the whole experience, as if I'd been swept into one of those Twilight Zone stories where I was in an alternate universe that looked just like ours but where people had died out instead of the dinosaurs.

Pulling into the little niche across from the steep drive, I clicked off the engine. My brain was playing good cop bad cop, or in this instance, Good Lynley—the one who goes on about her business and maybe mentions the sign to Special Agent Paris when she gets back to town—and Bad Lynley who compulsively noses around in places she has no business being. I had already come to the conclusion that following the sign could lead to danger; even if it weren't the Claw murderer, it might be some other crazy person who could get the wrong idea about a woman alone on a lonely road. At the very least, and most realistic of all, I'd get stuck at the bottom and have to wait three hours for Triple A to find me. I could walk down, but who knew how far it was to the breeder's house? I had a bad knee, a sore hip, and my balance wasn't that great; it wouldn't take a lot for me to slip and hurt something, and then what? No, it was drive down and take a chance that my cute little car would make it or give up and drive away.

My logical mind said drive away.

My heart said, Aw, the poor little last kitten; if I wait for the investigations team to get mobilized, it might be too late!

I started the car, took a deep breath, and down I went.

Chapter 23

Bleach, detergents, and many other household cleaners do not have to be ingested by your pet to cause caustic reactions to the skin and lungs. When using bleach to clean kennels, make sure it is properly diluted and followed by a thorough rinsing and airing out before kitty comes anywhere near.

Actually I was a pretty good driver: I'd maneuvered the snows of Canada, the sands of Arizona, the gravel backroads of the Pacific Coast. I knew to hold it in low gear, tap the brakes only lightly, and keep going no matter what until I got to safe, flat ground. As it turned out, only the first leg of the access road was the muddy incline, and after a fifty-foot thrill ride, it evened out into a level if still somewhat bemired stretch of rutted lane.

Once safely down, I rolled to a stop and peered ahead into the gloom. Despite the beautiful day, it was dark under the canopy of hemlock and Douglas fir. The air was dank and smelled primordial. To my right, the carcass of an old car sat moldering in the trees, shoots of alder and blackberry piercing the rusted frame; to my left and up ahead there was nothing but bush. The way itself curved out of sight a little farther on. I noticed moisture beading on my windshield and realized I had sunk into a patch of fog. Inadvertently I shivered and grabbed my pink wool jacket from the back seat. There was still time to turn back, Good Lynley urged. Bad Lynley gave her a poke in the eye and told her not to be such a wuss.

I started to pull ahead, then paused. The least I could do as a nod to personal safety was to call someone and apprise them of my whereabouts. That way they'd know where to begin the search once I'd been gone for forty-eight hours and was deemed a missing person. I pulled out my cell phone and checked the bars; there were none but that wasn't surprising. I punched in Frannie's number and watched the display as it was roaming.

And roaming.

And roaming...

After a minute or so, counted to the second by my phone, it disconnected itself. I tried again with the same results. Until I'd thought of calling home, I hadn't worried about being alone; now that I couldn't get through, I suddenly felt the panic of isolation.

Buck up, I told myself sternly. Since the road was too narrow to turn around, and there was no way I could have backed up the incline I came down, I had no choice but to go on. I rolled up my window and locked my car door. Feeling the panic quell just a touch, I proceeded into the dim.

There were several switchback turns and one more sign with the cat face and arrow, reassuring me this twisted gauntlet was not all for naught, then I saw a bright patch up ahead. It swelled as my car lumbered nearer, and suddenly I was out of the trees.

The sunshine burst down on me in a blaze of glory; I blinked like a mole in the brilliance. As the white coalesced into colors and shapes and distinguishable objects, I found myself staring at a scene that startled me more than anything I could have envisioned.

It was as if I had stepped back about a hundred years into Oregon history. No rundown shack or cabin left to molder—this was a lovely Victorian cottage, freshly painted and pristine. There was a garden patch, dark with loam, where winter chard pushed up red and white stalks topped by glossy green leaves. Budding rhododendrons dotted the lawn with every shade of purple and pink imaginable. Beyond the yard lay a small field with a split rail fence, and beyond that, the spectacular Columbia Gorge. Scraps of gauzy mist wafted in the lower valley, but the sky above was cloudless and blue as the eyes of a Siamese cat.

I breathed a sigh of relief. A place so beautiful could not possibly harbor any ills. Would a serial killer keep such a nice garden? Would a cat thief maintain the old house in such an immaculate manner? I knew logically that the answer could be yes as easily as no, that serial killers often exhibited symptoms of OCD—obsessive-compulsive disorder—but our culture is so influenced by appearance that without a second thought, all my red flags fell.

In front of the house was a wide, graded turnaround; it would be easy as pie just keep rolling right around and go back the way I came, but now that I knew escape was a simple matter, my need for it abated. Besides, it would be rude to leave now; whoever lived there was sure to have seen or at least heard me pull up and would be expecting a visitor.

I crunched to a stop and surveyed the house. The curtains were drawn. There were no other cars in the turnaround though one might have been parked in the small garage out back. Or maybe the breeder wasn't home. I laughed. All that worry for nothing. Still, I figured I'd better try the bell, just to make sure. I got out of the car, leaving my purse under the seat and locking the doors. I dropped my keys in the oversized pockets of my jacket and walked along the brick path, up the front steps to the ebony door. If they were home, I'd check out the little kitten; though the chances of me purchasing a breed cat were less than nil, I could at least examine its condition to make sure it was being properly cared for. If they were out, I'd head back to town and maybe stop for lunch in Corbett at the little café that overlooked the river, though even its stunning panorama could hardly compare with the view from where I stood.

For a moment, I gazed at the Columbia sparkling deep below like a silken thread. Wrapped up in thoughts of how wonderful it would be to see this lovely sight out the kitchen window, I didn't notice the door swing open until I heard a small cough. I wheeled around to see a large man in a white lab coat and a floppy straw hat pulled down around his clean-cut face standing in the shadow of the doorway.

"Are you here about the kit?" he asked flatly, then turned before I had a chance to answer and moved back into the darkened house. He paused when I didn't follow. "Well, come on. You want to see it, don't you?"

"Well, yes...," I began, but he was already on the move again. This time I followed.

"Please close the door behind you," he said without stopping. "We wouldn't want any catastrophes, would we?"

I shut the door quietly, wondering to what sort of catastrophes he might be referring, and hurried to catch up with the man whose name I had yet to know.

"I'm Lynley," I said to his back. "And you are..?"

"Ben." He turned just long enough to briefly give my hand a limp shake.

The rooms were dark, all shades pulled and all curtains

drawn, but in the darkness I could see the outlines of beautiful antique furniture, vintage glassware, and large framed artwork on the walls. Somewhere a grandfather clock ticked mellow time.

Once a dealer, always a dealer. Though I rarely dabbled in the collectible trade anymore, I still felt that old compulsion to see what treasures there might be. Maybe Ben wanted to sell a bit of it. Sometimes people inherited pieces from their family and then kept them merely because they were there. Maybe he was the type who would gladly swap the chintz and Roseville for chrome and Plexiglas. It would do no harm to ask once I saw the kitten and got a little more friendly with the guy.

We had come through the front hall, living room, and dining room and were now entering the large farmhouse kitchen. I found the lack of light a little disconcerting. Granted it was easy enough to see; the golden glimmer that filtered through the old-fashioned Venetian blinds created a pleasing half-light, but on such a beautiful day it seemed almost a crime to block out that gorgeous spring sunshine.

Ben stopped by a slim door at the far end of the room and turned to me. "It's down here." Swinging it wide, I could only see the first few steps descending into the black void of what I assumed would be the basement.

I looked at the hollow and then at Ben's veiled form. "You keep the kitten in the dark?" I blurted.

He laughed. "Certainly not. It's nappy time, that's all." His use of baby talk seemed at odds with his low, flat voice.

Ben reached to the wall and flipped a switch. The lower chamber lit up harsh and glaring as a hospital operating room. He didn't wait for me but started down the stairs.

"It's very important to keep kittens on a tight routine," he said, his manner slightly more animated as he touched on a subject that obviously interested him. "Grown cats too. They're creatures of habit, cats. There's mealtime and exercise time and slumber time—lots of slumber time—all on a carefully calculated schedule. It's posted on the wall if you care to look it over. If you purchase the kitten, you will get a copy for your own—I suggest you keep to it."

I took a few steps down and bent to see what I was getting myself into. All the bad things happen in the basement—another fact I'd gleaned from TV—but what I saw was reassuring. This space was light and airy, completely renovated from the cellar drear it had undoubtedly been when the old house was built. Sheetrocked walls were painted eggshell white; the linoleum floor, also white, was waxed and shiny. A narrow bank of windows ran across one side. They had been fitted with soft ecru cloth that let in a diffused luminosity.

The only color in the white room was a series of feline anatomical diagrams posted on one wall, the red of muscle and blood in stark contrast to the otherwise monochromatic decor. Beside them was the chart Ben had mentioned, a laminated Excel printout that looked way more complicated than it should be. On the far side of the expansive room stood a bank of kennels, not quite as large as I could have wished for the poor cats, but adequate. I sniffed the air; no trace of litter box odor, though there was a strong smell of bleach. I hoped Ben wasn't using the bleach inside the kennels since even a little of the caustic chemical could be unhealthy for the cats.

"Excuse the odor," he said as if reading my mind. "I did the floor a little while ago. The disinfectant has to sit for forty-five minutes, then I rinse it with fresh water. I was just about to do that when you came. But it can wait a while longer." He pointed to a timer clipped to his belt. The blinking black numbers read zero-zero-four. "It's dry now so it won't hurt to walk on it."

"Don't you worry about the bleach smell being bad for your cats?" I asked as I descended the rest of the way into the white room.

"We have to keep things clean—antiseptically clean, don't we? Otherwise corruption will grow." As if to make a point, he picked up a cloth and an unlabeled spray bottle half full of yellowish liquid. He made a display of squirting an imaginary spot on the wall, wiping it vigorously, inspecting his handiwork, then dabbing at it again for good measure. He put the cleaner down and tossed the cloth in a plastic bucket on the floor, then crossed to the one occupied kennel. A burst of tiny mews rose from inside as the kitten roused from its nap.

As a cat to catnip, I was over to the cage in a heartbeat. The tiny kit could have been no more than eight weeks old. The little points at nose, ears, toes and tail were almost silver. The ears seemed far too large for her small, frail body. She contemplated me with huge, pale blue eyes though she never moved from the pile of fleece blankets that comprised her bed.

"Lilac Point," he said proudly.

"What's her name?" I asked, sensing she was female; so far Ben had only referred to the little animal as "it," a habit which I deplore.

"Buyer gives the call name,"

"Call name?"

"Whatever they're going to call it. That's added after our cattery name on the registration papers when it's sold."

"What's your cattery name then?"

"MoonDiamond. All one word."

"That's pretty," I said, trying to break the tension with a

compliment.

"It's accurate."

"Accurate?"

"Moon Diamond is Thai for Siamese."

"Oh." I remembered hearing the term, Moon Diamond, but I was under the impression the breed was not quite the same as Siamese. Still, what did I know? He was the breeder, and I was the shelter advocate with six decades of miscellanea rattling around in my head. "So do you call her Moon Diamond?"

"I don't call it anything."

I shrugged, guessing the subject was closed. "May I see her?"

He pulled his hat down farther on his brow, and I swear I heard a growl, but he flipped open the grid door, reached in and extricated the kit from her nest.

I took the small being and cuddled her close. She squirmed for a moment and then settled in, purring as loud as a cat twice her size and nuzzling into the crook of my arm.

"So how long have you been breeding Siamese?" I asked, feeling that even though I wasn't going to buy the cat—*was I?*—I should at least sound like a prospective client.

Ben turned and busied himself with her kennel, straightening her covers and returning stray kibble to its stainless steel cup. "Oh, long time."

"*How* long? I hope you don't mind," I added with a gracious smile, though he wasn't watching, "but this is my first experience with a purebred, and my veterinarian made me promise to buy only from an experienced breeder."

"Good advice," he conceded. "Good you have a vet

already. Who is he? Maybe I know of him?"

"Uh, *she's* in town, in Portland."

Ben paused in his work. "Portland?"

"Yes, that's where I live."

Picking up the water dish and taking it to the sink for a refill, Ben mumbled. "Well, I hope it's a good one. We wouldn't want anything to happen to the little beast."

I looked at the kitten who was now asleep in my arms, wondering at Ben's choice of word since I'd never seen anything less beast-like in my life. Maybe he was being facetious. I noted that he still hadn't answered my question, so I pitched another one. "Has she had all her shots?"

"All immunizations are current," Ben affirmed. "We can't have it getting sick. But it will be due for the next set in a month."

"Do you have the report?"

"Of course." He refolded the blankets in the kennel for the third time. "You will get all that with the sale."

"What about her parentage?" I looked around the bare walls and empty kennels. "I should probably check out their pedigree," I said as if I knew what I was talking about and hoping my jargon was at least slightly plausible. "You are the breeder, aren't you?" I added when he didn't respond.

"The sire's not here. It's a nuisance to keep a whole male," he grumbled. "The dam is elsewhere."

"Elsewhere?" I pursued. "Elsewhere here in the house? Or elsewhere at another location?"

He turned, pushed his hat back on his forehead, and stared me in the eye. "Look, lady. This is a top show-class kitten. It's guaranteed to be a champion, nationally recognized, very rare. You may have the breeding rights as well. This is what it costs." He took a pencil and a small notebook out of his shirt pocket, dashed off a number and handed it to me. "Now if you're not interested, go buy a pussycat from a pet store and quit wasting my time."

An ear-splitting beep cut through the quiet room. I recoiled in shock, but not at the timer alarm which Ben shut off with a grunt, nor at his abrupt manner. It wasn't even the four-figure number he had written on the pad. My panic was triggered by something else entirely.

What with the darkened rooms, the floppy hat and his constant tendency to fiddle, this was the first time I had clearly seen Ben's face, a face I recognized instantly though I had come across it only once before and then for no more than a moment. That face was burned on my memory: the narrow, brown eyes; the waxy complexion; the perpetual disapproving frown. There was no doubt in my mind it was the man who had assaulted me in the holding kennel at Friends of Felines.

The man who stole the Siamese.

The criminal responsible for the breed simulation scam.

The killer whom I had come to call the Claw.

I backed up another step and made a strangled sound before I could gather my wits. There was only one thing to do and that was to get out of there as fast as my little feet could carry me. I thought about making a break with the kitten but knew I'd never get away with it. A better plan would be to continue to play innocent, get the hell back to my car, and call the police the minute I made it somewhere my phone could get a signal. The kitten would be alright for a while longer; it was me I needed to worry about.

"Oh, yes, well," I stammered. "This is a little more than I was thinking of spending," I said with a forced smile. I placed the kitten gently back in her bed and closed the kennel door. "I'm sorry to have bothered you. I can find my

213

way out."

I slipped cautiously across the white room toward the stairs; Ben the Claw grumbled irritably but made no move to stop me. I took the steps at a quick trot, something I probably hadn't tried for at least a decade, but adrenaline is a great lubricant, and neither knees, hips, nor back could compete with the fear that pushed me forward as I fled.

At the top, I considered closing the basement door and slipping the bolt, trapping him in while I made my getaway, but decided just to keep going instead. He hadn't seemed to have caught on that I'd caught on. I sped across the kitchen, through the twilight dining room, the murky living room, the gloomy entrance hall. I felt as if I were running in slow motion. The ticks of the grandfather clock seemed to come long seconds apart, then the clock chimed, a low base boom that resonated throughout the house like thunder. I didn't know what time it was, but the bursts went on forever, negating all other sounds.

Finally I was at the front door. I glanced behind me, afraid I'd find him in pursuit, claw raised to rip me to pieces like a wolverine, but I was alone. With great relief, I flung the door wide and ran outside, straight into the arms of Detective Garrison.

Chapter 24

Cats are one of the oldest mammals on the earth. Fossils of African wild cats from as early as thirty-eight million years ago have been found and documented.

For a millisecond I stood, amazed at how situation can alter attitude, then grabbed the big man's hand with the joy of a long lost friend.

"Detective!" I exclaimed. "Am I ever glad to see you! I found him—the killer who's been counterfeiting the breed cats! He's in the house..." I paused to catch my breath, then began to giggle uncontrollably. "But then you must already know that or why else would you be here? Not to buy a Siamese kitten, I'd bet."

I looked around the parking, then drew back. "But where's your backup? Oh, goodness," I gasped. "Are you under cover? I'm so sorry! I certainly wouldn't want to mess things up for you. It's probably alright." I glanced behind me through the vacant room, then whispered, "He's in the basement. I'm pretty sure he didn't realize I was on to him."

Garrison frowned and squinted into the shadows but remained inert.

"It's him alright," I added. "I recognized him from the time at the shelter when he knocked me out. You remember? You must. You thought I'd taken the Siamese, but it was this guy." I pointed inward. "I'm sure of it. I'll never forget that face..."

Still the stony silence, but I could accept that; where I was overjoyed to see Detective Garrison, he was probably less than thrilled to see me.

I took a deep breath and pulled myself together. "Well, I'll just slip off and you can get back to your business. And don't worry, I won't say a word about the break in the case until you give me the okay. If you need my statement, you know where to reach me." I hesitated. "I know we've had our differences, Detective, but I would do anything to get this demon off the streets, away from people *and* cats."

With a final, obliging smile, I stepped onto the walk and edged past the big detective. As I started toward my car, I felt his hand on my arm. "Not so fast, Cannon."

The fingers tightened. Garrison swung me around, none too gently, and I gave a surprised yelp. Expecting him to loosen his grip and possibly even apologize for his rough treatment, I got a second surprise when he stepped into the house, pulling me along with him. Indignantly I tried to shake free, but the hand squeezed tighter. His substantial fingers dug into my biceps, and I yelped again.

"Let go, you're hurting me!" got no response at all, so I flipped into all out tantrum mode. By this time I wasn't as concerned about Ben the Claw hearing my ruckus as I was with not setting foot back in that killer's lair… ever. "Let me go!" I whined, peppering my plea with one-syllable expletives just to prove I was serious. I tugged with all my strength, then braced my free hand against the door jamb. I spread my feet and dug in my heels, a move I'd learned from cats being shoved into carriers. For those of you who've done it, you know what I mean; for those who haven't, let me just say that if kitty doesn't want to go through that little wire door, she will suddenly become a huge, multi-legged blob equipped with sharp, pointed hooks that catch on anything in range. Unfortunately for kitty, we are bigger and more determined; inevitably she ends up in the box. And unfortunately for me, this situation was no different.

I cried out in pain and frustration as Garrison finally shoved me into the room, minus a fingernail or two which remained embedded in the door jam. Now I was mad. I hadn't thought about police brutality since I was marching for peace in sixty-eight, but this bully brought it all back to me in one *Hell no, we won't go!* moment.

Clutching my torn fingers, I turned on the man, but instead of yelling *%#* *fascist pig*, I adopted my best respectable old lady façade: shoulders set, back straight as a rod, nose in the air. I glared down my glasses at the object of my disdain and in the most commanding tone I could muster, I clipped, "This behavior is unacceptable, Detective Garrison, and completely uncalled for. If you wanted something from me, you need merely ask. Even though your jurisdiction is in another state..." I paused to let the dig sink in. "...I would have respected your wishes as an officer of the law."

Noting no change to his expressionless face, I shifted tactics and added with a shrug and a smile, "Hey, we're both on the same side, aren't we?"

The smile dissolved. "Aren't we?"

That was when the revelation hit, and I had the sudden, disheartening hunch that maybe we weren't. It made no sense that he, a policeman, would be in cahoots with a crook, but it would explain a lot—everything from why he was there to how the simulator continued to get away with his scam.

I heard footsteps behind me and turned to see Ben come in to the room, wiping his hands on a towel. He looked briefly at me then his gaze slid to the man standing in the doorway. A strange look came over his face. I couldn't be sure in the half-light, but I could have sworn it was a look of fear. The unease was replaced by a forced smile. It was the first time I'd seen him do so, and the wide grimace didn't look comfortable on his pancake features.

"Robert! Fancy meeting you here."

"You're not the easiest man to find, Bannock."

"There's a reason for that, as you well know. But come in, come in. Would you like a refreshment? Coffee, beer? And you, ma'am? I have tea as well. You should have mentioned you were friends with my estimable cousin here. I would have given you a much better deal on the kit."

"She's not with me," Garrison growled. "She's a no-good busybody cohort of the Portland Police."

Ben's dark eyebrows knit. "Oh, well, that's a horse of another color."

"Yeah, no kidding," the detective agreed, "and what's more, she thinks she's got you made. I told you to get out of town before it came to this."

Ben locked eyes with me, but his words were for the man he called cousin: "I am out of town, Robert. If you hadn't noticed."

"Not far enough, obviously."

Ben began to circle me, all the time staring like the cat with a cornered mouse. "So you're not really looking for a Siamese kitten?"

I shook my head.

"And you know who I am?"

I nodded. "I think so."

"Then this could be a problem."

"No problem," Garrison grumbled as he took a few

strides closer. Before I could wonder what he meant by that, his fist came up and zeroed in on my face.

"No!" I began when I saw the appendage begin to fly at me like a fleshy asteroid. I heard the crunch from inside my head and felt a whole boatload of pain, then the world went white and I felt nothing.

* * *

I was floating. Below me, the watercolor landscape stretched away in a fusion of greens and grays and purples. Forest and field, not a sign of civilization, and the beauty of it was breathtaking. The firmament in which I sailed like a barn swallow was the deep blue of twilight, just after sunset. Venus twinkled in the north, heralding the night to come.

Effortlessly I swooped and spiraled, feeling free and light. The soft atmosphere caressed and cooled my wings...

Wings?

But I didn't have wings.

And without them, how could I fly?

How could I be skimming the treetops and riding the jet stream? The answer that popped into my head like an ugly electric billboard was that I could not.

Instantly the air was sucked out from under me. I began to plummet, head first toward earth. No longer pastel and misty, the ground began to coalesce into a camouflage of brown and black. Rocks bared jagged edges; branches protruded like swords.

Then I hit, face first, an explosion of agony that went on and on. Pain pulsed with every heartbeat, and I realized I wasn't dreaming anymore.

I was sitting, knees bent, on a hard, cold floor. My nose was running, adding insult to the injury. I moved to get a

Kleenex from my pocket and found my wrists were bound behind my back. I had a difficult time collecting my thoughts between the drumbeats of my misery, but intuitively I knew I was in a world of hurt that went far beyond a busted nose.

I squinted my eyes open just a slit, just enough to see through my lashes without letting anyone know I was awake and ready for further punishment. We were back in the white basement, and from the corner where I'd been deposited like so much dirty laundry, I could distinguish Garrison and Ben—Bannock—standing across the room with their heads together. I remembered that name from Garrison's cryptic email. What had it said? I strained to recall, but the substance escaped me.

I noted without much satisfaction that I hadn't been wrong all those months ago when I thought I'd seen a resemblance between the two. Side by side, the familial relationship was obvious. Both men were tall and brawny, the same oval build with barrel chest and smallish head. I guessed both to be in their forties, with Bannock on the younger side and the detective passing forty-five. Bannock still wore his hat so I couldn't tell if his hair resembled Garrison's tousled sooty scruff, but the faces held similarities. The eyes were almost identical, close-set and beady. Though Garrison's complexion was tanned and rugged and Bannock looked as if he never went outside unless it was required of him, the general structure was alike.

They were speaking quietly, but with the pounding in my ears that rivaled the ocean during a winter squall, I couldn't make out the words. Closing my eyes, I concentrated on a mantra or two and, after a few cleansing breaths, was elated to find the pain diminishing to a dull but tolerable roar. My senses quickened, and the conversation became audible.

Garrison was angry, but what's new? I don't think I'd ever seen the man in any other mood. Bannock seemed placating, odd if he were the brutal butcher and not the other way around. For a moment I debated the possibility that Garrison was the Claw but dismissed it. Detective Croft had implied they had a suspect; if it had been the Montana detective, she would hardly have sat down at the table with him. No, gruff, unpleasant, and the dirty cop that Garrison might be, I didn't peg him for the killer.

Then again, mild-mannered cat aficionado Ben or Bannock or whoever he was didn't really fit the persona either. Of course I'd only met one bona fide murderer in my life (that I knew of), and I would have never guessed it in a million years had I seen her in the local grocery store buying onions.

I caught myself; it was obvious I still wasn't thinking straight because I was doing far too much deliberating and not nearly enough listening. My best hope was to get some idea what the men were up to so I could plan my miraculous escape.

"Well, you've really done it this time," Garrison was admonishing Bannock. "I'm not sure I can pull you out of this one."

"Look, Robert. Just a few more and I can start working on my own. You know I'm good at what I do."

"You came to the wrong state, cousin. That was your big mistake. Didn't you know that Oregon has its own set of real live kitty-cops, just watching for people like you?" Garrison charged. "Let me tell you, those guys will track you to down like bloodhounds. They don't give up. You'll never get away unless you leave the region altogether.

Which is what I told you before, though I see you didn't listen."

"I was going to go. I had it all planned out, but then I found this place. An old man in a nursing home needed a caretaker. It's perfect, Robert!" Bannock effused. "Just look around. You know me, I love these old homes. And the view! Have you seen the view? Even a spot for the kennels." Bannock flung his arms out zealously, then the moment was over and he hung his head. "I figured it would be obscure enough, at least while I sold off the last of the kits."

"You figured wrong; this is still Oregon. You should have got your butt to Timbuktu, then we wouldn't be having this problem."

Garrison's head swiveled toward me, and I quickly shut my eyes, both irritated and scared for my life that *Problem* seemed to have become my new nickname.

As I feigned unconsciousness, I heard footsteps coming toward me. They stopped within inches of my body. I sensed him draw even nearer, bending down; felt his breath on my face. Inadvertently I flinched, and it was all over.

He finger-jabbed me in the shoulder, and I let go a whimper of pain.

"You awake, Cannon?"

I opened my eyes and glared up at Garrison but kept my mouth shut.

"We should clean her up, Robert," Bannock murmured. "The wound should be disinfected before it goes septic. And besides she's getting blood all over my nice clean walls and floor. Toxic, dirty blood." He said it almost as a curse.

Garrison ignored him. "Lynley Cannon," he ruminated.

"You should have stayed home safe with your knitting circle, not come out here sleuthing like a crazy old lady."

"I'm not crazy, yet," I coughed before the pain set in again.

Garrison glanced over at his cousin, a grin of amusement contorting his thin lips. "Listen to that. She doesn't think she's crazy." He turned back to me. "And do sane people walk into dangerous situations of their own accord? Situations that can get them hurt?"

"I just came here to see the kitten."

"We both know that's not true, Lynley. You came because you had a hunch you might find the notorious breed counterfeiter, didn't you? You thought you'd stick your nose into police business instead of leaving well enough alone."

"By police business, don't you mean your own?" I spat, my anger outshining my pain. I looked the man in the eye as best I could and added, "Why, Robert Garrison, are you really even a policeman at all?"

Garrison's face turned an angry shade of burgundy, like the wine I used to swill in my younger days, but instead of bopping me again for my insolence, he pivoted on his heel and stalked over to the stairs where he flopped down, putting his head in his hands. "Blast it, Bannock. What do we do with her now?

"You know I'm going to have to alert Thomas," Garrison added pointedly.

For the second time, I saw Bannock cringe. Whoever this Thomas was, the big man was certainly afraid of him.

"No!" Bannock cried. "We can handle this on our own." He straightened his shoulders. "I can take care of her. We needn't bother Thomas just yet, need we?"

Garrison harrumphed but didn't disagree.

Bannock took a deep breath and approached me. As he loomed over me, digging in his lab coat pocket for what I was sure would be the weapon of my demise, I found myself suddenly calm.

"You won't get away with it, you know," I stated matter-of-factly. "Detective Cross is on to you. She'll find me. I have a GPS locator in my car. I called her just before I came in and told her everything. She should be here any minute."

"You're lying."

I grinned. "Are you sure?"

Bannock looked at Garrison, but the detective was deep in his own little pity party and paying no attention to the dialog.

"So you should probably get moving before she comes and arrests you for murder," I urged.

"Murder?" Bannock blustered. "What do you mean, murder?" He took a step backward and stared at me with an expression of shock. "You didn't think I was going to kill you, did you?"

"Why not? Why not claw me to bits like you did the others? Or would that take too long? Maybe another punch in the face?" I paused, then nodded toward his pocket. "Or a knife?"

"A knife?" He pulled out his hand; he was indeed holding something—not a weapon but a handkerchief. "I don't have a knife. I was only going to wipe the blood off your face."

Bannock turned to Garrison. "Killing? A claw? What's she talking about, Robert?"

"You know exactly what she's talking about," he growled, looking up. "Don't you read the news?"

Bannock began to visibly shake. "You mean,

Londale...?"

"That's right."

"But after the raid on the old mill, I thought he'd left for the Everglades. That's what you told me. You said I wouldn't have to worry about him anymore."

"He did, and I did. But he came back."

Chapter 25

A cat is considered feral if he has grown up in the wild without human contact. These cats are terribly afraid of humans and rarely adapt to being pets. To cut down on rampant feral populations, many communities have adopted a Trap, Neuter, and Return program. With TNR, the ferals can live out their normal lives without adding to the homeless cat population.

Bannock began raging like a feral cat caught in a live trap. "What if he finds me? What do we do?" he bawled, more to himself than to the detective or me. "I've got to get out of here. I've got to pack and run!"

"Who is Londale?" I asked.

"Londale's crazy! He's spent too much time around that toxic colorant. He thinks it's funny. He even uses it to dye his own hair. It's gone to his brain."

"He never had much of a brain to begin with," Garrison grumbled. "And neither did you, getting involved with that crook."

"I'm sorry, Robert. It seemed like such a good plan at the time."

"And look where it got you? Running from both the police and your own partner."

"I hate to interrupt," I interrupted, twitching my nose where the blood had dried and was itching something awful, "but if you're not going to kill me, could I please have that handkerchief, Ben? My face is driving me nuts."

Bannock stopped in the middle of the room and stared

at me. "Oh, misery!" he cried. "What am I going to do?"

Garrison stood up. "Oh, give her the hankie. I shouldn't have struck her so hard."

Did I hear a hint of remorse?

Bannock came over and offered the pristine white linen. I wondered if he expected me to take it in my teeth.

"And untie her hands, for pity's sake!" Garrison added. "She's not going anywhere. Are you, Cannon?"

I started to shake my head, but at the resultant dizzying pain in my cranium, I thought better of it. "I'll be good, I promise, but please just let me clean up. Is there a bathroom I could use?"

"There's a sink over there. You don't want to see yourself in a mirror anyway."

Bannock squatted meekly and did as he was told, turning me so he could remove the binding, an elaborate strip of gauze-lined surgical tape, from my hands. I rubbed my wrists, then grabbed the hankie and held it to my face, giving a little gasp when my fingers hit the sore spot. Using my other hand to help shove my cramped body up from the floor, I staggered to my feet. A wave of vertigo hit, and I leaned against the wall, breathing hard. Still, I was determined not to show weakness. They had let me free; I wasn't going to do anything to make them tie me up again. The thought of another fist in the face was too painful to even consider.

Bannock was back to his helpless pacing, and Garrison was yammering away about who knew what. I didn't care. Until I got the drippy, oozy feeling in my nostrils staunched, nothing else mattered. I ran the water in the spotless sink until it was as hot as possible, then dipped the hankie under the faucet. The feel of the warm cloth against my face was instantly soothing. I stood for uncounted seconds just soaking away the pain.

I was rinsing out the linen for the third time, watching the reddish stain tornado down the sparkling drain, when I sensed a presence behind me. I turned to see Garrison, his hands stuffed in his coat pockets, looking what I thought seemed rather sheepish, if that glowering face could ever show such an anomaly. Instinctively I stiffened, preparing to run or duck or fight—whatever his next onslaught would require of me.

"Okay, here's what's going to happen now," he announced.

I wiped my face with the dry corner of the handkerchief. "I'm listening."

"Bannock is going to disappear. Like he should have done a long time ago," Garrison added over his shoulder to his cousin. "You never saw him, and you never saw me."

"Okay..."

"Before he goes, he's going to clean up—he's very good at that as you may have noticed. There won't be a useful shred of evidence—not a cat hair, not a kibble—left in this house to tie either of us to a crime. You're going to wait here until he's finished and gone. Then you and I are going to leave together. You can go your way to whatever it is you do in your retirement life, and I'll go mine, back to catching the bad guys—I *am* a law enforcement officer, by the way, and I'm not dirty, no matter what you might think you know."

Garrison sighed. His shoulders slumped. "Ben's family, you see. And he's going to go straight from now on. He really is a cat breeder, and he's good at it. He just got off to a bad start."

"Because of Londale?"

"That creep!" Garrison fumed. "He got Ben into this

breed counterfeiting scam, convinced him it would pay off faster than being an honest breeder. Ben already had a little business going back in Montana, but it's tough at first to build the kind of reputation that attracts affluent clientele. Horace Londale had the knowhow to fake a client list, the pedigrees, then finally the cats themselves, but it came with a price nobody expected. The special combination of chemicals he used to color the cats' coats is highly toxic in its liquid state."

"I know about the chemicals. It's a terrible thing to do to a cat. Can the breed cat business really be lucrative enough to go to all that trouble and risk?"

"Oh, definitely, if you are selling a high-end product. Show-quality cats go for thousands."

"I gathered," I said, recalling the figure Bannock quoted for the kitten.

"Thing is, those true top quality cats are hardly ever sold outside the breeding and show community, and almost never to novices. They're way too rare."

"Then how did Ben and Londale get away with it?"

"Oh, Londale did the sales, and he was very careful who he sold to. He would feel out the buyer, looking for people with no experience, people he could scam into thinking they needed a top show kit to break into the business. Lure them with promises of glamour, fame, and huge cash prizes. He'd supply them with fancy lists of surefire, step-by-step instructions how to succeed. I think he even made a DVD."

"Then he passed off a cat or kitten for thousands of dollars that was worth a hundred at best?"

"Probably less because of all the tampering they had done, which could compromise the cat's health and well-being down the line."

I walked over to the kennel where the Siamese kitten slept in its little pile of blankets. Opening the wire door, I took her in my arms. Gently I felt her fur for the telltale stiffness. "Has she been dyed?"

"I doubt it. Bannock promised me he was going to stay out of trouble after he split from Londale. At worst, it's someone's pet with forged papers. The colorant can kill a cat that age."

Garrison broke off, shaking his head. "Londale did the coloring, but even so, just being around the stuff was beginning to give my cousin anxiety attacks and hallucinatory paranoia. Ben wanted to get out, but Londale didn't care. He's a madman. He blackmailed Ben, both emotionally and physically. Ben's a follower, good at heart but easily led. I tried my darnedest to help him. I'd thought maybe this time..."

"So let me get this straight. Detective Cross was wrong, or at least partially wrong—there are two criminals, not just one. Two people running the breed scam, but only one doing the killing? I'm guessing that's this Londale person."

"Right, he's the one. My cousin couldn't kill anything bigger than a flea, and then only if it was threatening one of his precious cats. The more Londale worked with the chemicals, the crazier he got; the crazier he got, the more he worked with the chemicals. He began to be unpredictable, then downright violent. He assaulted Ben on numerous occasions—I had to come pick up the pieces, try to convince Ben to give it up, but Ben couldn't. It was a classic abusive relationship: the beating; the apologies; the promises; the forgiveness. Everything's hunky-dory until the next time. Except this was between men.

"Londale worked so close with the cats that he began to think he was a cat. That's when it went really nuts. He made up a glove with claws he carved from bone and would threaten people with it, just to see their reactions. He thought it was funny. He tried it with me one time," Garrison growled, "but only once. He never made that mistake again."

"But he murdered people! He clawed them to shreds!" I shuddered, recalling the scene outside my window that black, stormy night: the upstretched arm, the scythe-like claws; the ripping, over and over while I watched helplessly...

"Yeah, as time progressed the threats turned deadly real. He never went after Ben that way, but anyone else who riled him was good as dead."

"Then the victims weren't random, like the police thought?"

The detective shook his head. "They don't have a clue who they're looking for."

"And you're not about to tell them."

He turned on me, the anger back in his mousy eyes. "You bet I'll tell them! I'll lead them right to his door and laugh while they put him in cuffs."

Like a toy with a dying battery, he sank in on himself. "But not till I know Ben is safe. Soon. It's gotta be soon."

"And now your cousin thinks Londale will be coming to get him, too?"

"That's the paranoia talking," said Garrison, regaining his composure. "Londale has no idea where Ben is. Ben's fears aren't without basis though."

"But you told Ben that Londale was back."

"He is, or at least he was earlier this month. Those grisly headlines in the Portland papers about the Panther killer confirmed it. Look, Lynley." Garrison lowered his voice even though Bannock had disappeared up the stairs, ostensibly to begin his exit strategy. "I'm a cop. I want my cousin to get right and stay right, but he can't do that in Oregon. The law's too close on his track, and I don't mean me. I can't hold them off forever. He needs to disappear, to start over. I've got him just about convinced this time, and maybe a little fear will be the push he needs to make the right choice."

"And what about Londale? How do you propose to get him once Ben is safe?"

"I've been chasing Horace Londale all across the United States, but he's elusive. So far, I haven't been able to catch up with him, but I won't stop until I do. I already told you, he's going to get his, for the murders and for screwing up my cousin's life."

"It all sounds good, Detective Garrison, but how do I know you're telling the truth?"

Garrison's face went grim, back to the visage I knew so well. "You'll just have to take my word for it."

"And what if I don't?" I ventured before I could stop myself.

He just shrugged. "Your word against mine. A respected police detective and a crazy old cat lady—who do you think they'll believe?"

He had a point. If his only deviation from the law had been to cover his cousin, it would be nearly impossible to prove that anything I'd heard or seen in the past few hours had ever really happened. I could send a forensic team back to the house to try to uncover some evidence, but I was pretty sure Garrison wasn't underestimating his obsessive cousin's ability to sanitize the scene. Besides, they don't just send those crews out on the whim of an old lady. There needs to be some pretty reliable evidence to warrant all the trouble and expense of forensics.

And what was the point, if this Londale was the killer and Bannock only a pawn in his vicious game? Fact was, I felt sorry for the big man who wanted so desperately to breed kittens. I didn't think he should get off scot-free—after all, he had his part in a terrible scheme—but he wasn't a killer.

First things first, I reminded myself. Getting out of there was mission enough for the moment.

"What's going to happen to the kitten?" I said impulsively.

"Take it," Garrison said. "Take it to your cat shelter and sell it. I'm sure it'll bring in a few bucks, even without papers."

I held the small kit whom I had come to think of as Mab, the Faerie Queen from Celtic folklore. (Had she *communicated* that name to me, or had I just made it up?) "Mab," I said softly, stroking fur softer than silk.

"Huh?" Garrison grunted.

"Nothing," I said, turning away from him before he could change his mind.

Suddenly through the open window over the kennel, I heard the crunch of gravel. Garrison heard it too. Instantly he tensed, head turned to listen.

"Are you expecting somebody?" I asked.

"You wait here," was all he said as he bounded up the stairs, two at a time.

I heard his heavy footsteps cross the floor above; a car door slammed, then the babel of voices, loud but not loud enough for me to tell what was going on. I prayed that the visitor was someone who could get me out of that madhouse—a contingent of FBI agents with flak vests and automatic weapons would fit the bill nicely—but I had a feeling that I might not be so lucky.

Someone stomped into the living room, and a sharp, metallic clatter hit the floor. The hubbub continued: voices raised in anger; a high pitched bawl; the trample of feet resonating throughout the old house.

Then I caught a different sound, the wild wail of a Siamese cat. Mab pricked up her ears, the first real interest I'd seen in her since I came. Without thought, I sprinted toward the howl, taking the kitten with me. It was a reflex, with no clear brain-work behind it—very feline, as cats will often run to the cries of their kind. I did have the presence of mind to hang back once I reached the kitchen, not wanting to announce myself until I knew what I was getting into. The wail came again, then another and another—my goodness, how many cats did they have in there?

I crept in the half-light, now thankful for the drawn curtains, and hunched behind the door between kitchen and dining room. I could see a narrow vertical strip of the scene through the crack: there were indeed cats, at least five carriers within my range of visibility. They were tipped at odd angles as if they had been dumped willy-nilly, and the cats weren't happy about it. The smell of excrement was undeniable. I cringed, wondering how long those animals had been kept in those filthy little jails for them to be fouling their own space.

Bannock was running back and forth, shouting and screaming about the mess on his nice clean floor. Garrison stood motionless, hands in the air, talking quickly to someone—I presumed it was the newcomer who was still out of my line of sight. The new man was talking too, a strange voice that seemed to range from a shrill cry to a low, gruff growl.

"Yes, I followed you, Robert," the voice was saying. "I

sniffed you out like an old fish. Then I waited. I have all the patience in the world when it comes to my prey. I knew you'd flush out your cousin sooner or later." The man turned to Bannock. "I shouldn't have had to do that, little partner. You should have let me know you were moving. But I'm sure it was an oversight, am I right? I wouldn't like to think you've been avoiding me."

Bannock just stared and whimpered.

"Quit worrying about the stupid floor and look what I brought for us? Eh? Eh? Look at these beauties!"

"No more," Bannock stuttered. "I can't do it anymore. I just want to breed the cats, really breed them—no more scams."

"That's no attitude, little partner," the voice crooned. "You know I can't do it without you.

"I tried!" the man suddenly yelled at the top of his lungs, making everyone jump including Mab and myself. "Goodness knows I tried!"

He crossed to Bannock, and I caught my first glimpse of the dreaded Panther killer.

The picture was somewhat disappointing; not the rampant, gorilla-like monster from my imagination, Londale was short and slight, gangly in movement. The fact that he'd referred to Ben as his *little* partner now seemed ironic since he was at least a foot shorter than the breeder. With his nice gray business suit, blue tie, slicked black hair, and thick-rimmed glasses, he reminded me of a nineteen-fifties game show host only in miniature. I noted that his left hand was wrapped in a not-so-clean bandage. My heart skipped a beat; my mother's shot hadn't missed after all.

He threw his arms around Bannock; the larger man seemed completely cowed by this mini Jack the Ripper.

Suddenly he hugged the man back. "I'm sorry," he whimpered. I'm so sorry."

"Don't listen to him, Ben," Garrison charged. "Remember what I told you. He's a liar and a very bad man. He'll hurt you, make you do things you don't want to do. You know he wants to dye these cats. Your delusions will come back, and this time they could kill you."

"Shut up!" Londale shrieked over his shoulder. "There, there," he crooned to Bannock. "Everything's going to be fine. It'll be like old times."

"You leave him alone. Horace Londale, I'm placing you under arrest on suspicion of murder." Garrison took a few steps toward the killer. "You have the right to remain silent..."

Londale whirled around, holding something in his good hand. Even though I couldn't make it out in the shadows, I knew from his stance exactly what it was.

He brought the gun up, aiming at Garrison's chest. "You're the one who's going to remain silent."

Garrison pulled back as the shot rang out. The detective spun and toppled. Bannock made to run to him, but Londale gripped him tightly. The echo of the report faded away, and aside from the ticking of the grandfather clock, the room was still.

Then there was a sound. One sound, faint and tiny after the explosion of gunfire but equally audible. My breath caught in my throat, but it was already too late.

Mab mewed again.

Londale's head whipped around like a terrier's; I could almost see his narrow ears prick up. "What was that?"

Bannock's stupefied gaze slid slowly from his downed cousin to the man who held him. "Wha..?"

"That noise. It sounded like a kitten."

"There is a kitten," Bannock stated slowly and without comprehension. "One left in the kennels. In the basement."

"That mew didn't come from the basement. It was way closer than that."

I was amazed at how quickly the slippery little man made it across the room. I turned to run but he was already on me. He paused, gun up in my face.

"Who the hell are you?"

Chapter 26

Depending on what sources you reference, ailuromania is defined as: a passion for cats; an abnormal love of cats; an addiction to cats; an unhealthy obsession with cats; a desire to have many cats, even when conditions are not suitable for health.

It was a rhetorical question; I knew that the moment he said it, but something stemming far back into my formative years required that the polite thing to do was to answer. "I'm Lynley," I said as if I were introducing myself to any stranger. "Lynley Cannon. And you are...?"

The small man harrumphed. "I'm the man of your dreams, sister. Who do you think I am?"

He grabbed me by the elbow, and I caught an unmistakable whiff of the noxious dye. I stared at his hair, only inches away from me; its wetness was no product-induced illusion. He must have touched it up recently and with great gusto. Oily droplets still clung to the short locks and dripped down onto his collar, making Rorschach dots on the white fabric.

With a rough twist, he ushered me back into the dining room. There, I finally got the full effect of the nightmare tableau. Garrison, dead or still clinging to life—I couldn't tell—lay face down on the floor in his pooling blood; Bannock stood in the center of the room like a statue—only his eyes moved, tracing an endless triangle between his felled cousin, Londale, and me.

"Where did this come from, little partner?" Londale

urged, giving me a poke in the shoulder.

Bannock's gaze never strayed from its relentless rounds.

"Bannock!"

The dark eyes lingered on Londale. "Huh?"

"Where did this woman come from?" the small man articulated as if to a child. "And what is she doing with our kitten?"

"That's Lynley," Bannock said so softly I could barely hear him. "She came to look at it. Well, no, not really," he added. "She just pretended to. Robert said she was some sort of snoop for the police." He began to giggle wildly. "She thought I was you! She actually thought I had killed all those people. Me! Can you imagine?"

Bannock's laughter escalated, building toward full hysteria. Londale crossed to him in two long strides and slapped him hard across the face. The larger man crumpled into a heap on the hardwood beside his cousin, his laughter dissolving into tears.

"You shut up about that, little partner, or *Maahes* will come after you next."

It took me a moment to realize I was free, that the uproar had taken Londale's attention off of me. It was a long shot, and the odds were bad, but it was possibly the only chance I would get. In a heartbeat, I was off and running.

I dashed back into the kitchen and slammed the old oak door behind me. It wouldn't stop him long, but every second counted. At the far side of the cavernous room was another doorway. It was shut, its small four-paned window revealing only dusk. An enclosed back porch? If so, that would certainly mean a way outside.

I made for the shadowy rectangle. Once through, I saw

I was in the right place. The narrow sun porch ran the length of the house. Bamboo blinds covered the broad windows, but down at the end was a square of pure, unadulterated sunshine. Through it, I could see a blooming cherry tree and the gray-green of firs—my destiny, so close I could almost taste the sweet gorge air.

The dining room door crashed open and shoe clicks approached across the smooth oak planks. I made for that sunny square as if my life depended on it, which in fact, it probably did.

I glanced back to see the diminutive shape of Londale materialize in the entry like an animated Ken doll. That was okay though. My hand was on the doorknob; my keys were in my pocket. I had only to get to my car and get gone.

I turned the knob and...

Nothing!

I tried again, this time yanking so hard that pain shot from my wrist to my shoulder, but it still didn't give. I squinted in the dim for a latch to turn or a bolt to slip, but all I saw was the round brass outline of a deadbolt lock. Lightning fast, my eyes skimmed the nearby wall for a key—after all, wasn't it prudent to leave a key nearby a locked deadbolt in case of fire? That's what I did at home. But this wasn't my home. Not even close.

I pivoted and backed into the door. I stared at my predator. In the light from the window, I could see the hateful, crazy look on his face. The good news was he had put the gun away somewhere and was no longer holding it on me; the bad news was it took him only moments to cross the small space. Then his hands were around my neck, shaking and pressing, pressing and shaking.

I fought him one-handed, the other clasping the kitten to my chest. I scratched at his arms and face, stomped on his leather shoes, and tried my best to knee him in the groin, but each move brought only more anger, more pain. I felt my consciousness slipping, white galaxies exploding in my sight, the roar of the ocean growing ever nearer...

I reached out for something to grab, something I could hit with that had more clout than my arthritic fist. I felt along the dusty sideboard: a plastic flower pot; a bag of clothespins; a near-empty box of who-knew-what. Then I found it; my fingers closed around the smooth iron surface; I grasped it hard and struck.

I had been aiming the antique sadiron for his face but missed, instead hitting his hand—the left one that my mother's gunshot had grazed. Londale screamed like a girl and let go of me. I didn't wait but shoved past him, knocking him against the wall where he collapsed, gasping and whimpering, into a little pile of hurt.

I was still groggy from my brush with asphyxiation, staggering and banging into things as I fled. I wasn't thinking straight either, because instead of zipping out through the front room and running to my car, which had seemed such a good idea a mere moment ago and probably still was, I found myself scampering up a long flight of stairs to the second floor of the old cottage. My footsteps echoed through the house like the proverbial herd of elephants. If I'd wanted to get away and hide, I was off to a bad start. Of course, I could hope I had incapacitated Londale with my bash on his injured hand. (Thank you, Mum!) I could also hope an alien spaceship would come swoop me away to safety. I knew realistically, even through my stupor, that hope wasn't going to do much to save my life if Londale stayed on the hunt.

I paused at the top of the stairs and hastily weighed my options. There was a short hallway with three doors, all shut tight. At the end was a bathroom, its door flung wide, displaying an ancient toilet with an overhead tank. The bathroom should have a lock on it—I could run inside and pray Londale didn't decide to blow it away with his gun. I pictured the tiny, ancient latch hook; I envisioned the sleek, black gun. I looked around for a better prospect.

One of the doors was narrower than the other two. I knew these old houses, knew that one would lead to the attic. I listened for footsteps, but all I could hear was the fitful wail of a Siamese cat.

Glancing down, I gazed at the kitten. She blinked up at me with clear blue eyes and gave a little mew. It seemed like she was saying, *I trust you with my life; don't disappoint me.*

I'll try not to, I sent in return as I slipped through the attic door and up the steep stairs, this time as silent as a cat.

The attic was dim but not much more so than the rest of the house. Shadowy shapes hunched against the sloping rafters: boxes; piles of magazines and papers; large pieces, probably furniture, shrouded in sheets like lumpy ghosts. A light bulb hung on its twisted wires from the eaves in the middle of the room. Quickly I unscrewed it and for no good reason, shoved it into the left pocket of my coat. I slipped Mab into the right one where she settled deep within the warm pink folds. Now I had both hands free in case I had to fight again, though I hoped I wouldn't. For a moment, I wished I'd kept hold of the sadiron and quickly scanned the room for something else with weapon potential. I saw a broom lying on the floor—good for poking but not much weight behind it; a timeworn Webster's dictionary—heavy as a barbell but unwieldy; and a set of fireplace tools. I seized the blackened shovel since the poker seemed to be absent and ventured on to my second goal: finding a place to hide.

Again I listened. This time I thought I could hear movement below but wasn't sure where it was coming from or even if it were human. Assuming the worst, I slithered behind a spectral mound that turned out to be a folding bed covered by a tattered linen tablecloth. The top edge of the bed was shoved up against the pitched rafters as far as it would go, leaving a small triangle of emptiness behind it. I shrugged myself in as far back as I could get, realizing that if he did manage to find me, I'd be trapped. I ran my hand along the squared iron handle of the fireplace shovel, hoping I wouldn't have to use it.

Now the wait; it was the hardest thing I'd ever had to do. Within a minute, my leg cramped; my face had begun to throb again where Garrison hit me; I couldn't breathe through my mangled nose which had decided to run like a mother bear. Trying not to wheeze, I rummaged in my coat for a Kleenex, found a small pack, and crammed the whole lot of them against my nostrils at once. Though thankfully silent, Mab was squirming, and I wanted to, too, except there was no place to shift in that tight, dusty cubby of cover.

Then I heard the rattle of the doorknob at the bottom of the stairs and pain was replaced by adrenalin terror. My heart beat so fast I was sure I would pass out; I gulped for air, then held it, certain he would be able to hear my hoarse breathing. The kitten went still, lying like a dead weight against my side as if she knew what was at stake.

The door scraped open. Soft footsteps progressed slowly up the stairs, one excruciating tread at a time, so like a scene from a horror movie I almost giggled. Then he was on the landing; the old floor creaked once and all was quiet. The silence stretched into eternity. Seconds? Minutes?

Years? Finally there was a sound, but not the ominous footfalls I was expecting.

I strained my ears, trying to identify what I was hearing: a soft, padding shuffle made by more than two feet. At first, I wondered if Bannock could be with the killer, but that didn't make sense. Only one person had come up, I would have bet on it. This tread of clump-clump clump-clump more resembled beast than man.

Inching forward, I strained to see around the edge of the bed frame. I watched until the thing came stalking into view. With an inadvertent gasp, I jammed my eyes shut, but the image was imprinted in my mind as surely as a sunspot. I looked again; this time, both fascinated and horrified, I couldn't take my eyes off it.

It was Londale, alright, but Londale as I could never have imagined. Down on all fours, he was slinking across the dusty floor like an animal.

Like a cat, I realized. Like the panther or whatever wild *Felis* he had chosen as his alter ego. I had to say, he'd got it down. His emulation of the side to side, one-step-in-the-other stride of a cat was so authentic that I couldn't help but admire it.

But that wasn't where the pretense ended. Gone were the business jacket, tie, slacks, and slip-on Oxfords, replaced instead with a black one-piece cat suit, complete with cowl. No wonder he had taken his time to find me—he had to change into his super-villain guise. Thing was, it worked. What had been a little man in a big world, had, through that costume, morphed into a creature to be reckoned with.

Swinging his head from left to right, he uttered a low growl. He paused in front of an old waterfall dresser, then with a gravity-defying leap, sprung to the top where he turned and looked out over the room like the king of beasts. His reflection rippled, wraithlike in the round mercury-glass mirror.

That was when I saw it. On his right hand—the uninjured one—he wore a skin-tight elbow-length glove of ebony fur with razor hooks protruding from the tip of each finger: the Claw, itself! Posing it in the air like a malevolent Maneki-neko, he opened his human mouth and gave a convincing, panther-like hiss.

"I know you're in this room," he continued in human-speak. "You might as well come out and face your fate. I warned you not to get on the wrong side of *Maahes.* You should have listened while you still had the chance."

When would that have been? I wondered briefly. *When you were holding a gun in my face or when your hands were around my neck, choking me to death?* But the question was irrelevant. He knew I was there; I had two choices—hide like a scared feral or come out and face him like a man.

Not being a man, I opted for staying where I was. He still had the disadvantage of the damaged hand; maybe I could whack it again before he tore me to ribbons, then jump out the attic window and fly away like Peter Pan. Yup, that just might do it.

To my surprise, instead of launching into a full scale search and destroy mission, Londale sat back on his haunches—I mean his thighs—and began to talk. This was the voice I'd heard when he first came in the house, the peculiar range of tones that ran from keening to a near-snarl. Beginning with a high-pitched yowl, he offered his story.

Chapter 27

In ancient Egypt, cats were important members of society. Because they controlled vermin, including snakes such as cobras, they were elevated to divinity. In the event of fire, men would stand guard to make sure no cats ran into the flames. When a cat died, its household would go into mourning, shaving their eyebrows to signify loss. Killing a cat, even accidentally, incurred the harsh penalty of death.

"I am Maahes," the creature who had been Horace Londale howled. "Maahes, son of Sekhmet and blessed in my own right. My soul was born in the deserts of Kmet, the Black Land, but my frail human body was spawned elsewhere. I came to the understanding of my true nature only a short while ago. When I found my terrible purpose, my life took on meaning. I knew I had a duty, a destiny. No longer small and fragile, I am Maahes, Miysis, Mios, the lion-headed god of war!"

He paused briefly, and I could swear he turned and gave a short lick to his shoulder, the way a cat might do when nervous. Then the proud head went back up, sniffing the musty air.

"I am the last of my kind," he hissed. "I live only to avenge the extinction of my people. Whosoever crosses me shall feel the brand of my claw."

His words gave me goosebumps. I was absolutely sure he believed his tale, and he nearly had me convinced, too. There was something about the innate longing, the utter loneliness of his plight that touched my heart, and for whatever reason, for that moment in time, I pitied him.

He took a deep breath, opened his mouth and *flehmened* like a cat. In a heartbeat, he bunched his muscles and sprang, hitting the floor at a run. He seemed to sense exactly where I was, though I swear I'd made no sound. With a roar, he swiped the clawed glove across the sheltering bed, caught the old mattress and flung it away. I cowered, exposed like a snail ripped from its shell, staring into the wide, yellow eyes of a madman.

He brought up the claw, ready to strike. As I began to tremble, I felt Mab's tiny squirm against my body. Suddenly I knew I had to protect her; I couldn't give in to this aberration without a fight.

There has always been a little bit of cat spirit in me, though thank the powers that be I'd never felt it driving me to dress up and kill people. Still, there it lurked, my inner tiger, waiting for this moment when it would be needed to defend the puny, furless body in which it was housed.

Pulling the kitten from my pocket and placing her gently in a box of old blankets, I bounded. Londale clearly wasn't expecting that; he crouched, frozen, mouth open, watching as I skimmed right underneath his arm and out the other side. I didn't bother with the clumsy authenticity of using all fours; whatever inner beast was urging me on, it was not above utilizing all my assets, human and otherwise.

It didn't take long for Londale-slash-*Maahes* to regain his senses. He sprung after me as I sprinted across the room. I slipped behind a chest of drawers, Londale only seconds behind. I braced my shoulder against the back of the heavy piece and heaved. It crashed onto its side, raising up a cloud of antique dust. Londale hesitated, then cat-like, scrambled up and overtop.

I zipped behind the dresser that had been Maahes' podium. Again I pushed at the cumbersome furniture. It tumbled, blocking his path. Amidst the tinkle of breaking glass and the howl of the frustrated maniac, I raced for the stairs. I made it to the landing when a furry hand grabbed my ankle. As surely as a tree topples to the logger's axe, I went down.

There was a loud, firecracker-like bang. I screamed, and he wavered. I knew it must have been the light bulb in my pocket, but he didn't have a clue. His hand loosened, just the slightest, and in that moment of hesitation, I jerked from his grasp.

I scrabbled forward like a crab, feeling a splinter from the old floor dig into my hand. The pain didn't slow me; if anything it pushed me to move faster. There was a window in the peaked dormer, and I made for it. It was instinct; I had no real illusion I could get out that way, and even if I did, there was little chance of climbing down from there in a manner that didn't kill me. Still, I honed in on the flyspecked glass as if it were the gates of Heaven.

I heard a scuffle behind me. Londale leapt and landed hard, knocking me flat. His knee dug into my spine. For a moment I was conquered, but the cat in me wasn't finished yet. I executed a twist worthy of a Siamese and flipped over onto my back, knees bent and feet up in the defensive stance I'd seen cats assume in both fight and play. I caught him in the stomach with my solid granny shoes and heard the breath *oof* out of him. The claw hand, which had been coming up for the kill, flopped impotently to his side.

I kicked him off me and fumbled to rise, but this time I wasn't quick enough. That last move, though effortless when done by a feline, had taken its toll. My cat-self evaporated, leaving only a tired and hurting old lady. Londale pulled me back and straddled my torso, clasping my arms to my body with his knees. With a low, guttural growl, he raised the claw once more. He did it leisurely and with pleasure, drinking in the fear that mounted in my eyes, relishing my helplessness as if it were food. Powerless, I watch it ascend as if it were the only thing in the world.

Suddenly two other elements registered, instant and electrifying. The first was an explosion so loud my eardrums throbbed; the second, nearly synchronous, was a sticky mist that peppered my face like hot rain. Londale's eyes opened wide with surprise, as did his mouth. A thin trickle of blood traced a dark scar from the corner to his chin. The claw descended like a flag being lowered to half mast, then Londale began to list. Ever so gradually, he leaned, until finally gravity took hold. He fell to the side where he lay motionless, that look of absolute amazement still haunting his hollow, lifeless gaze.

Like a broken robot, I sat up and pushed the remaining leg off me.

I knew the man was dead, that I was safe.

I looked around for the kitten.

* * *

There was a jumble of sounds now: boots on the stairs, cars in the drive, a siren blast, the crackle of a police radio. A soft blanket slipped around my shoulders, and I looked up into the cat-green eyes of Denny Paris.

"Special Agent?" I managed through chattering teeth. "I thought you only rescued four-legged victims."

"You know you're a special case, Lynley," he smiled back. Then in all seriousness, he began to look me over,

"Are you hurt? I mean, aside from the obvious."

For a moment I had to ponder what he meant, then I reached up and touched my face. "Ouch. It aches, but I think it looks worse than it is. No, I'm okay, but I'm really ready to get the hell away from this house."

"The paramedics will be here in a few minutes. Let's just wait and have them check you out before we go anywhere."

"Oh!" I exclaimed as my brain began to function again. "I need to find Mab so she doesn't get lost among all these people!"

"Mab?"

"She's only a baby kitten, you see."

Denny smiled. "Leave it to you, Lynley, to get yourself a cat in the midst of a crackdown."

I struggled to rise but found it was more than I could do. I sank back with a sigh. "I'm serious! A big boot could hurt her, and I can't think what might happen if she got outside. I have to find her now," I added in a whimper.

"Okay, okay. Don't worry, Lynley. We'll get her for you."

Denny stood up and called attention. The half dozen officers and EMTs looked his way. "Somewhere up here is a kitten," he announced in his no-nonsense cop voice. I would have sworn he was pronouncing a manhunt instead of a misplaced kit. "We need to find her pronto. Okay?"

There was a round of *Sure things* and *You bets*, and everyone except for the man tending to the body of Horace Londale began to search.

"I put her in a box under the eaves." I pointed. "Over on that side of the room."

A wiry policewoman stepped up to the jumble of cartons and looked, then turned to me and shook her head.

"She's got to be somewhere," Denny encouraged. "If we don't catch her up here, start looking downstairs."

Sure enough, it wasn't two minutes before she was discovered hiding in the corner of a half-open drawer. A firefighter the size of a football player brought me the little cat. I was touched to see the delighted gleam in his eye.

"Thank you," I told him as I took the kitten in my arms. She proceeded to chatter for a few minutes, telling me all about it, then settled down to a loud, rumbling purr.

"He's the Claw murderer, you know." I said to Denny, nodding toward the remains of Londale that was being tagged and photographed from all angles. "He was crazy, I think. Partially from the chemicals he used to dye the counterfeit cats, but it wasn't just that. Otherwise Bannock would be crazy, too, instead of just anxious and paranoid. Londale seemed more..." I searched for the word. "Pathetic, I guess.

"Bannock!" I exclaimed. "Did you get him? He didn't hurt anyone, but he did help run the breed simulation scam."

"We got him."

"And Detective Garrison? Is he...?" I faltered, picturing him unconscious on the hardwood floor with his life's blood flowing red around him.

"He's alive. Looks like the bullet passed right through his shoulder. It's going to require some pretty fancy surgery, but he'll be back to his old grumbly self in no time."

"I'm glad. We never saw eye to eye, but he was trying to do right by his cousin, even if it turned out all wrong."

"Cousin?" Denny shook his head. "I don't think we know anything about that. You'll have to give a complete statement, bring us up to speed." Denny paused and frowned. "But Lynley, what were you doing here in the first place?"

"Looking for a kitten." I held Mab out for him to see.

"You were looking for a kitten," he repeated dryly, "and just happened to pick the one breeder who's on America's most wanted list?"

I nodded. "It's all part of the story, but I really don't feel up to telling it right now. Is that okay?"

Denny acquiesced. "Sure, Lynley. Whatever you need."

Something had been bothering me, annoying and illusive as a buzzing fly. But then I caught it. "How did you find me? When I first got here, I tried to call out, but my phone wouldn't work. What was it—an anonymous tip? Were you having me tailed? ESP?"

Denny gave a little laugh. "Do you remember the victim in the assault earlier this month? The one that just happened to take place in front of your house?" he added pointedly. "Well, he was in a coma for a while, then when he woke up, he remembered next to nothing. Over the weeks, it's been coming back to him, a little at a time. This morning he finally recalled the whole horrific thing.

"Seems he's a service station attendant at the place on Belmont where Londale goes to buy gas. The two had talked on several occasions, waiting for the fill-up. He knew the make, model, and color of Londale's car, as well as the first part of the license plate. It was enough to begin a search. The wonders of modern technology did the rest. Traffic cams caught Londale heading toward I-84. The police copter traced him here."

"Wow!" I mused. "So it's actually a wild coincidence you got your information in time to save my life? Aren't I the lucky one?"

"I'd have to agree that you are."

"Did you find out why the Claw... why Londale attacked that man? And why on my street? Was it something to do with me?"

"No, but in a way, yes. Does the name Kale Cole ring a bell?"

I thought. "I know a guy named Kyle. He's my neighbor down the street. He moved into the apartments sometime last winter."

"That's the one, except his name is Kale, like the vegetable; not Kyle. That's our victim. According to his story, he was coming home from work and caught Londale lurking around the neighborhood. Londale was in full regalia—black leotard, hoodie, fur gloves." Denny gestured to the corpse nearby. "Like that, I guess. It took Mr. Cole a moment to recognize him. Cole asked what he was doing there, and Londale answered with some gibberish about being the descendant of Egyptian kings. He ranted about how the gas station attendant had shortchanged him and how the station, itself, was evil and run by serpents of chaos. Cole made the mistake of laughing. That was all it took. Cole, though bigger than Londale, wasn't anticipating any violence. He figured it was just some innocent dress-up thing, a role-playing game, you never know—this is Portland, after all. Londale jumped him and he went over, hitting his head on the asphalt. Londale had just begun to tear into him with the poison claw when your mother took her shot. Saved Kale Cole's life, for sure."

"So it had nothing to do with me?" I mused.

"Nothing to do with you at all."

"Just coincidence?"

Denny shrugged. "Just coincidence, Lynley."

"What if I don't believe in coincidence?" I sighed, but

either Denny didn't hear me, or he chose not to respond.

The paramedics were finally ready for me, and after a once over, pronounced me safe to travel. As Mab and I were ferried out to the waiting ambulance, I had only one thought in my muddled, aching head, and it was a good one: my little family of cats had just grown to eight.

Chapter 28

In 2013, a Georgia family adopted a sweet white cat named Mr. Meowy from a local animal rescue group; the next day, Mr. Meowy returned the favor by alerting the family to a burning pillow thus saving the family's home from going up in flames.

I didn't want a sixtieth birthday party. Heck, I didn't want a sixtieth birthday, but the alternative wasn't that great either. So, like the proverbial lamb to slaughter, I let myself be led to the Governor Hotel where my wealthy daughter had arranged a gala celebration with a hundred of my closest friends.

I sat at the head table, making small talk and trying to hear over the music and chatter. I had a new outfit, a mandarin-necked black silk jacket over a shapeless bronze paisley dress. The high neck hid the fading bruises from Londale's strangulation. Heavy pancake foundation covered the purple butterfly slapped squarely over the bridge of my nose, greening wings spread across my cheeks—thank you, Detective Garrison. I had considered pressing charges against the Montana cop, but he had his own problems: a bullet through the shoulder, a criminal cousin, a nasty review board to face once he got well. I reckoned he would get his without any help from me.

Conversation was interrupted by the squawk of a microphone. I looked up and saw my daughter standing at the podium. I should have known she would get her two cents in sometime during the night. Oh, well, as long as she didn't turn it into a roast, I would deal. If they started cracking dirty jokes about my shortcomings, I'd be out of there faster than a cat on catnip.

"Friends, family," Lisa began. "Thank you for joining us tonight. Before they pass out the desserts and we all get hopelessly distracted, I'd like to say a few words." Lisa smiled indulgently at me from the stage. "We're going to take a step back in time, to nineteen seventy nine. I was five years old, but I recall it as if it were yesterday."

My hair prickled. Not the dreaded *Remember when...* I smiled up at her, thinking of ways to get my revenge once this whole fiasco was over.

It wasn't nearly as bad as I had feared. Lisa told a sweet anecdote about finding a stray kitten. After that, my granddaughter read a poem she had written for me, a haiku, also about cats. I was beginning to relax, thinking I might get off easy, when Lisa returned to the stage.

"I have someone here from Lynley's yesteryears." She gave a sly smile. "Someone who was very close with Mother but whom she hasn't seen for decades." She looked at me, her grin widening—she was definitely enjoying being in charge of my emotional destiny. "Can you guess?"

Faces were flashing through my mind as I tried to figure out just what crazy she might have dredged up from my sordid past. I gave a brief prayer that it wasn't some burned out druggie from my hippie days, days mostly forgotten and better left that way.

"I have no idea, dear," I managed far more calmly than I would have thought possible.

Lisa looked stage left; a tall elderly man approached her. Of course, I realized in a flash, he was probably not much older than I was. He stepped up to the microphone and turned his penetrating gaze on me. That smile, that rugged face, that rakishly curly hair, once brown, now silver—it took a moment, but it all came back to me in a flash of rainbow patchouli.

"Hi Lynley," Simon Bird said in a voice that hadn't changed in thirty years. "It's been a while."

* * *

We sat in the all-night café and stared at each other with silly grins on our faces. He looked the same, though the lush seventies mustache was gone and the long hair neatly trimmed. Simon Bird had always had the hardy good looks of a movie star, and he had aged like one as well. His physique was lean and well-muscled; where some three decades back, he resembled an artsy Magnum, P.I., he now suggested Tom Selleck's more recent character, Jesse Stone.

Simon had been by far the most attractive man at the Portland Community School of Art; too bad he was gay, all the girls had lamented. Not me, though. I loved him for what he was, and his sometimes flamboyant, sometimes moody sensuality was all a part of the complex persona.

We had been best friends, had some wild and crazy times and tried to keep it up after graduation, but he had moved out east. We'd lost track. As I basked in his presence, the years slipping away, I wondered why.

We'd been talking for an hour, and after the initial chit-chat, his *How are you doing, old girl* had opened the flood gates on my recent scrape with adventure.

"It sounds like you've been busy, Lyn. Catching cat criminals and crazy killers. But I must say it's not out of character. You always were fearless."

"Oh, I don't know about fearless. I was plenty scared when Londale had me cornered in that attic." I gave a nervous laugh as I thought back. "It's hard to describe the horror of it now—the little man in his cat suit creeping around on all fours. It sounds like some comic book scoundrel, but trust me, at the time it was nothing short of terrifying."

Simon's eyes twinkled as he put a hand over mine. "I believe you. I can see it in your face. Terror lingers."

"It's funny," I mused. "After it's all over, you begin to think of things."

"What sort of things?"

"Oh, little things that don't make sense, questions that were never answered. Like Thomas, for instance. That's been bothering me."

"Who's Thomas?"

"That's just it. I never found out. Detective Garrison and his cousin, Bannock, talked about a man named Thomas. They seemed to be afraid of him, afraid to tell him their plans got bungled. I never knew what it was about."

"Friend or foe? Good or evil?"

"Tinker, tailor, soldier, spy?" I shrugged. "It's probably nothing, but I can't help wonder if there's one more of the old gang still out there."

"Maybe I can help," came a familiar voice from behind me. I looked up to find Denny Paris standing in the aisle, a Grande to-go cup of coffee in each hand. He still had on the slacks and jacket he wore to my party, but he'd unbuttoned the neck of his shirt and his tie hung rakishly loose.

"Special Agent Paris! Fancy meeting you here."

"On my way back to Northwest Humane." He offered the coffee cups as proof. "I'm on administrative leave for the next couple of weeks, until Internal Affairs finishes their investigation." For a moment, his face clouded. "You know, into the shooting." He took a deep breath and reclaimed his smile. "I can't work, but there's nothing says

I can't volunteer in another department. I've been helping Andy Huff with the records scanning project. NHS is coming into the twenty-first century with electronic records, and all the old paper charts have to be scanned and indexed into the correct files."

I couldn't help but smile. "You're filing? Not quite the level of excitement you're used to, is it?"

"Hey, you never know what you might find in those old pages. I'd tell you about it, but I had to sign a statement of non-disclosure."

That got a laugh from both Simon and me.

"Your party was my lunch break. Extended," he added.

"Well, you might as well make it a little longer. Have a seat." I scooched over. "Denny, this is my friend, Simon Bird; Simon, this is Special Agent Denny Paris, humane investigator for the Northwest Humane Society."

The men exchanged how-do-you-dos.

Denny slipped onto the bench beside me and put down the cups. I turned to him. "So you think you can clear up the mystery of the illusive Thomas?"

"Yes, but it's going to be anticlimactic. Are you sure you really want the dull truth?"

"Absolutely!" I exclaimed. "After everything that's happened, dull is my new best friend."

Denny flipped the plastic lid off one of the coffee cups and took a sip. "Ah!" he breathed contentedly. "Verna makes the best coffee on this side of town." He gave a little wave to a jeans-and-apron-clad lady in her early thirties who was busy wiping down the counter with a bleach-white cloth.

I said nothing. I knew he was deliberately taunting me and was determined to wait him out.

He smiled and capitulated. "Okay, this is what I found

out at the inquest. Captain Raphael Thomas of the Missoula Police Department is Detective Garrison's superior. He was sympathetic to Bob's family attachment to the breed simulation case, and they had a working relationship, sort of on the down low when it came to the cousin. As long as Garrison was able to pull useful information out of Bannock, Captain Thomas would turn a blind eye. If that eye ever got opened, however, Bannock would surely go to jail. Neither he nor Garrison wanted that, at least not until Londale was safely behind bars."

"So he's a cop?"

Denny nodded and took another sip of his steamy beverage. "Bob Garrison wasn't a bad guy, Lynley. Just used some iffy methods. All detectives have their informants. And it worked out in the end—Bob did lead us to the perp."

"I thought Kale Cole gave you that information."

"Well, yeah. But Garrison did his part. Give the guy a break. He's pretty much lost the use of his right arm because of the bullet he took; probably will have to push paper for a long time."

I believed that not putting the bully in jail after he bopped me in the face was more of a break than he deserved, but I didn't push it. I wondered how much Denny knew about the Missoula detective's abusive bent. I'd been forthcoming in my statement after the incident at the cottage, but Garrison had been right when he said the scales of persuasion tipped to the side of the stalwart policeman over the crazy cat lady.

"So you see, Lynley, it all worked out. A psychotic killer is off the streets, and the simulation of breed cats is finished for good. I doubt we'll be seeing anyone try that again soon."

The conversation lapsed for a moment as we all thought our individual thoughts, the kind that only come to the surface sometime after midnight. Then I remembered something else.

"There's another thing I don't understand. The break-in at the shelter, when Bannock stole the four cats back and knocked me out—why on earth did he do that?"

"Which part? Steal the cats or knock you out?"

"Very funny," I scoffed. "All of it, I guess. Why did he bother?"

"I think Bannock's—how should I put this? He's a little *different* from the rest of us. Not insane like Londale, but truly obsessed with his cats. And don't forget, the exposure to the toxic dye made him paranoid."

"Paranoid enough to risk everything?"

"According to Garrison, Bannock's greatest desire was to be a serious cat breeder. Londale convinced him the only way he could make that happen was to pull the scams. Londale was a manipulator, and Bannock, not too smart. But he loved those cats, every single one. Couldn't stand them being beyond his control."

"But he sold his cats. Aren't they pretty much beyond his control when they go off to their new homes?"

"He had a say in who bought, and most assuredly kept the addresses."

I shivered. "That's creepy. Some weirdo lurking around to make sure you treat your kitty right?" Suddenly I thought of the attempted burglary at my house when I first had Meow in foster. Was it coincidence that the offender chose the cat room window? Could it have been Bannock, even then?

"Did you ever find out who was with him? The other man?" I pressed on.

"Other man?"

"Kerry said the security camera picked up two men. I remember Ben talking to someone."

"Oh, yeah. Right. We don't know, and Bannock isn't telling. It wasn't Londale—the build's all wrong. We'll find out though, count on it."

I had my own theory about the other man, but I'd be happy to let someone else finger Detective Garrison for that particular collusion.

"I do have some good news," Denny said, grinning like the Cheshire Cat. "I didn't get a chance to tell you at the party, but we found Bill Todd's cat, Bonnie. Both she and Zoom-aka-Meow are back home where they belong."

I nearly jumped out of my seat with joy. "You found her? How? Where?"

"A good Samaritan saw her wandering around the neighborhood, didn't recognize her and noticed she didn't have a collar. After several sightings, he decided she must be lost or stray and brought her to the shelter. She was microchipped so the rest was easy. No way of knowing where she'd been for the past month, but aside from a few fleas and a hunger that wouldn't quit, she's healthy. I wish she could tell us her story, though," he joked.

Instantly my mind flew to the Animal Communications Workshop Frannie and I had attended back in January. In a way, that was the start of the whole thing. How naïve Frannie and I had been; how eager to try out our new-found psychic skills! We couldn't wait to ask Meow his story, never guessing it would be a tale of cruelty and woe. Had Meow known he'd been kidnapped by a killer? Had he tried to warn us with his manic behavior, the only way he knew how?

"Sometimes ignorance is bliss," I said enigmatically.

Denny gave me a strange look but let it pass. Good choice, because I was far too tired to go into four months' worth of revelations.

"Well, I'd better be getting back to work. Those charts aren't going to scan themselves." Denny clicked the lid tight on his paper cup and rose. He leaned down and kissed me on the cheek. "Happy birthday, Lynley. I'm glad you're okay, even if it means doing files for the next few weeks."

"Me too. That was a brave thing you did," I said, recalling with stark realism the spray of hot blood across my face, the surprise in Londale's eyes when Denny killed him. Ending someone's existence, no matter how compulsory, is no small matter; it was something Denny would carry for the rest of his days.

Denny turned to Simon. "Nice meeting you, Mr. Bird."

"You too. Great to see Lynley's hanging out with a better crowd these days."

Denny raised an eyebrow but didn't pursue it. I gave Simon a dirty look. "Aren't old friends just the cat's pajamas?" I said with dripping sarcasm.

"He seems like a nice young man," Simon said once Denny had taken off.

"Oh, he is. He's come to my rescue a few times, in more ways than one."

Simon smiled; I remembered that smile from half a century ago. "But enough about me. What have you been up to for the last few decades? Wait; let me guess. You're a rich and famous artist? A rich and infamous recluse? A rich and..."

He laughed. "You got it right the first time, at least the art part. I'm not exactly rich or famous, but I manage well enough. For the last several years, I've been painting to benefit the Cloverleaf Animal Sanctuary in Washington State. I assume as a shelter volunteer, you've heard of us?"

"Of course!" I exclaimed. "On Clover Island, in the San Juans."

Simon nodded.

"Why, that's one of the most notable animal shelters in the country, in the world. I get their online newsletter every month." I paused. "I've seen some of the paintings they publish. Beautiful and thought-provoking, reflecting the plight of homeless animals. Those are yours?"

"Yes. Thank you."

"But Simon, why haven't I read your name on the credits then? Surely I would have noticed."

"I've chosen to remain anonymous. It's not about me, it's about the animals I paint."

I shrugged. "I guess but give credit where it's due. The original paintings must be gorgeous. You shouldn't keep your talent a secret." I paused. "Sorry, it really isn't any of my business. I'm sure you have your reasons. I just don't think I'd ever be capable of such humility."

He laughed. "It's a long story, Lynley. But why don't you see for yourself? I do a retreat each August at the sanctuary. Only a handful of participants. We talk and paint and meditate. We try other art forms, too. Whatever you're into. Pottery, beading, even writing. It's always a lot of fun and extremely rewarding, at least for me, and I'd like to think for my students as well. You should come. The slots fill quickly, but I'll save you a space."

"I'll definitely think about it," I told him, realizing that it wasn't just a line—it did sound fascinating, too rare an opportunity to pass up.

"It's interesting that we both have chosen animal welfare for our golden years," I mused.

"I don't know about *golden years*, but I'm not surprised you went into shelter work. You always were the crazy cat lady."

I thought about all that had befallen me in the last few months, beginning with foster Meow and ending—well, it really wasn't over yet. There was still Bannock's court date and after that, Londale's trial. The whole thing boggled my mind, but I wasn't quite crazy. Yet.

* * *

Simon and I talked the night away like a couple of teenagers and not the elderly people that we had become thanks to Father Time. We parted at sunrise, he to his northern island and me to my home and my cats.

I had a lot of things to think about, and among them, the possibility of a summer art retreat at a celebrated animal sanctuary. The more I considered Simon's offer, the more I realized I couldn't pass it by. It would take some finagling to arrange care for the cats, all *eight* of them, but it could be done. After what I'd been through, I deserved—no, needed—the reward.

The retreat was still four months away, but I found I was already planning for it. An entire week of creativity, serenity and peace! I could hardly wait!

A Note from the Author

Thanks so much for reading my second Crazy Cat Lady Mystery, *Copy Cats*. I hope you enjoyed it. If you did, please consider leaving a review on your favorite book and social media sites. Reviews help indie authors such as myself to gain recognition in the literary jungle. Thank you in advance for your consideration.

Want more cozy cat mysteries? Look for more books in my **Crazy Cat Lady** series. Don't worry—the books need not be read in order. Just pick a plot that interests you and start reading.

"…Each book drew me right into the story and kept me intrigued and guessing all the way." —Catwoods Porch Party

Or check out my **Tenth Life Paranormal Mysteries** involving a septuagenarian, a ghost cat, and a small coastal town.

"This is the sort of cozy mystery that you like to curl up with on a rainy day with a cup of tea." —Verified Reader

For sci-fantasy fans, there is my **Cat Seasons Tetralogy**—Cats saving the world!

"Mollie weaves a story that blurs the lines of mythology, spiritualism, mysticism, science and reality that took me into another world." — Ramona D. Marek MS Ed, CWA Author

About the Author

Cat Writer Mollie Hunt is the award-winning author of two cozy series, the **Crazy Cat Lady Mysteries**, featuring a sixty-something cat shelter volunteer who finds more trouble than a cat in catnip, and the **Tenth Life Paranormal Mysteries** involving a ghost cat. Her **Cat Seasons Sci-Fantasy Tetralogy** presents extraordinary cats saving the world. She also pens a bit of cat poetry.

Mollie is a member of the Willamette Writers, Oregon Writers' Colony, Sisters in Crime, the Cat Writers' Association, and Northwest Independent Writers Association (NIWA). She lives in Portland, Oregon with her husband and a varying number of cats. Like her cat lady character, she is a grateful shelter volunteer.